Tur

SONS OF LIBERTY

ALSO AVAILABLE

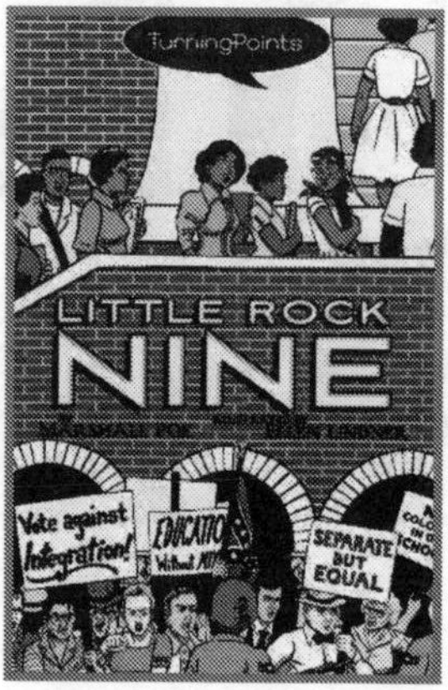
TurningPoints
LITTLE ROCK
NINE
Vote against Integration!
SEPARATE BUT EQUAL

COMING SOON . . .

A HOUSE DIVIDED

TurningPoints

SONS OF LIBERTY

BY MARSHALL POE
ILLUSTRATED BY LELAND PURVIS

ALADDIN PAPERBACKS
NEW YORK LONDON TORONTO SYDNEY

This book is dedicated to Julianna and Isaiah—M.P.

To my bride, Elizabeth, who makes my Life, Liberty, and pursuit of Happiness possible and worthwhile—L.P.

In this book, history is fleshed out with fictionalized details, and conversations have been added to make the stories come alive to today's reader, but every reasonable effort has been made to make the stories consistent with the events, ethics, and character of their subjects and the historical time period.

ALADDIN PAPERBACKS • An imprint of Simon & Schuster Children's Publishing Division 1230 Avenue of the Americas, New York, NY 10020 • Copyright © 2008 by Marshall Poe and Leland Purvis • All rights reserved, including the right of reproduction in whole or in part in any form • ALADDIN PAPERBACKS, Turning Points and logo, and colophon are trademarks of Simon & Schuster, Inc. • The text of the frontmatter and backmatter of this book are set in Turning Points, created by Dalton Webb • Manufactured in the United States of America First Aladdin Paperbacks edition June 2008 • 10 9 8 7 6 5 4 3 2 1 Library of Congress Control Number 2007937917 ISBN-13: 978-1-4169-5067-7 • ISBN-10: 1-4169-5067-2

ACKNOWLEDGMENTS:

MARSHALL POE

In writing *Sons of Liberty*, I felt a little like a traveler in an unfamiliar country. I needed a lot of guidance. Happily, I got it. First, from my agent, Bob Mecoy, who pointed the way. Next from Leland Purvis, who drew an excellent map. Then, when I was too thick to understand the said map, from the remarkable Carla Jablonski, who put me (and the book) firmly back on track. And finally from my editor at Simon & Schuster, Liesa Abrams, and from Matt Madden, who both greeted me when I arrived, at long last, safe and sound.

LELAND PURVIS

Special thanks to Bob Mecoy, Matt Madden, and Liesa Abrams; to my studiomates at Deep-Six Studio; and for the warm hospitality of Periscope Studios. And a deep bow and humble gratitude to Carla Jablonski for her reliably extraordinary contributions.

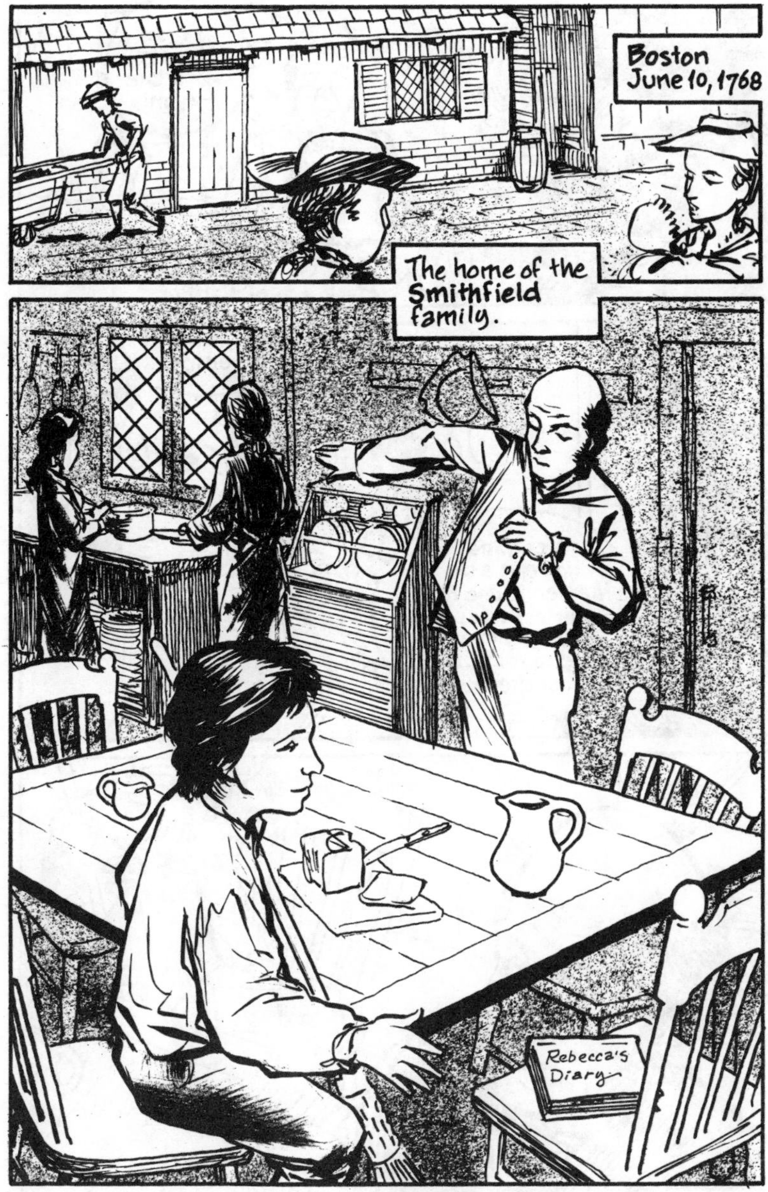
Boston
June 10, 1768
The home of the Smithfield family.
Rebecca's Diary

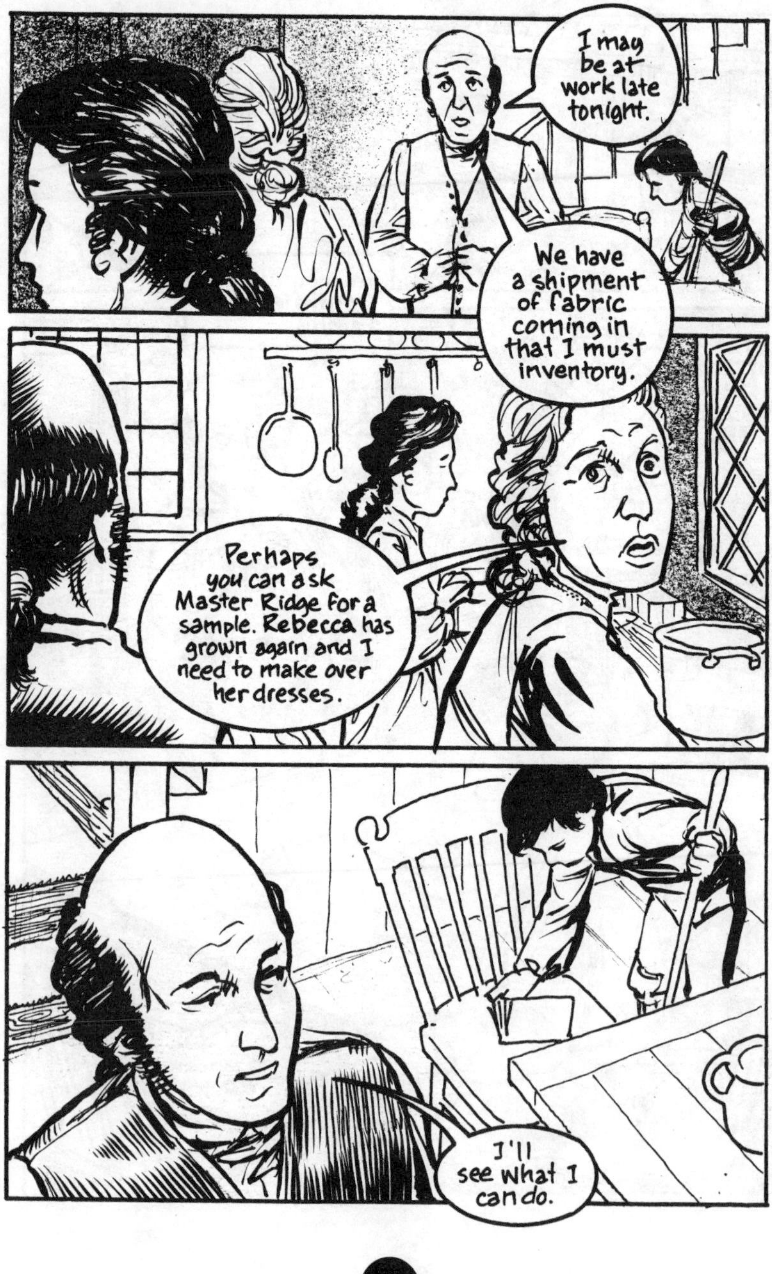
I may be at work late tonight.
We have a shipment of fabric coming in that I must inventory.
Perhaps you can ask Master Ridge for a sample. Rebecca has grown again and I need to make over her dresses.
I'll see what I can do.

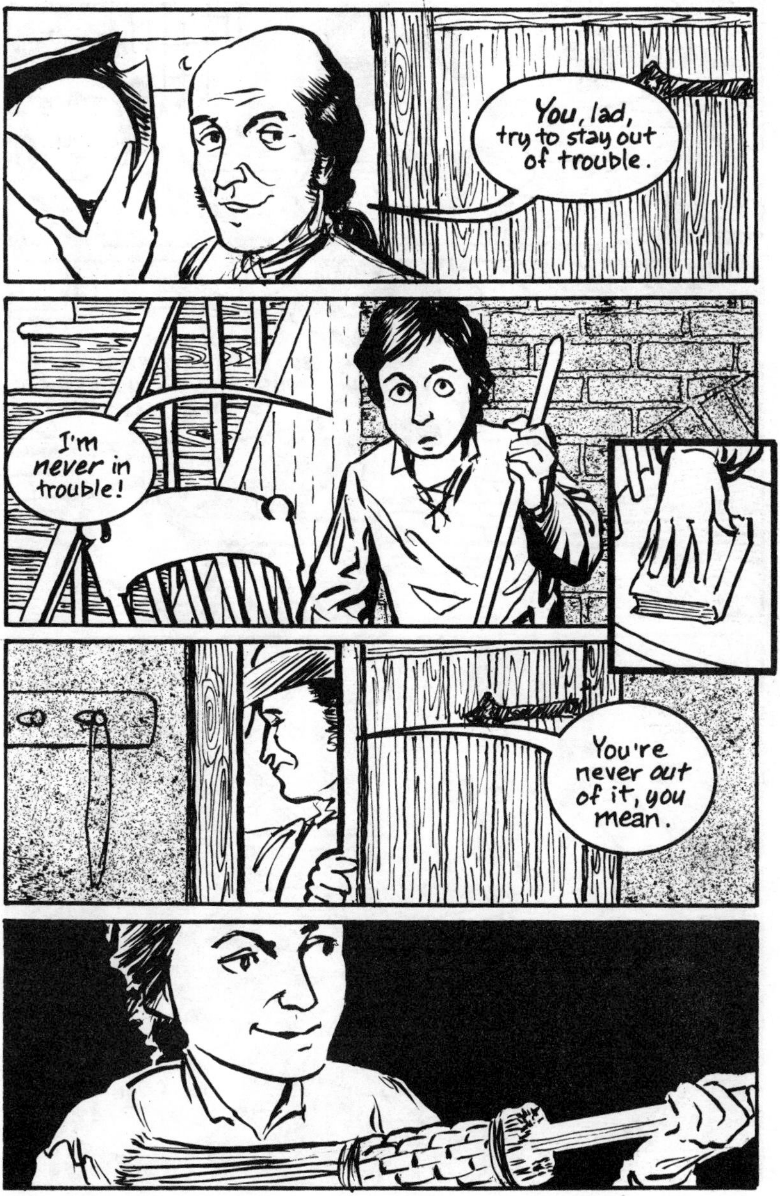
You, lad, try to stay out of trouble.
I'm never in trouble!
You're never out of it, you mean.

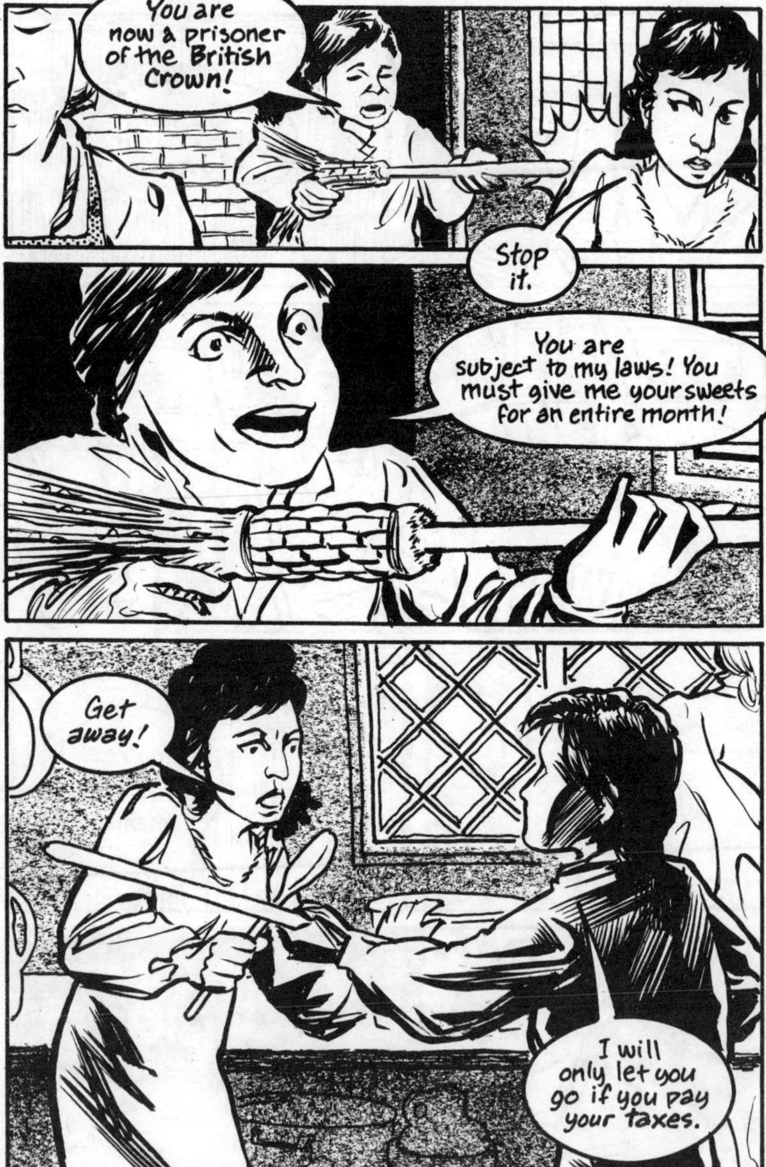
You are now a prisoner of the British Crown!
Stop it.
You are subject to my laws! You must give me your sweets for an entire month!
Get away!
I will only let you go if you pay your taxes.

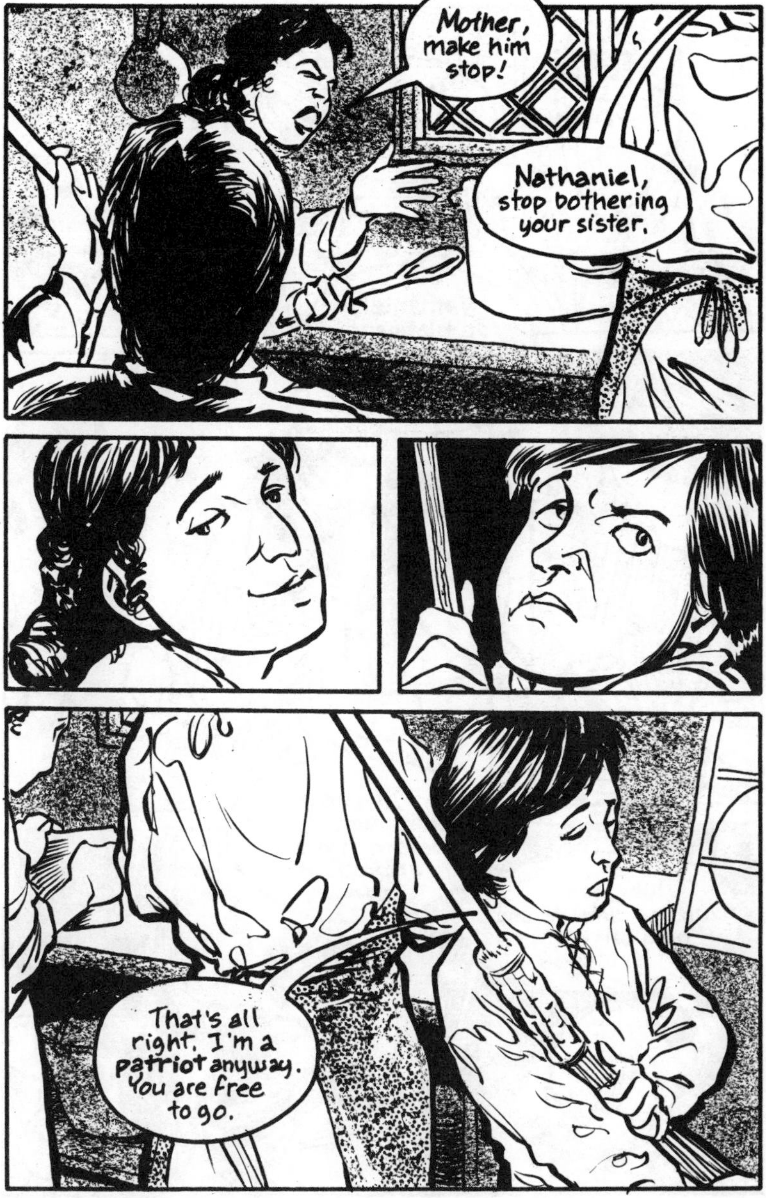
Mother, make him stop!
Nathaniel, stop bothering your sister.
That's all right. I'm a patriot anyway. You are free to go.

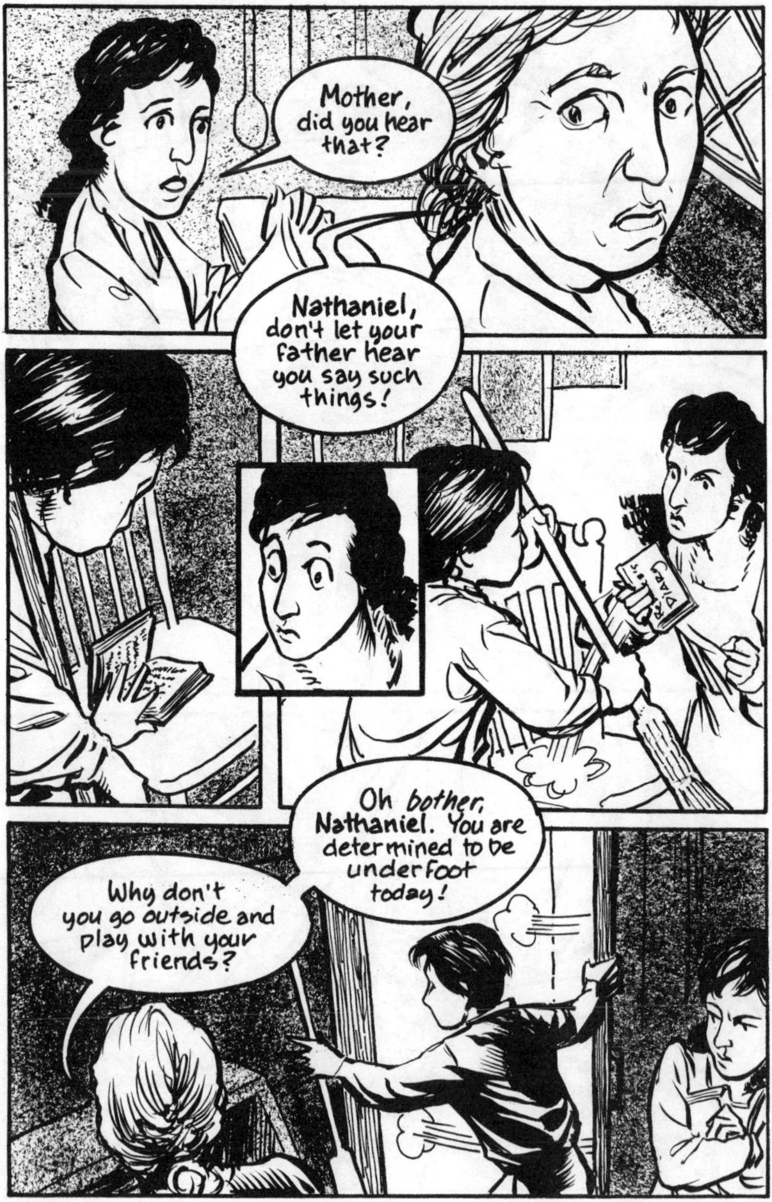
Mother, did you hear that?
Nathaniel, don't let your father hear you say such things!
DIARY
Oh *bother*, Nathaniel. You are determined to be underfoot today!
Why don't you go outside and play with your friends?

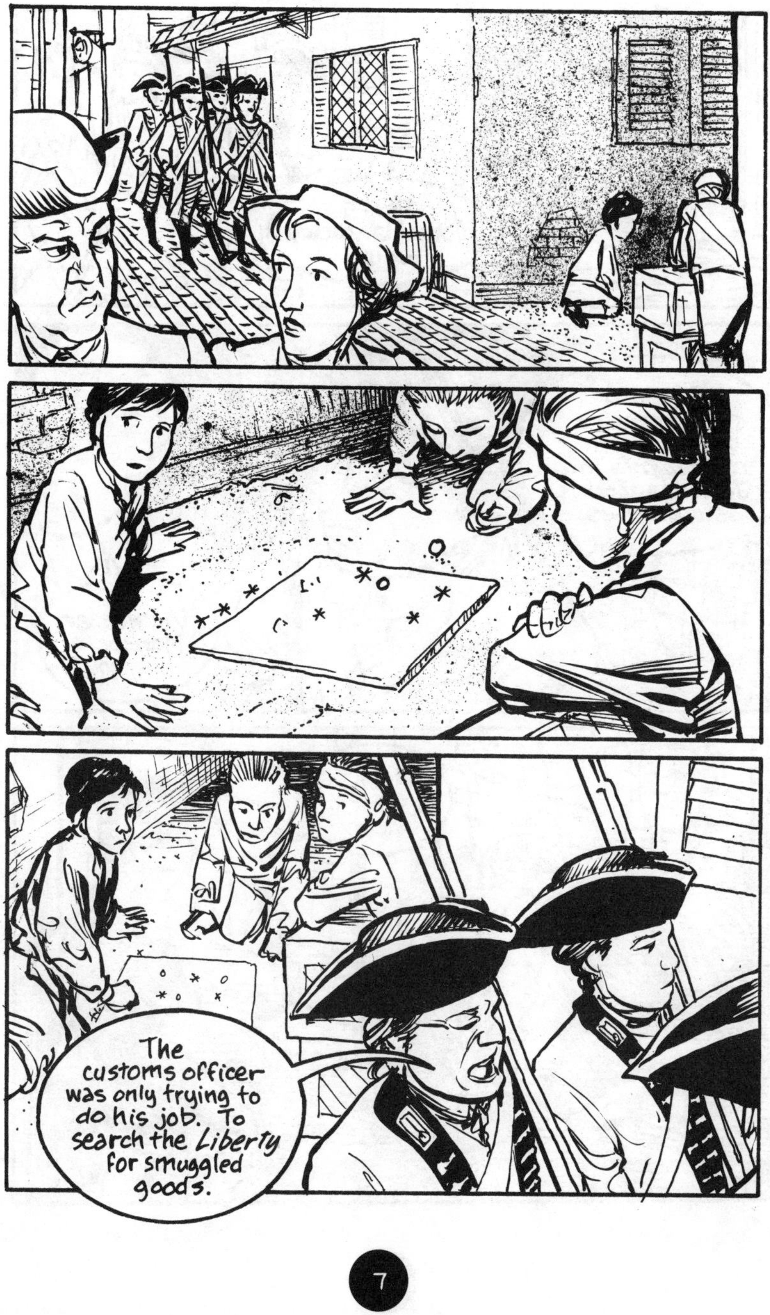
The customs officer was only trying to do his job. To search the *Liberty* for smuggled goods.

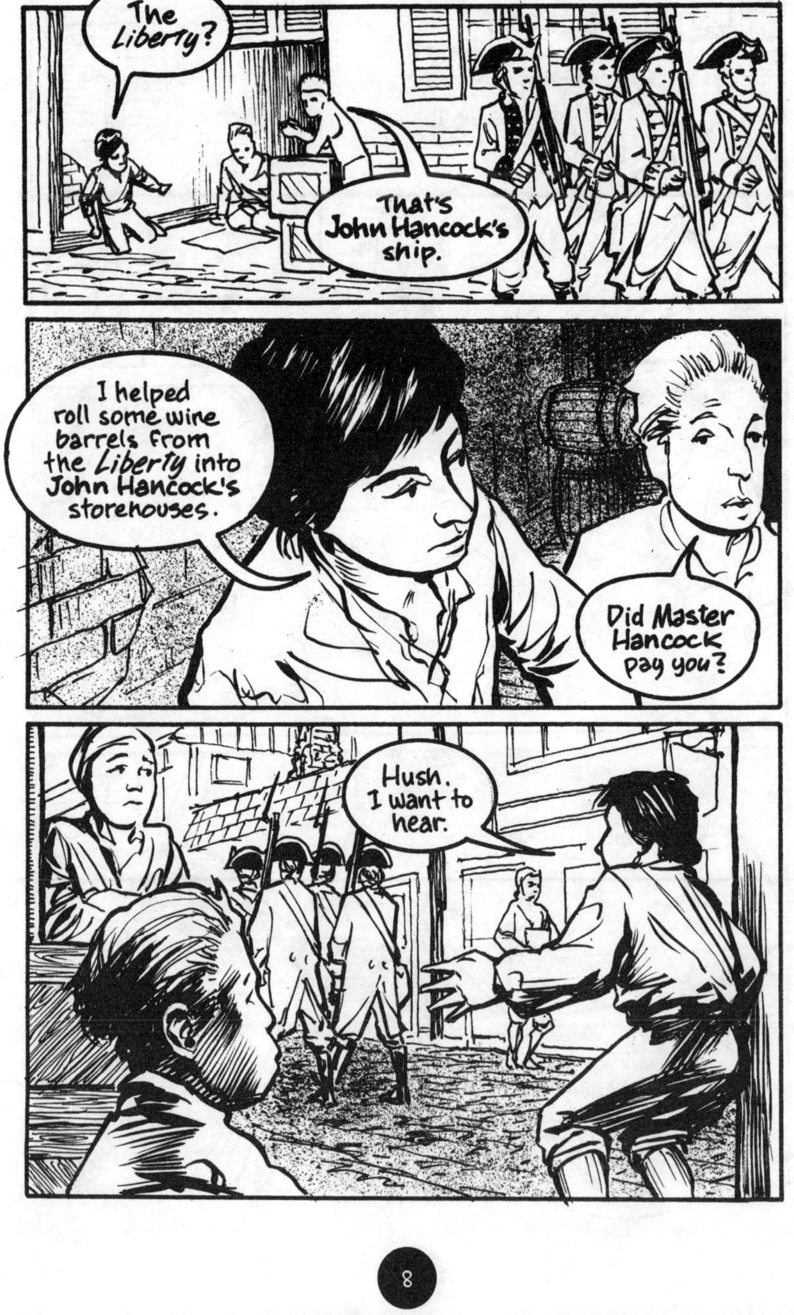
The Liberty?
That's John Hancock's ship.
I helped roll some wine barrels from the Liberty into John Hancock's storehouses.
Did Master Hancock pay you?
Hush. I want to hear.

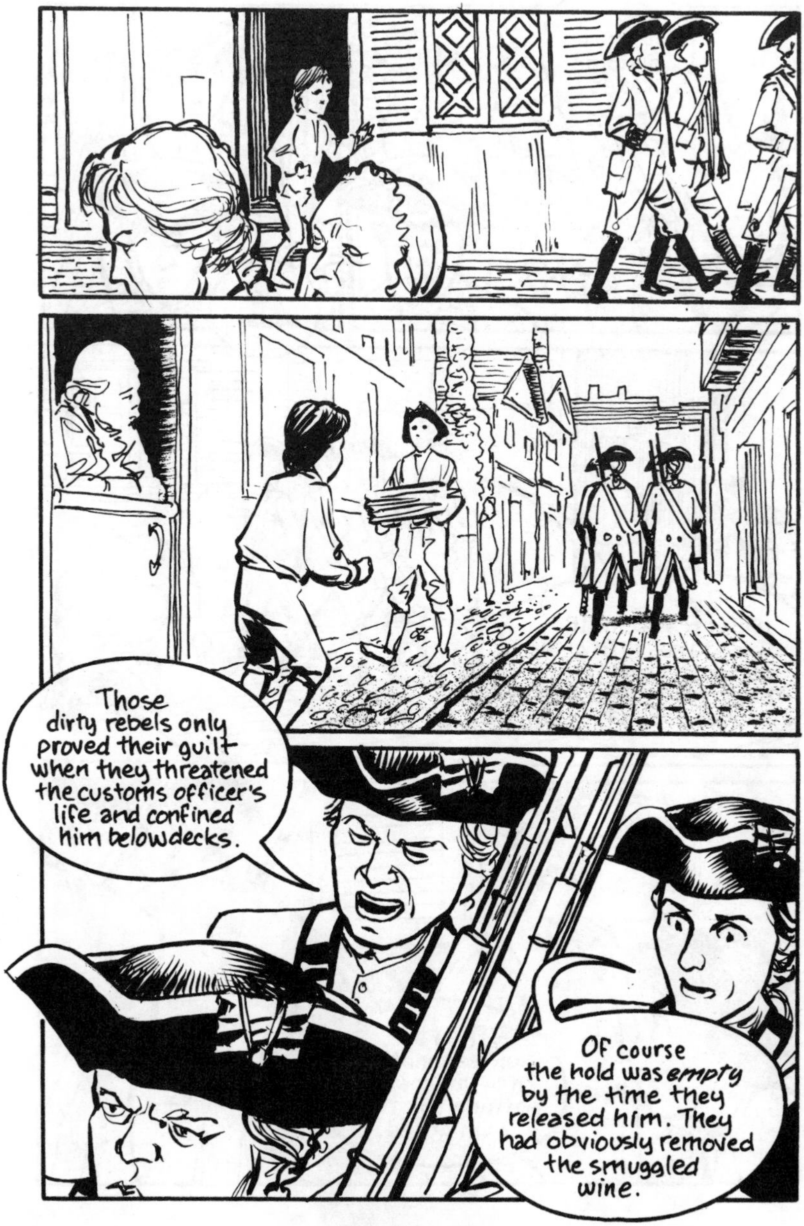
Those dirty rebels only proved their guilt when they threatened the customs officer's life and confined him belowdecks.
Of course the hold was *empty* by the time they released him. They had obviously removed the smuggled wine.

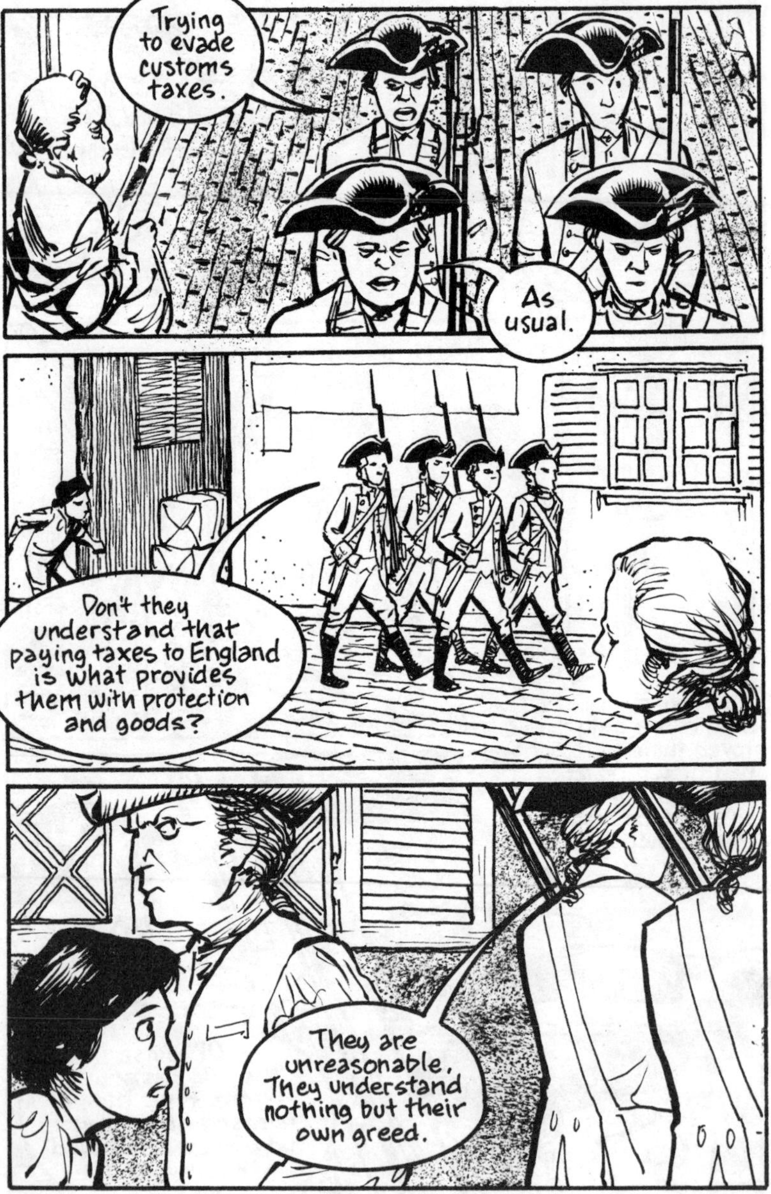
Trying to evade customs taxes.
As usual.
Don't they understand that paying taxes to England is what provides them with protection and goods?
They are unreasonable. They understand nothing but their own greed.

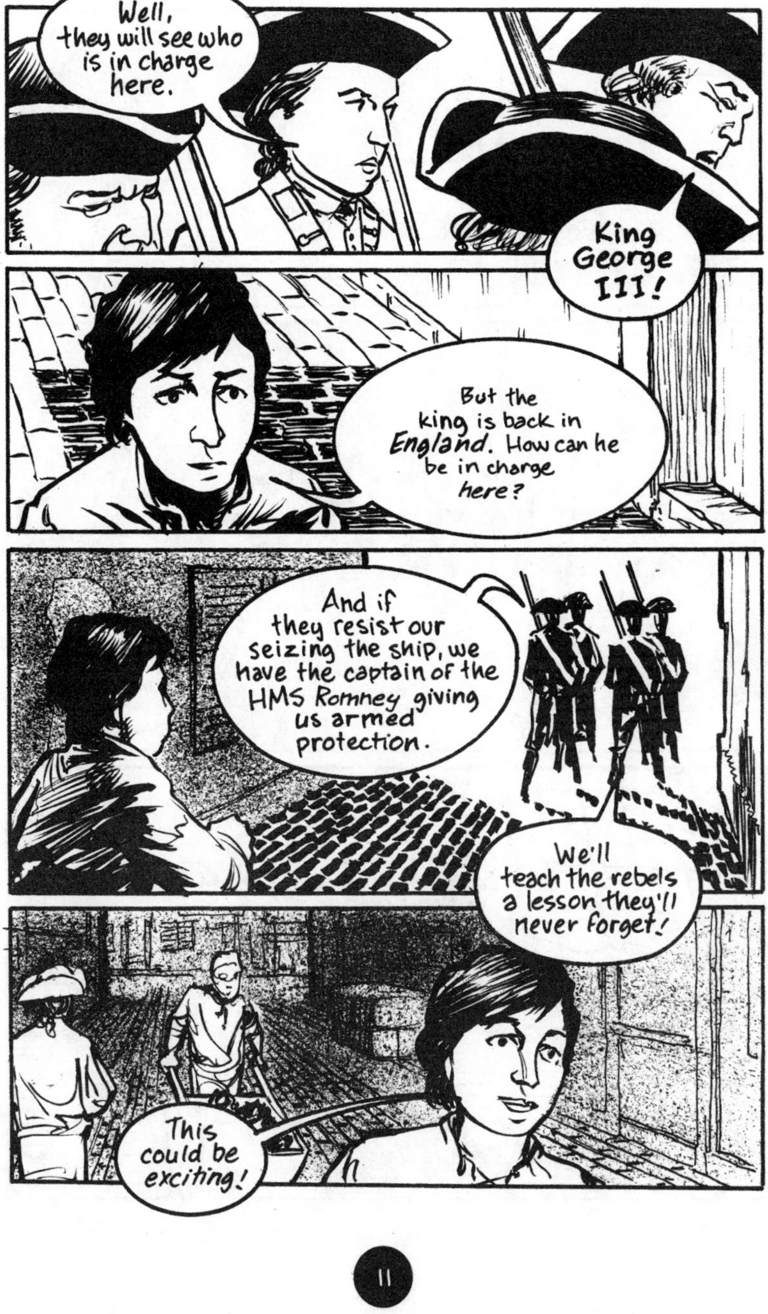
Well, they will see who is in charge here.
King George III!
But the king is back in England. How can he be in charge here?
And if they resist our seizing the ship, we have the captain of the HMS Romney giving us armed protection.
We'll teach the rebels a lesson they'll never forget!
This could be exciting!

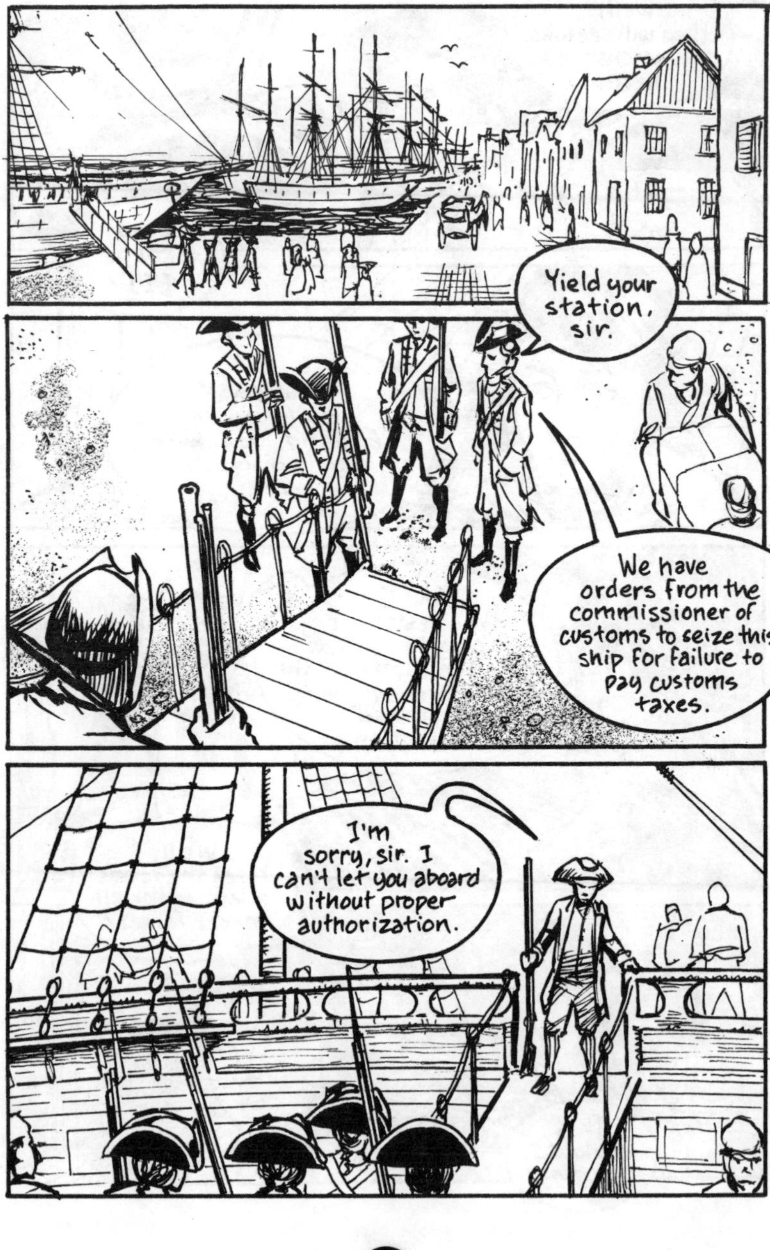
Yield your station, sir.
We have orders from the commissioner of customs to seize this ship for failure to pay customs taxes.
I'm sorry, sir. I can't let you aboard without proper authorization.

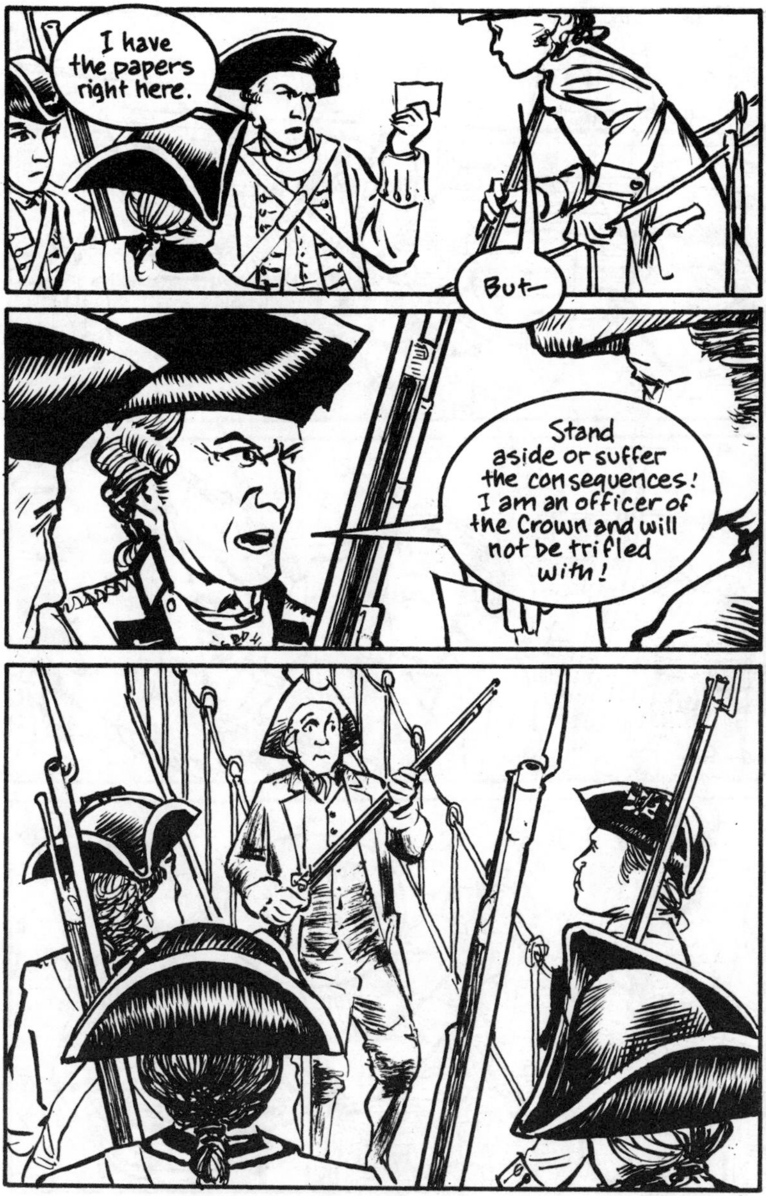
I have the papers right here.
But—
Stand aside or suffer the consequences! I am an officer of the Crown and will not be trifled with!

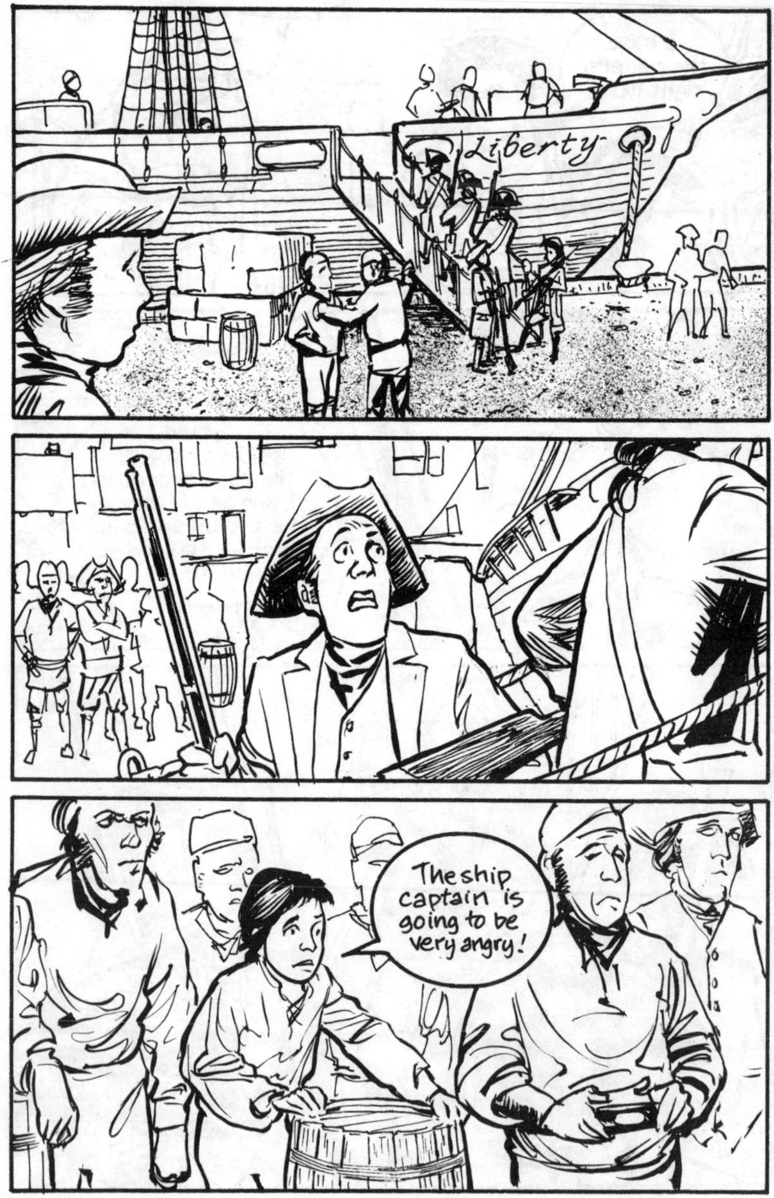
Liberty
The ship captain is going to be very angry!

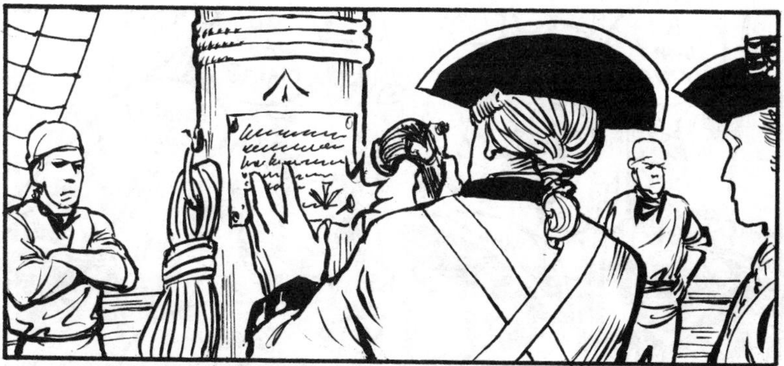

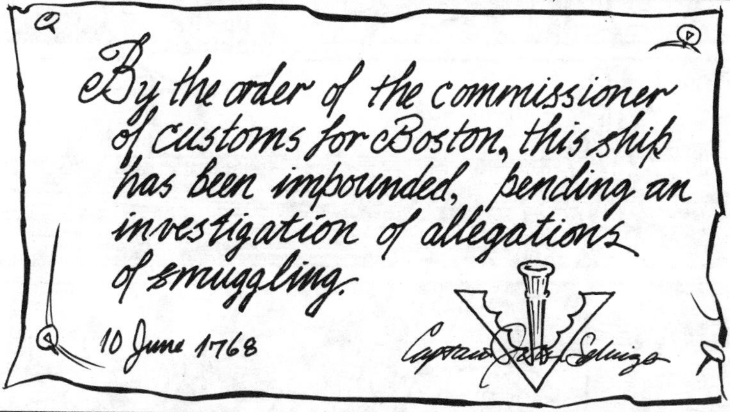
By the order of the commissioner of customs for Boston, this ship has been impounded, pending an investigation of allegations of smuggling.
10 June 1768

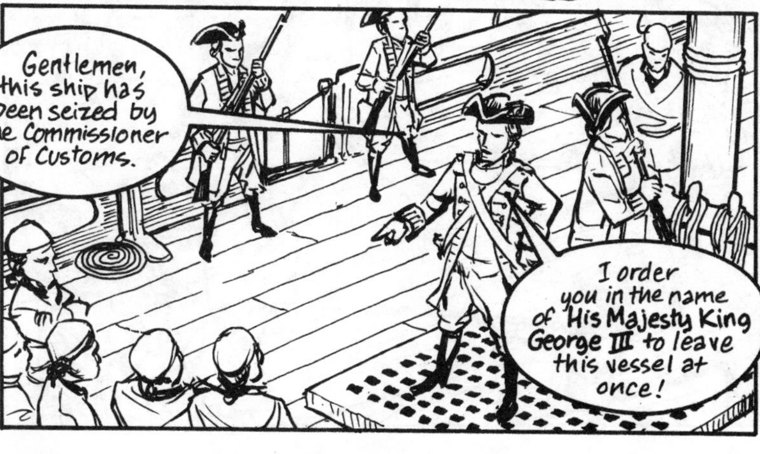
Gentlemen, this ship has been seized by the Commissioner of Customs.
I order you in the name of His Majesty King George III to leave this vessel at once!

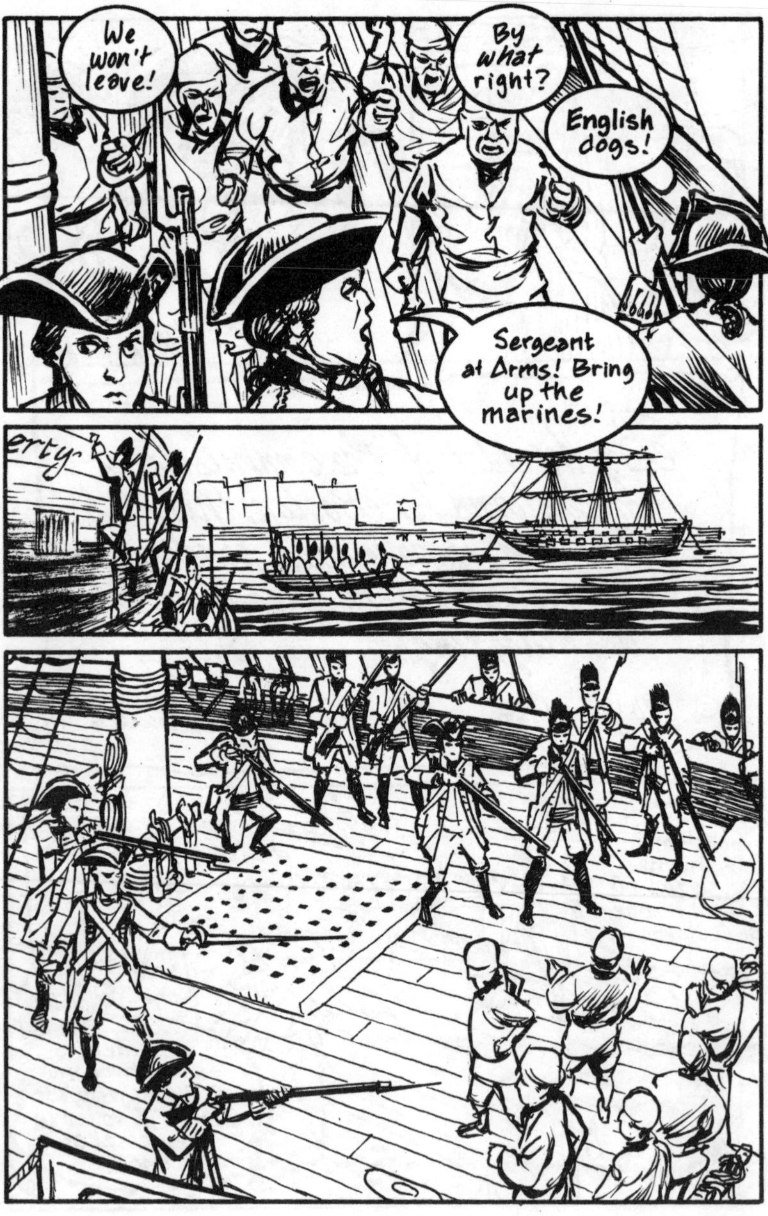
We won't leave!
By what right?
English dogs!
Sergeant at Arms! Bring up the marines!

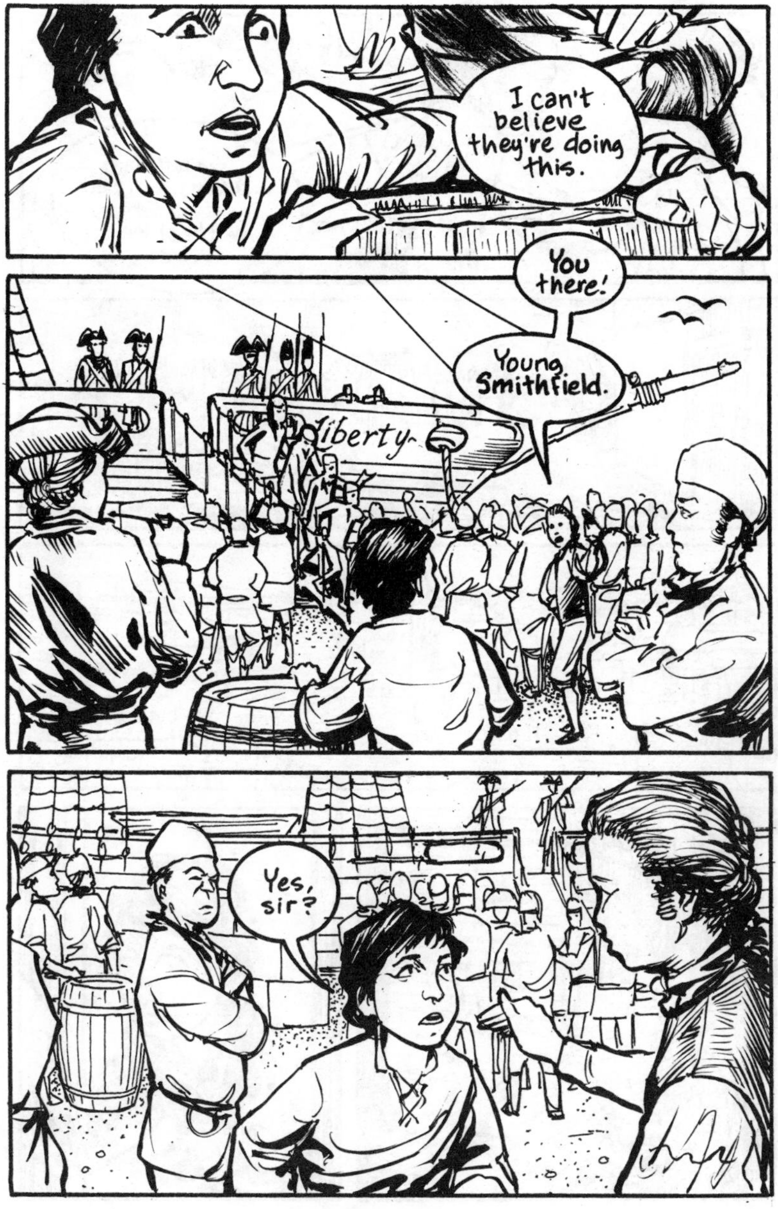
I can't believe they're doing this.
You there!
Young Smithfield.
Liberty
Yes, sir?

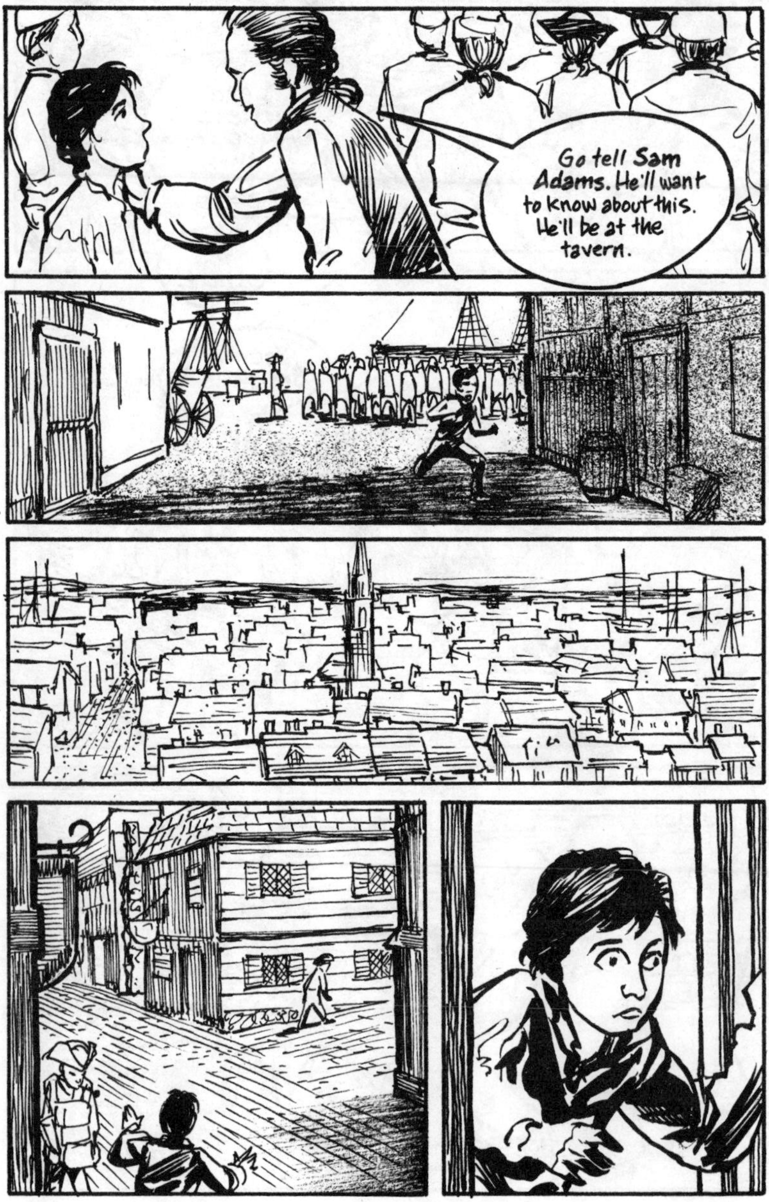
Go tell Sam Adams. He'll want to know about this. He'll be at the tavern.

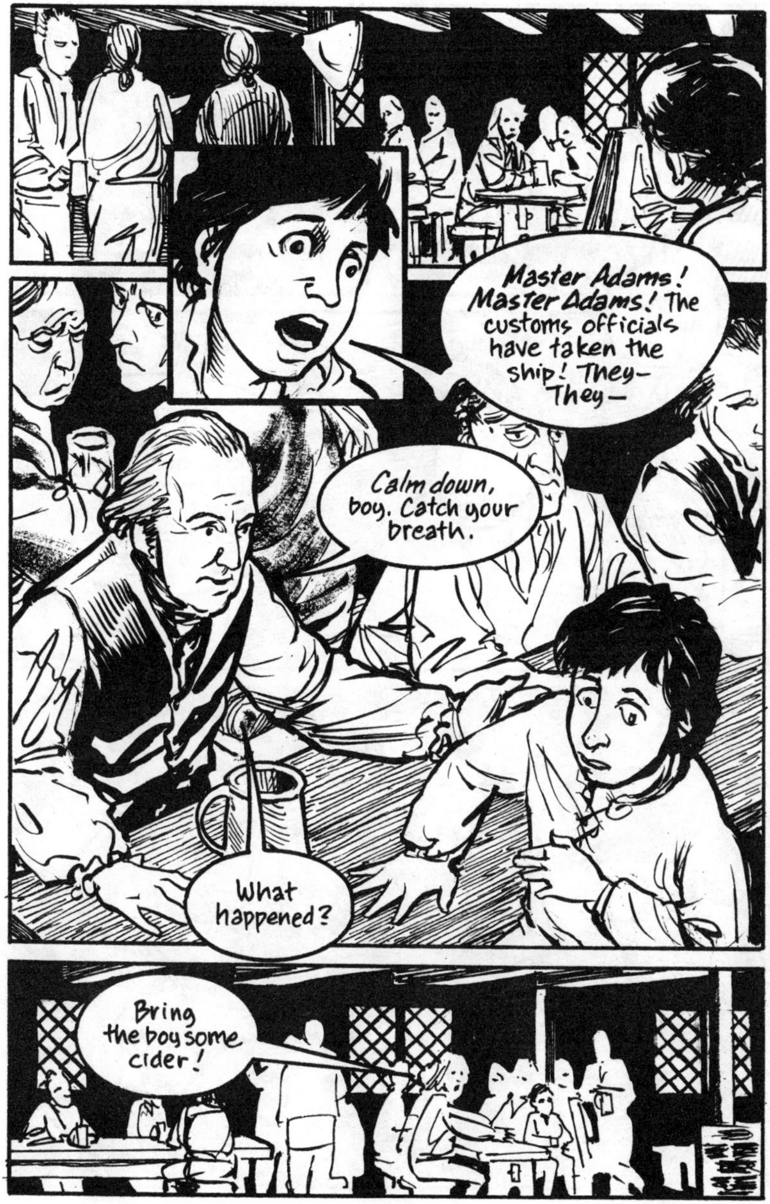
Master Adams! Master Adams! The customs officials have taken the ship! They— They—
Calm down, boy. Catch your breath.
What happened?
Bring the boy some cider!

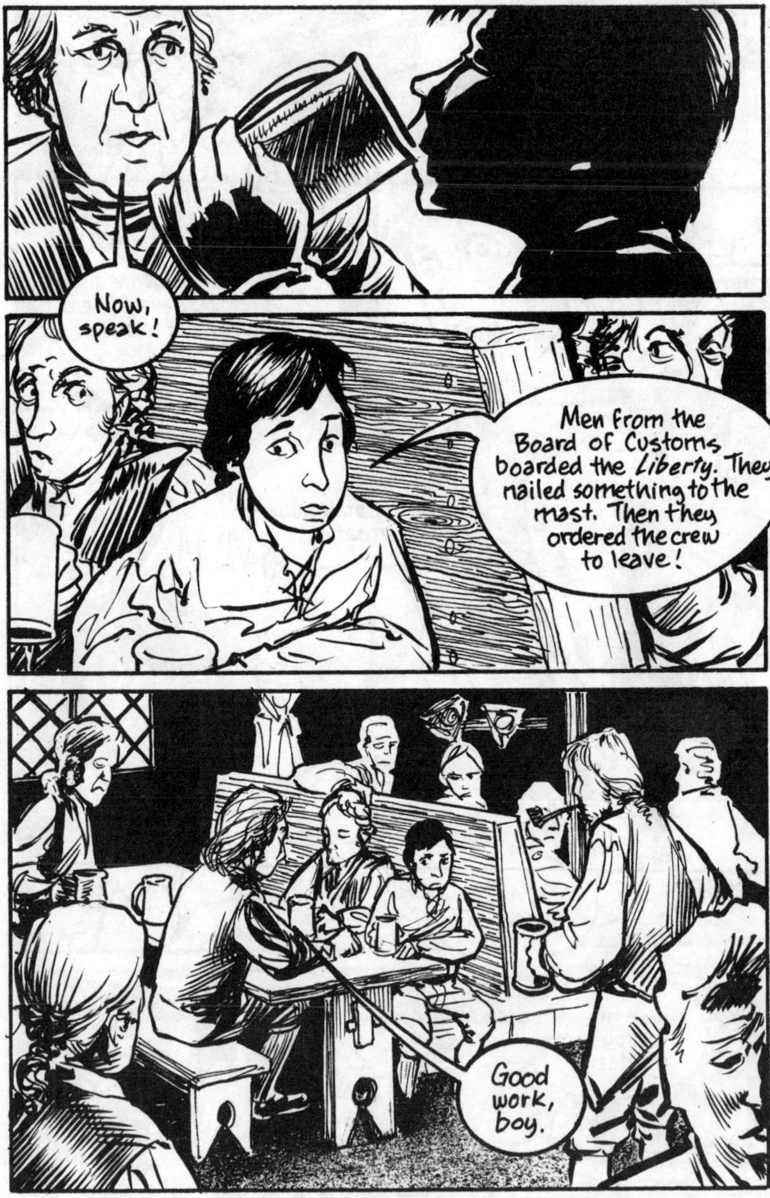

Now, speak!
Men from the Board of Customs boarded the *Liberty*. They nailed something to the mast. Then they ordered the crew to leave!
Good work, boy.

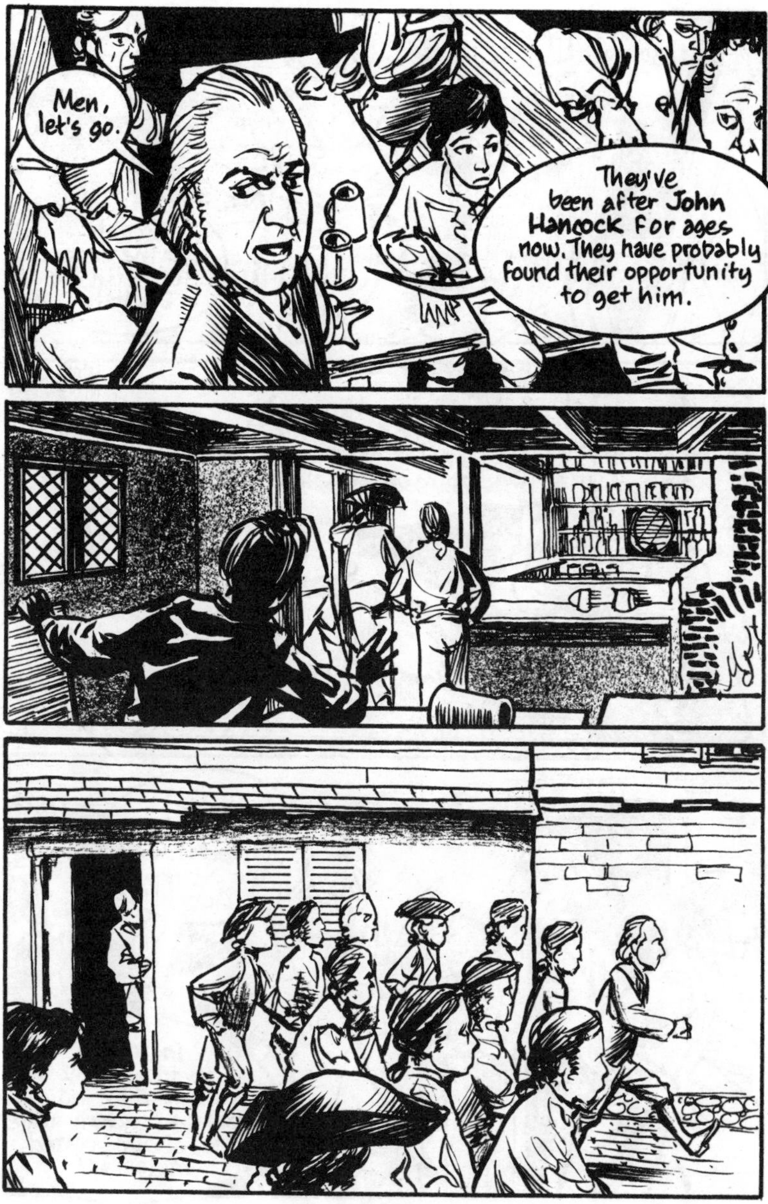
Men, let's go.
They've been after John Hancock for ages now. They have probably found their opportunity to get him.

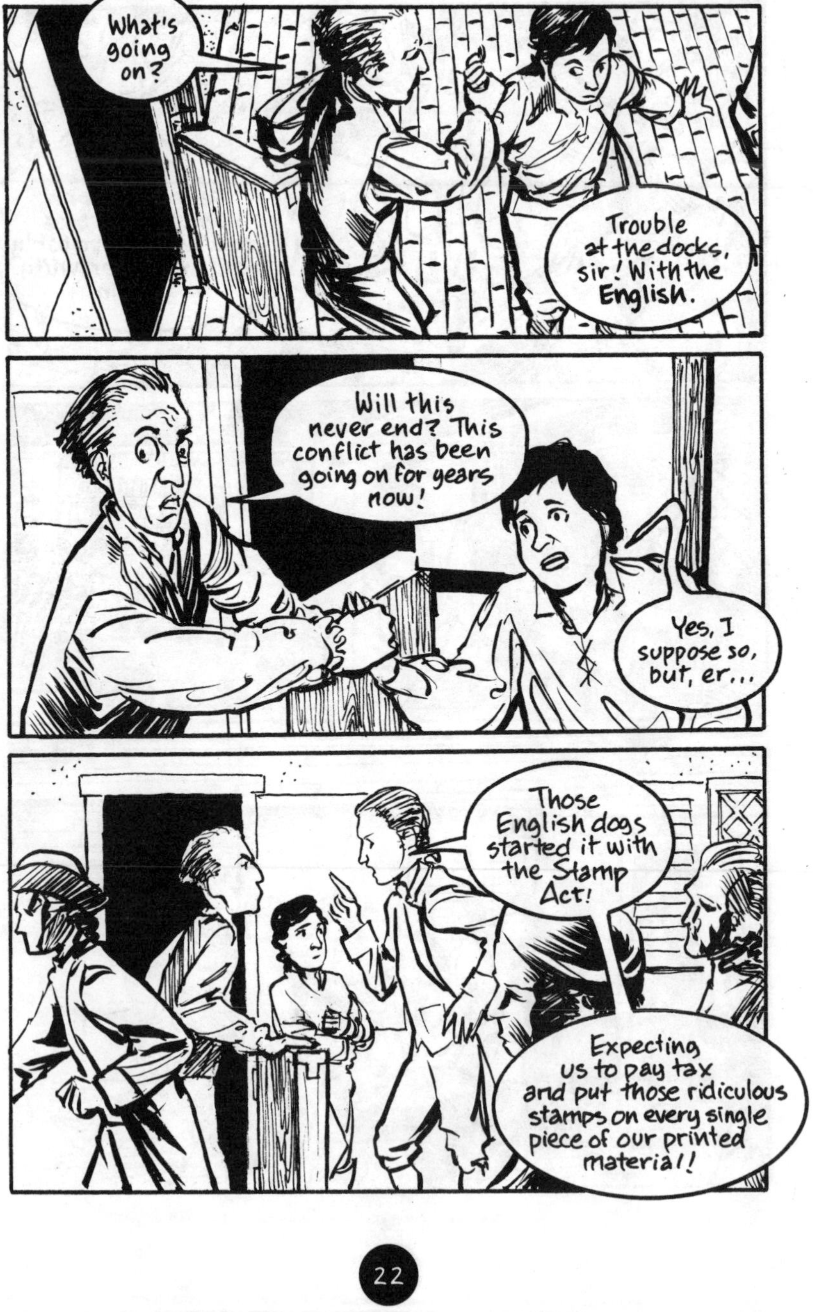
What's going on?
Trouble at the docks, sir! With the English.
Will this never end? This conflict has been going on for years now!
Yes, I suppose so, but, er...
Those English dogs started it with the Stamp Act!
Expecting us to pay tax and put those ridiculous stamps on every single piece of our printed material!!

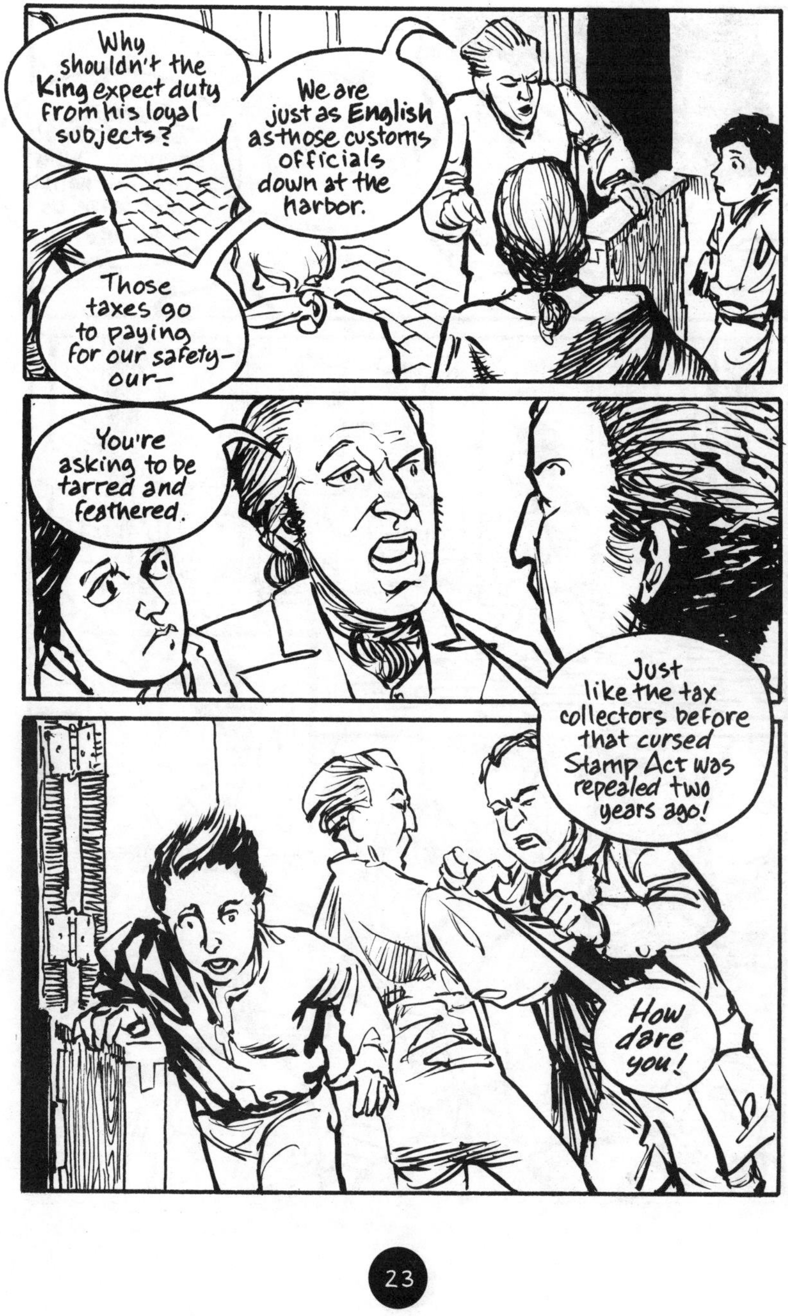
Why shouldn't the King expect duty from his loyal subjects?
We are just as English as those customs officials down at the harbor.
Those taxes go to paying for our safety-our—
You're asking to be tarred and feathered.
Just like the tax collectors before that cursed Stamp Act was repealed two years ago!
How dare you!

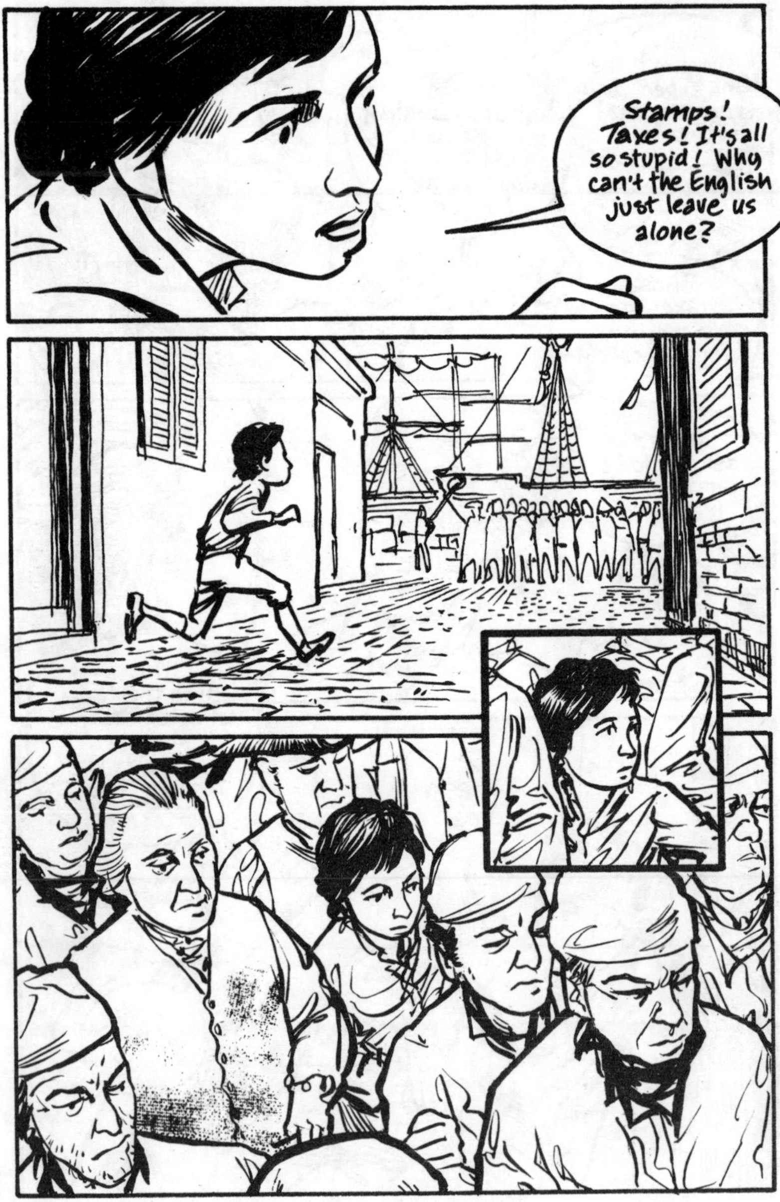
Stamps! Taxes! It's all so stupid! Why can't the English just leave us alone?

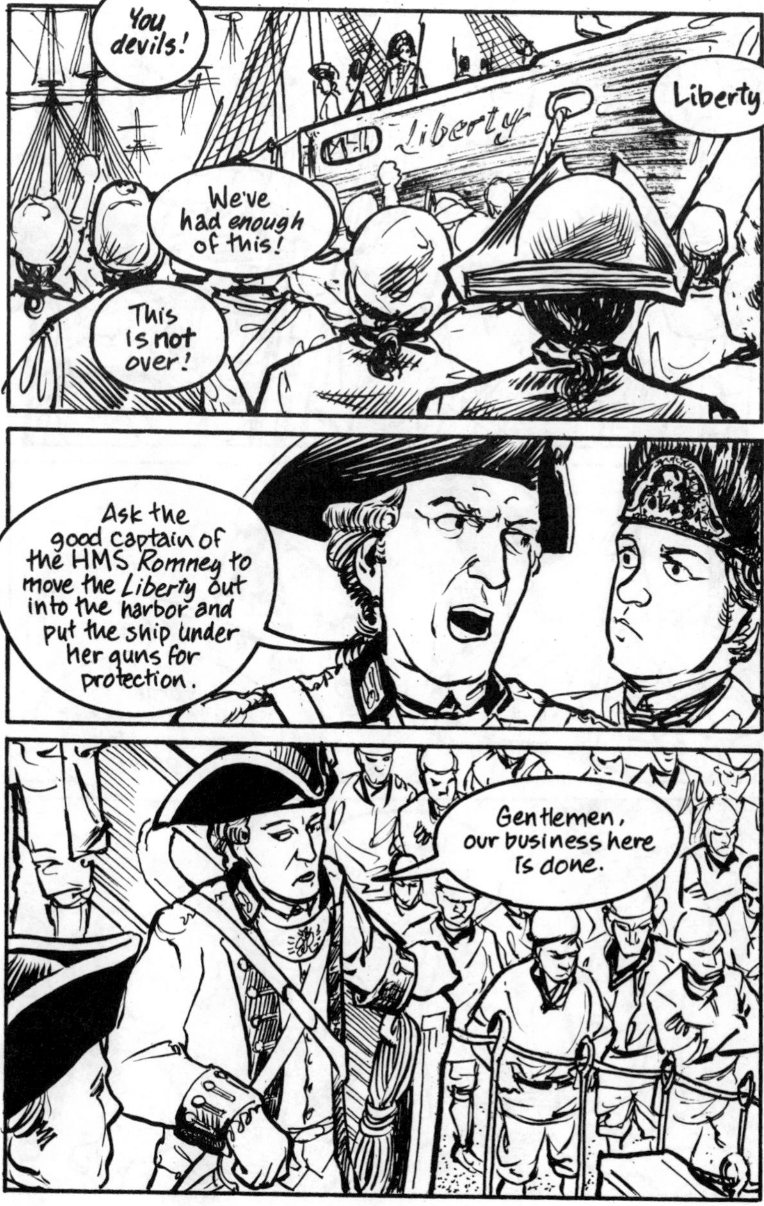
You devils!
Liberty!
Liberty
We've had enough of this!
This is not over!
Ask the good captain of the HMS *Romney* to move the *Liberty* out into the harbor and put the ship under her guns for protection.
Gentlemen, our business here is done.

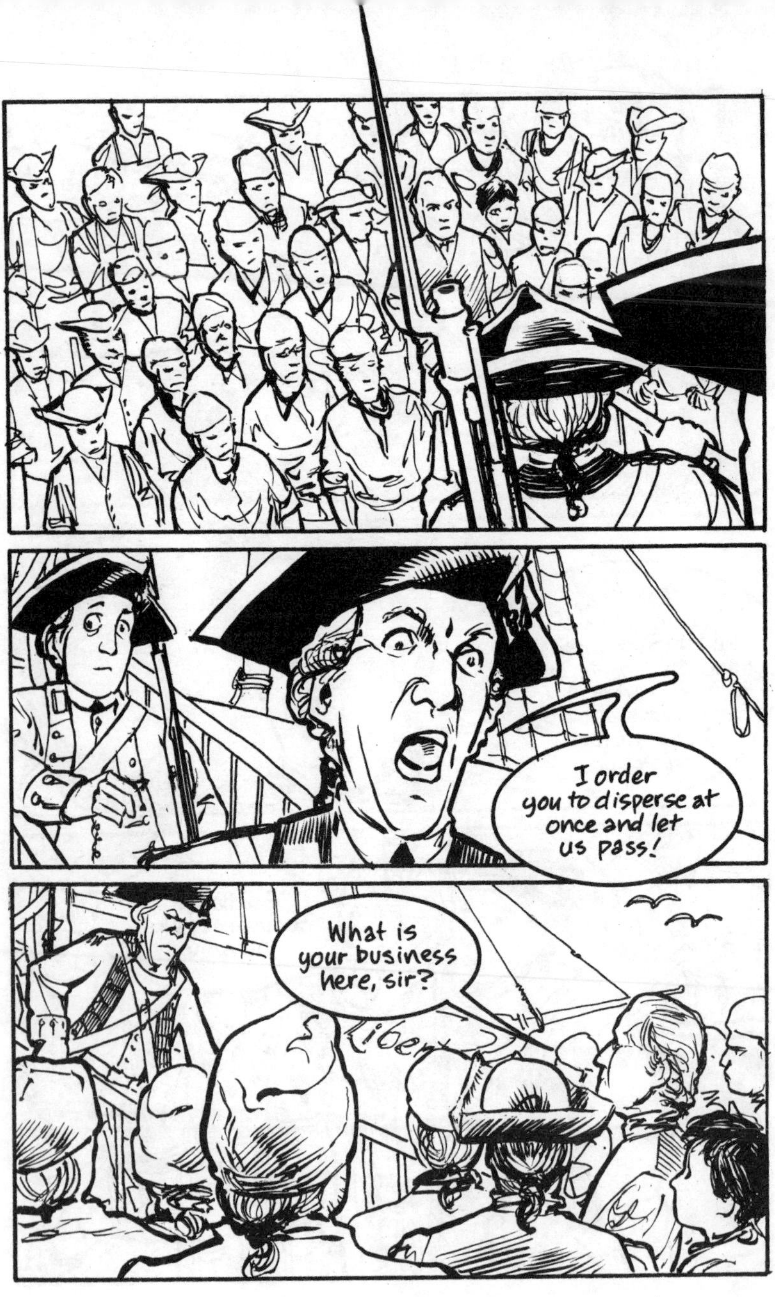
I order you to disperse at once and let us pass!
What is your business here, sir?

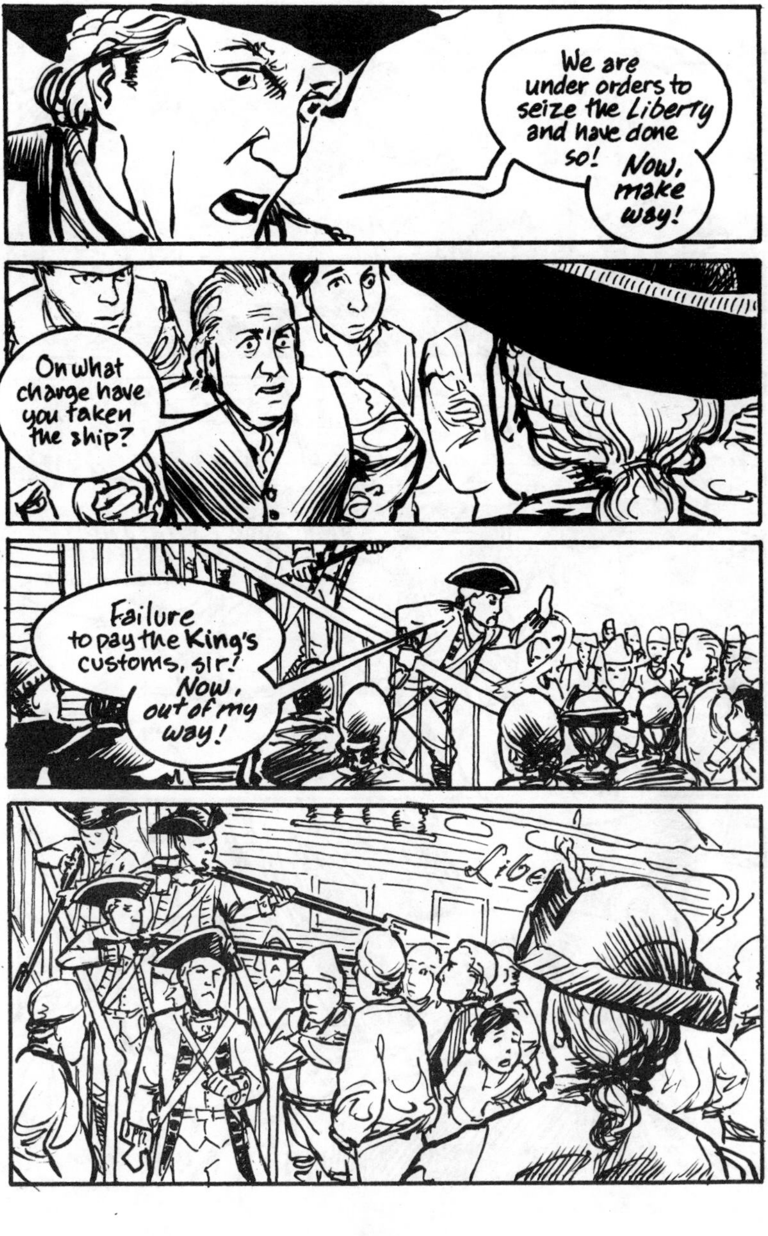
We are under orders to seize the *Liberty* and have done so!
Now, make way!
On what charge have you taken the ship?
Failure to pay the King's customs, sir!
Now, out of my way!
Libe

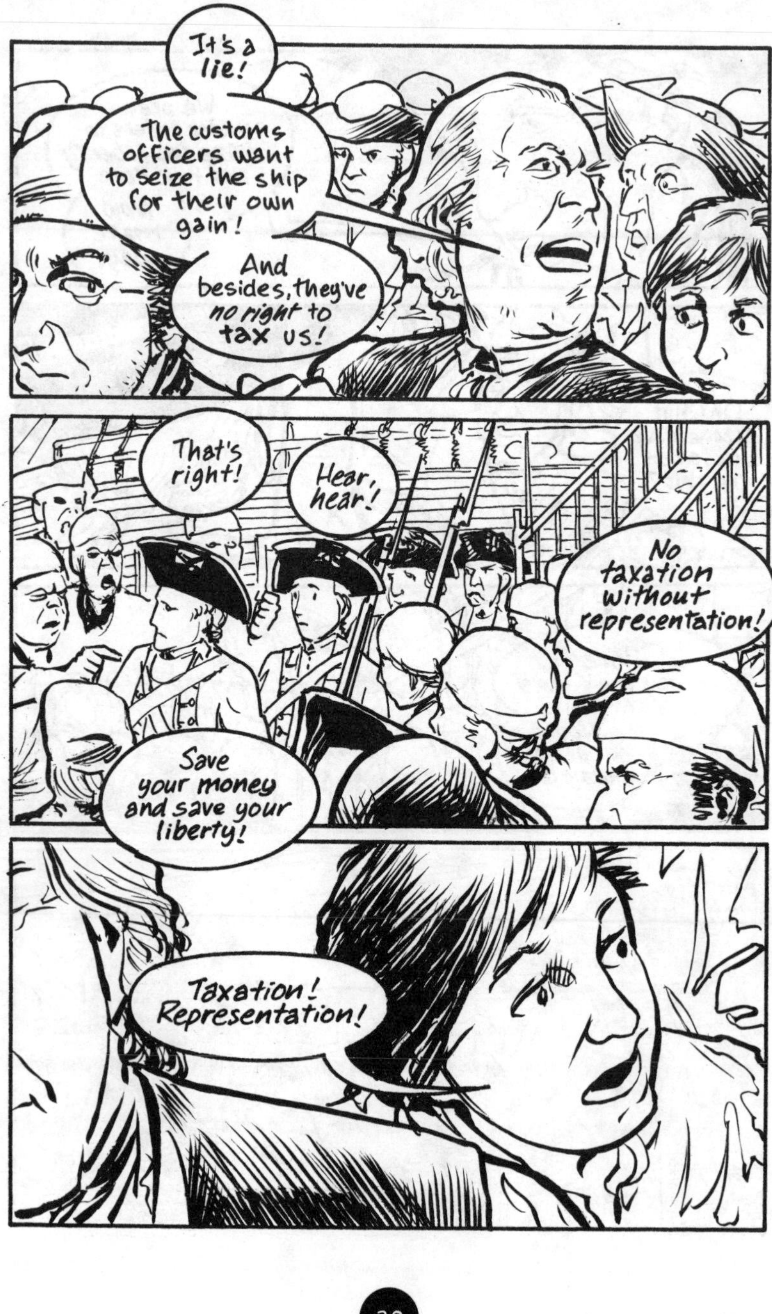
It's a lie!
The customs officers want to seize the ship for their own gain!
And besides, they've *no right* to tax us!
That's right!
Hear, hear!
No taxation without representation!
Save your money and save your liberty!
Taxation! Representation!

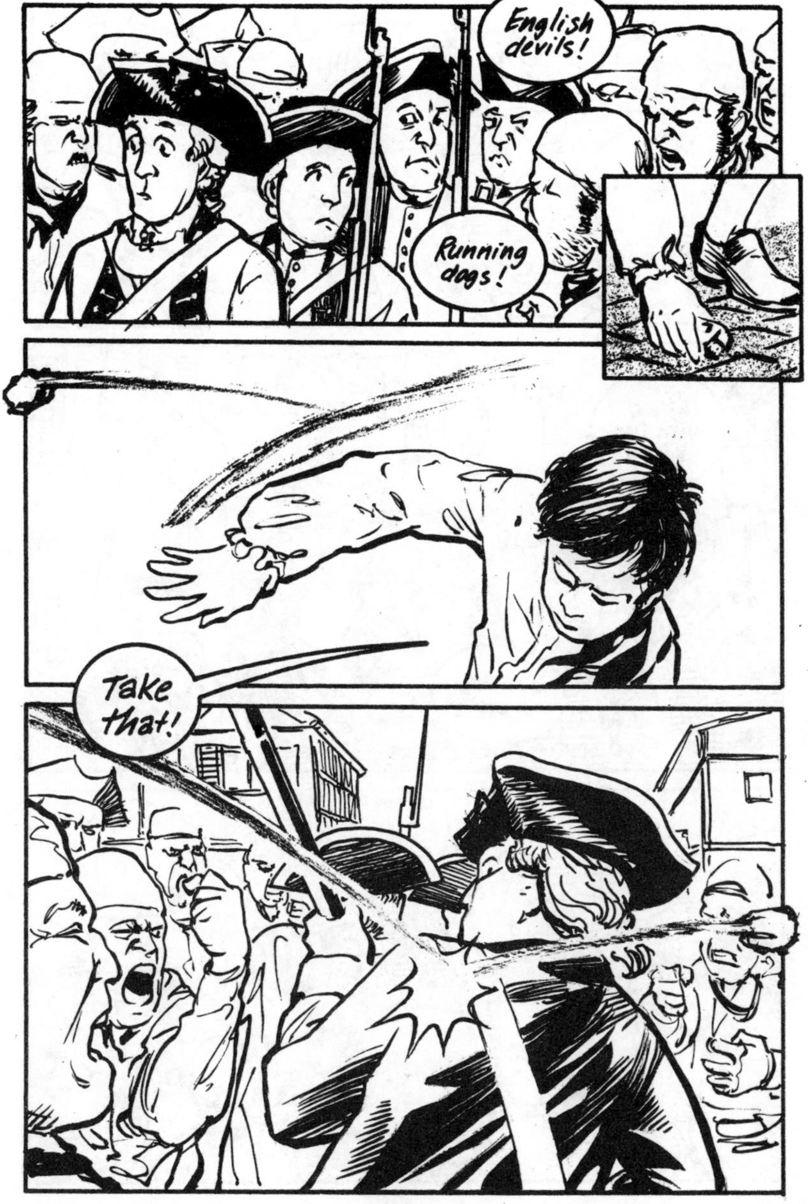
English devils!
Running dogs!
Take that!

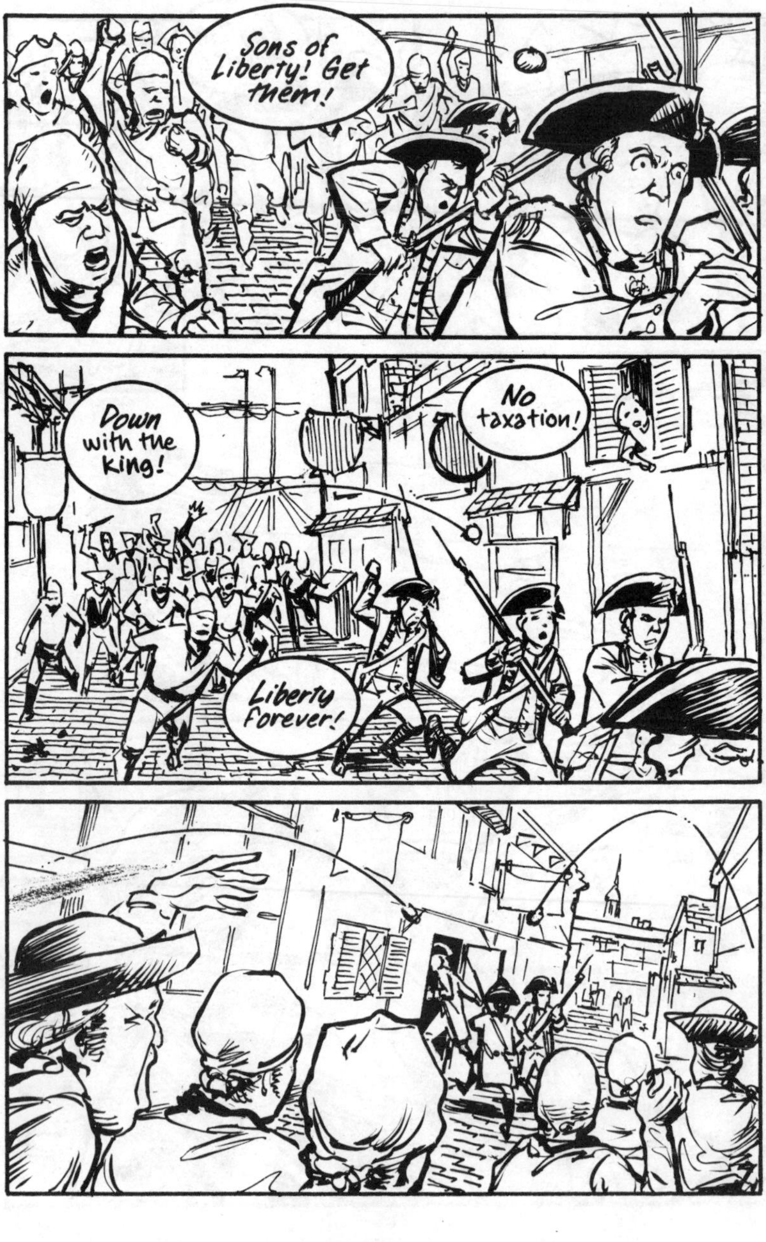
Sons of Liberty! Get them!
Down with the king!
No taxation!
Liberty forever!

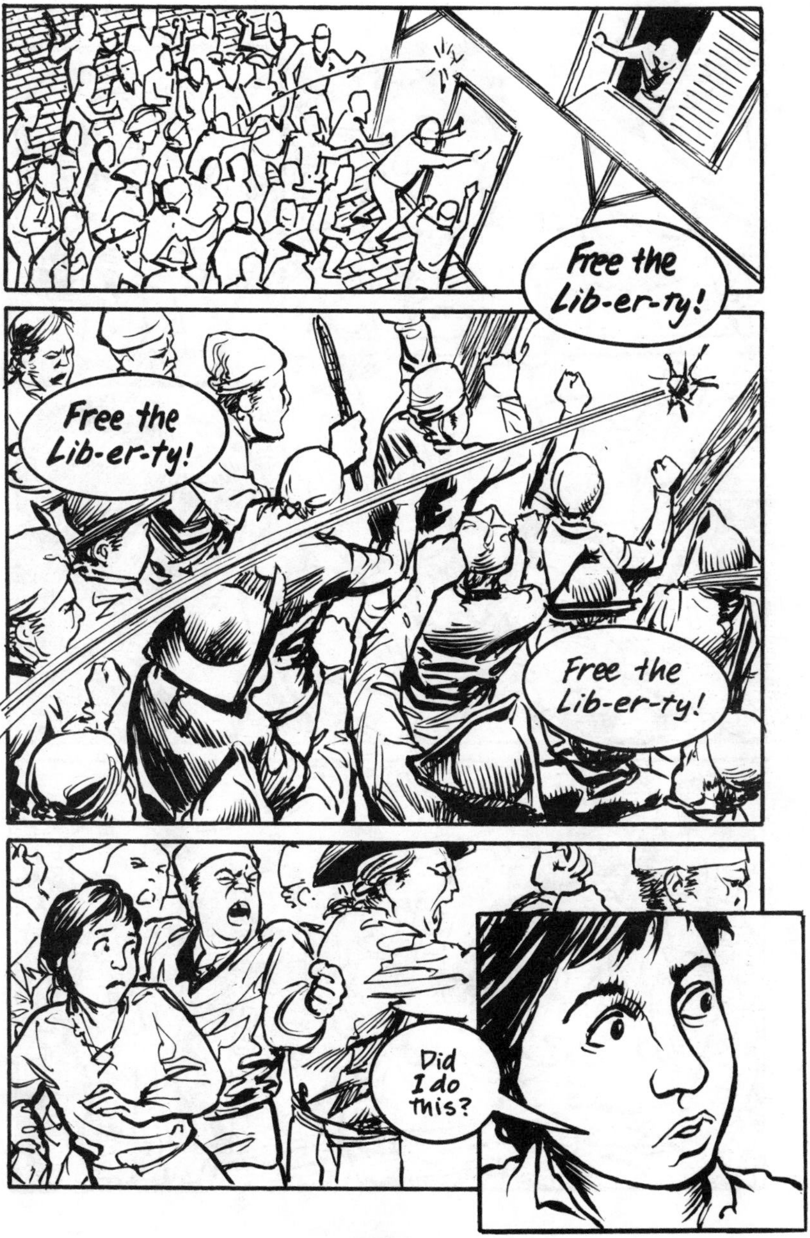
Free the Lib-er-ty!
Free the Lib-er-ty!
Free the Lib-er-ty!
Did I do this?

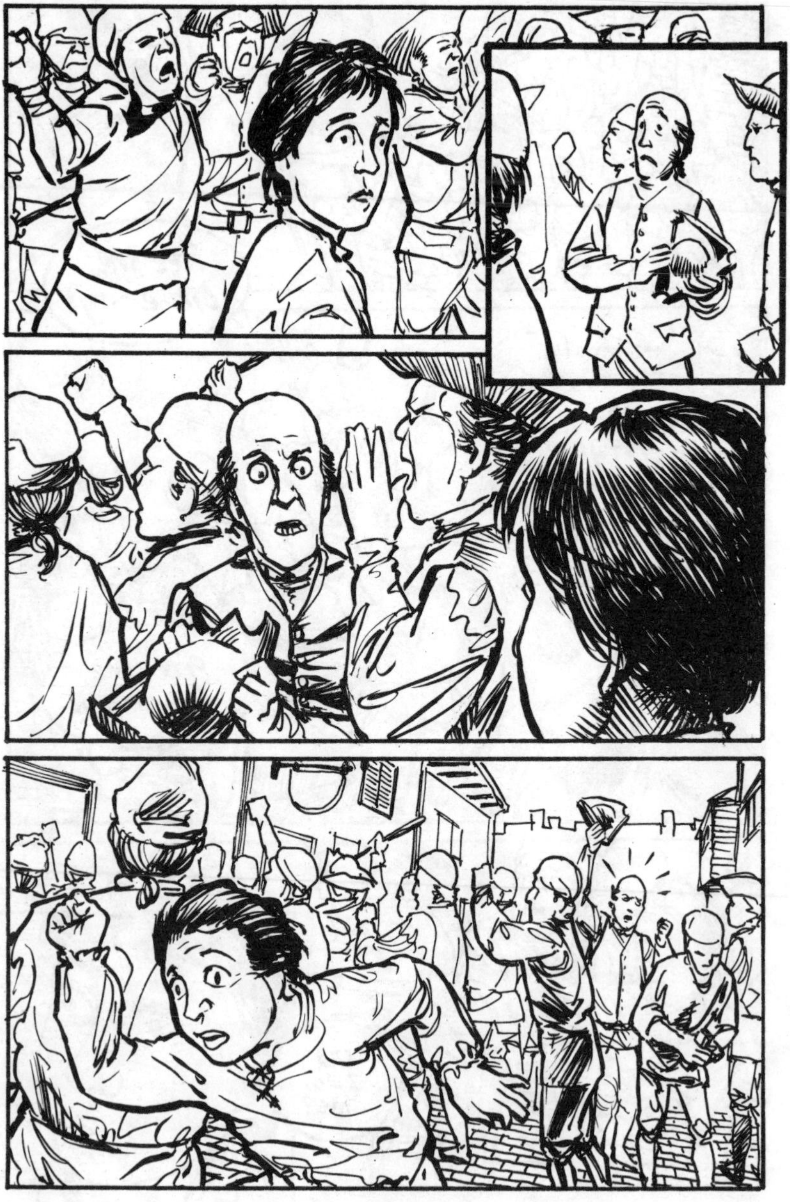

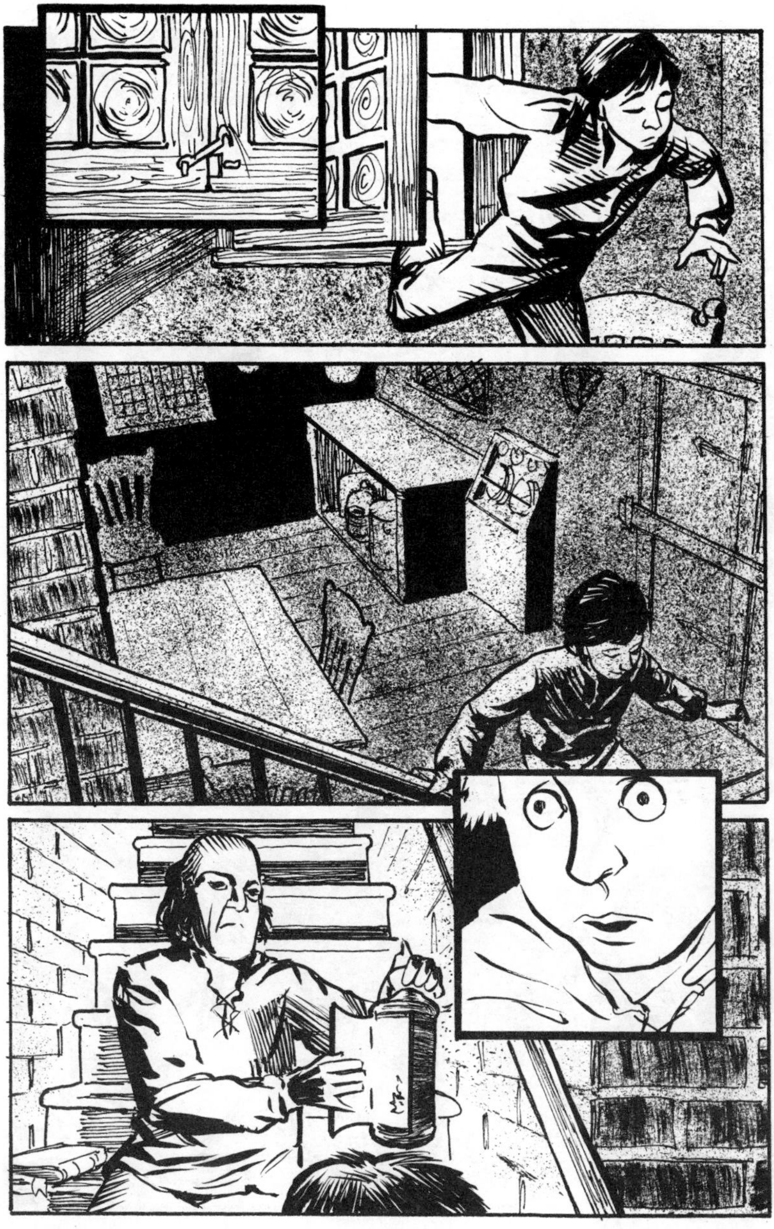

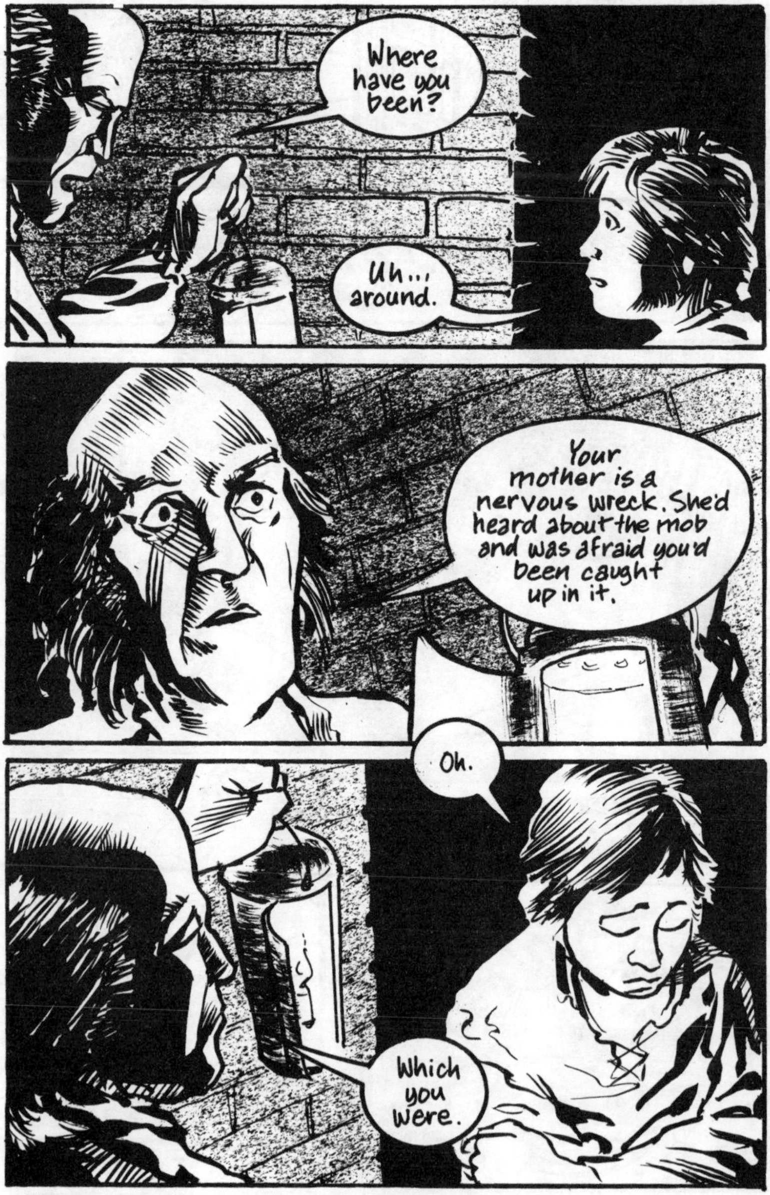
Where have you been?
Uh... around.
Your mother is a nervous wreck. She'd heard about the mob and was afraid you'd been caught up in it.
Oh.
Which you were.

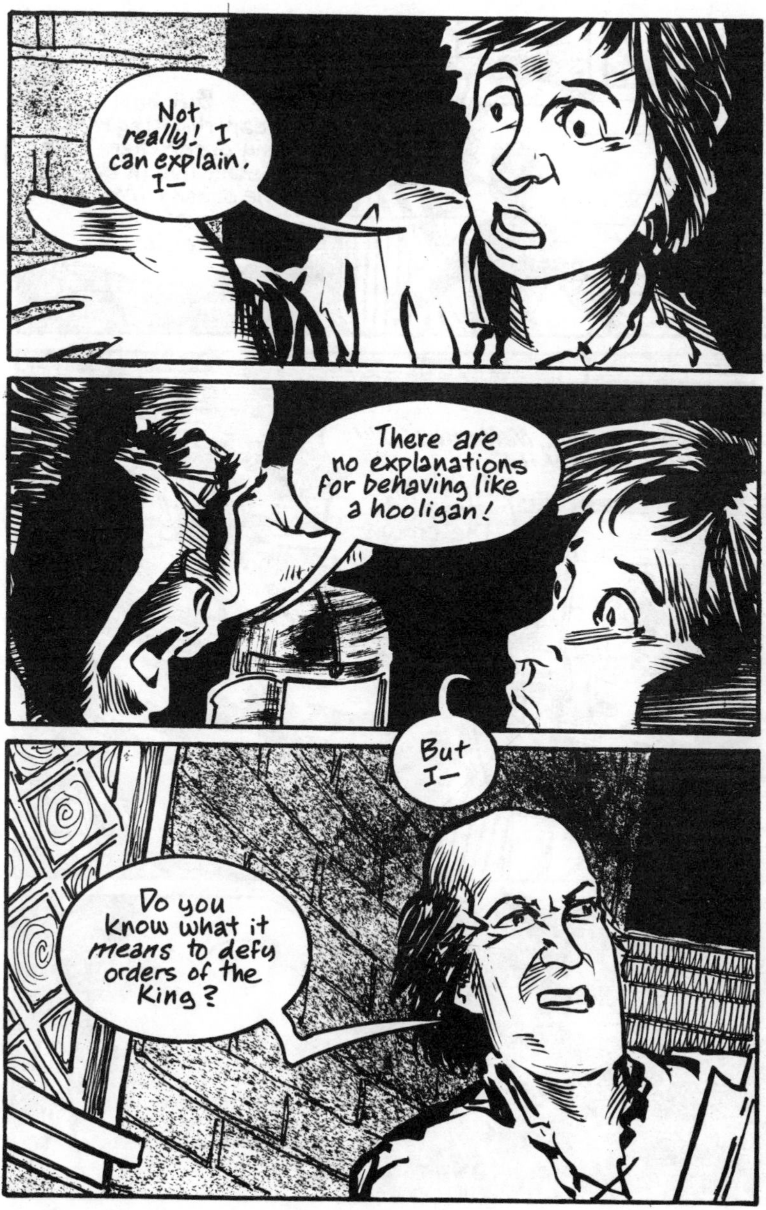
Not really! I can explain. I—
There are no explanations for behaving like a hooligan!
But I—
Do you know what it means to defy orders of the King?

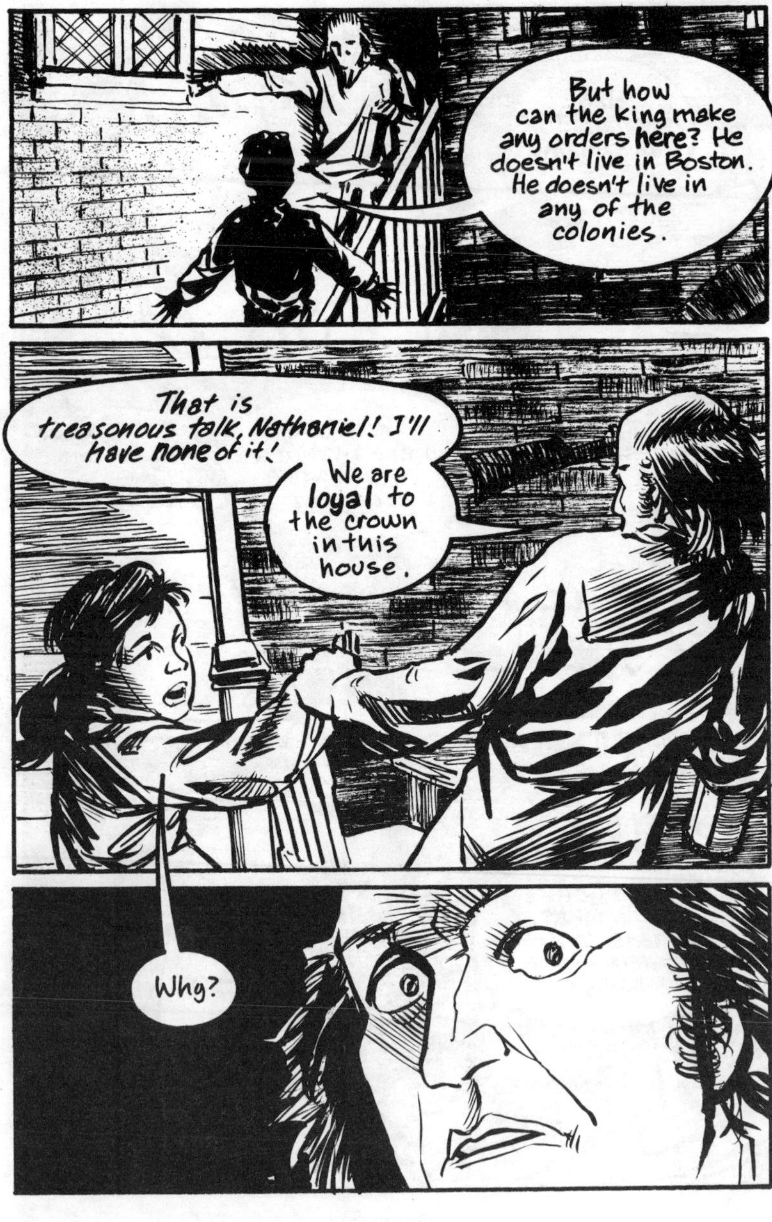
But how can the king make any orders here? He doesn't live in Boston. He doesn't live in any of the colonies.
That is treasonous talk, Nathaniel! I'll have none of it!
We are loyal to the crown in this house.
Why?

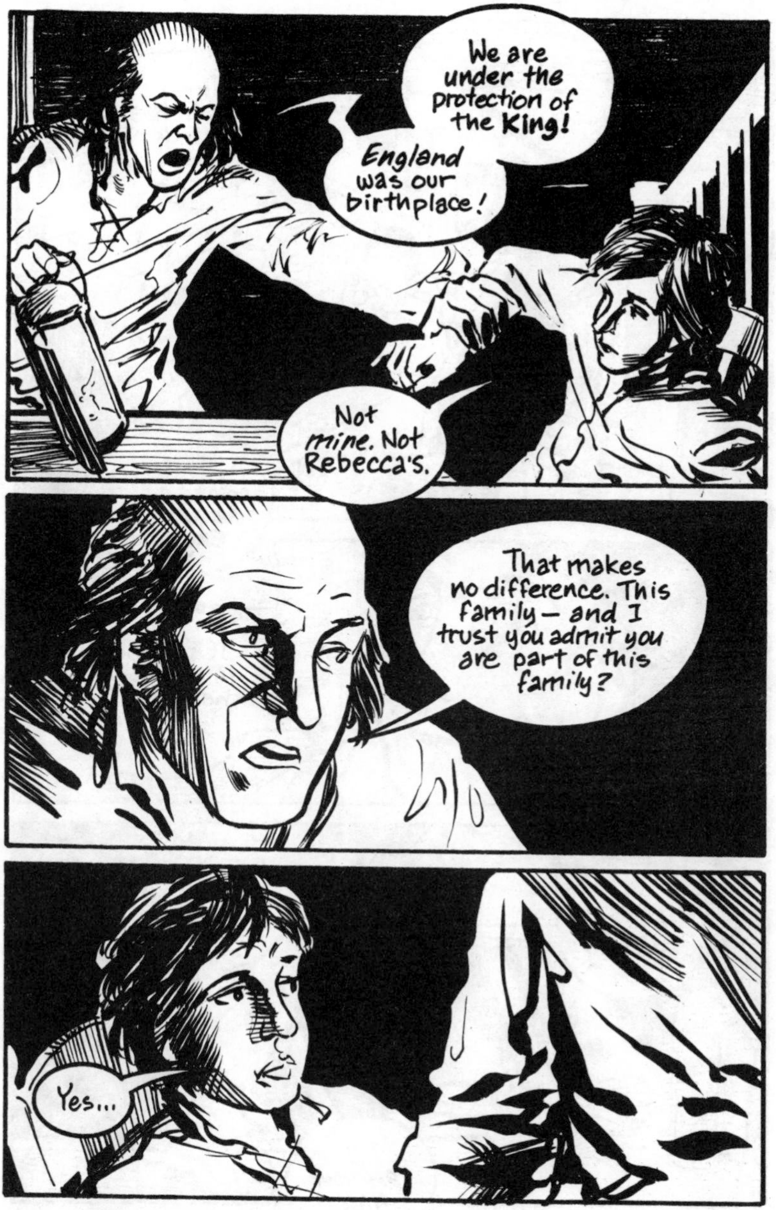
We are under the protection of the **King!**
England was our birthplace!
Not *mine*. Not Rebecca's.
That makes no difference. This family — and I trust you admit you are part of this family?
Yes...

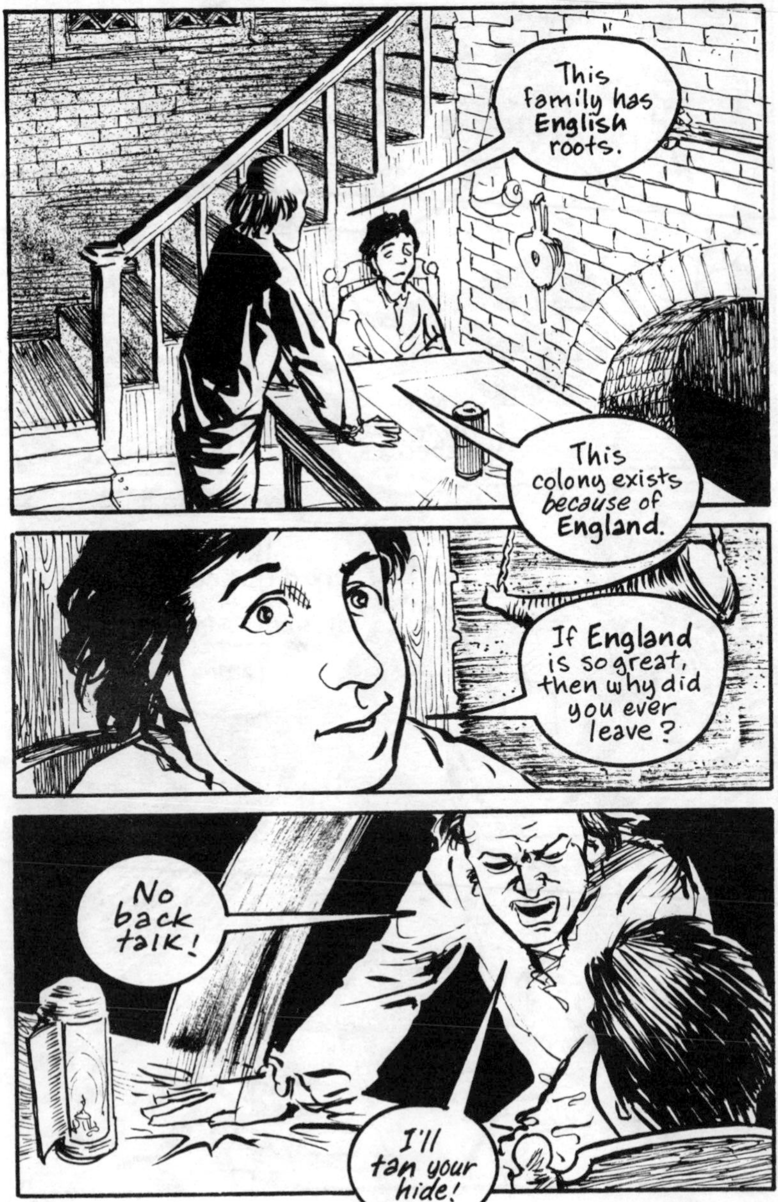
This family has English roots.
This colony exists because of England.
If England is so great, then why did you ever leave?
No back talk!
I'll tan your hide!

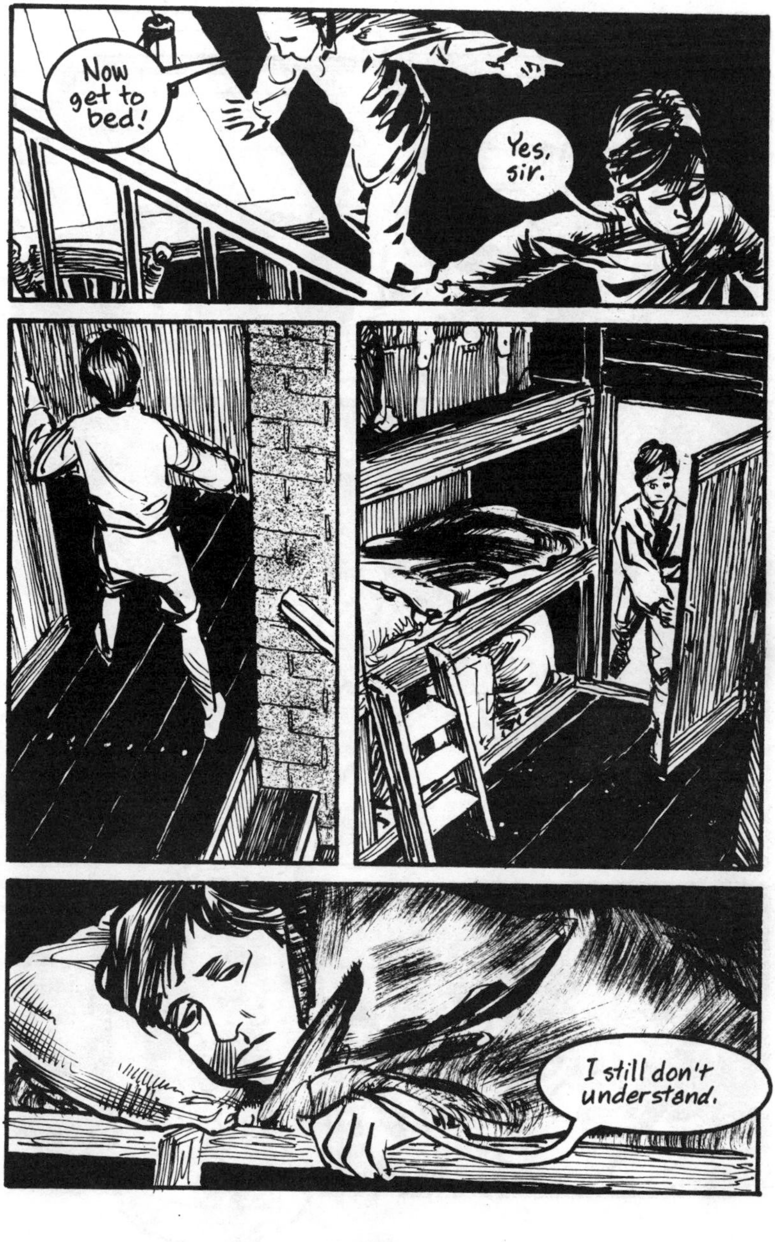
Now get to bed!
Yes, sir.
I still don't understand.

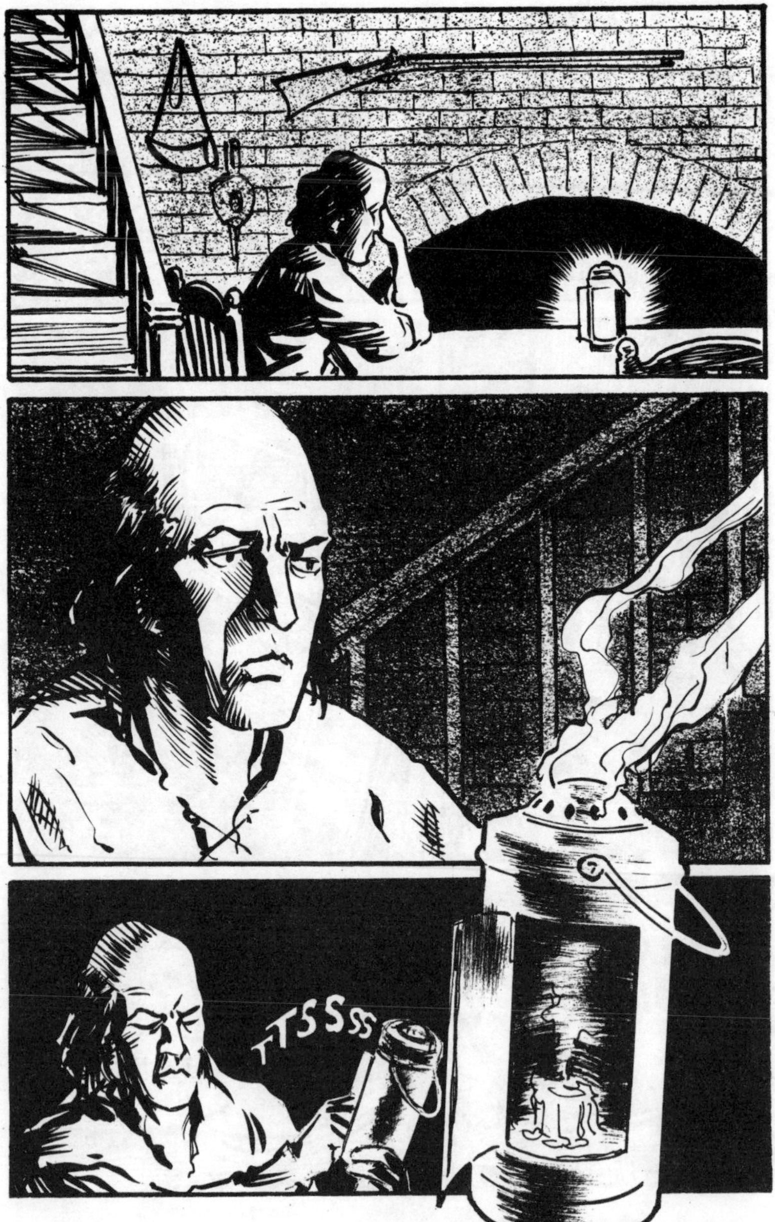
T-TSSSS

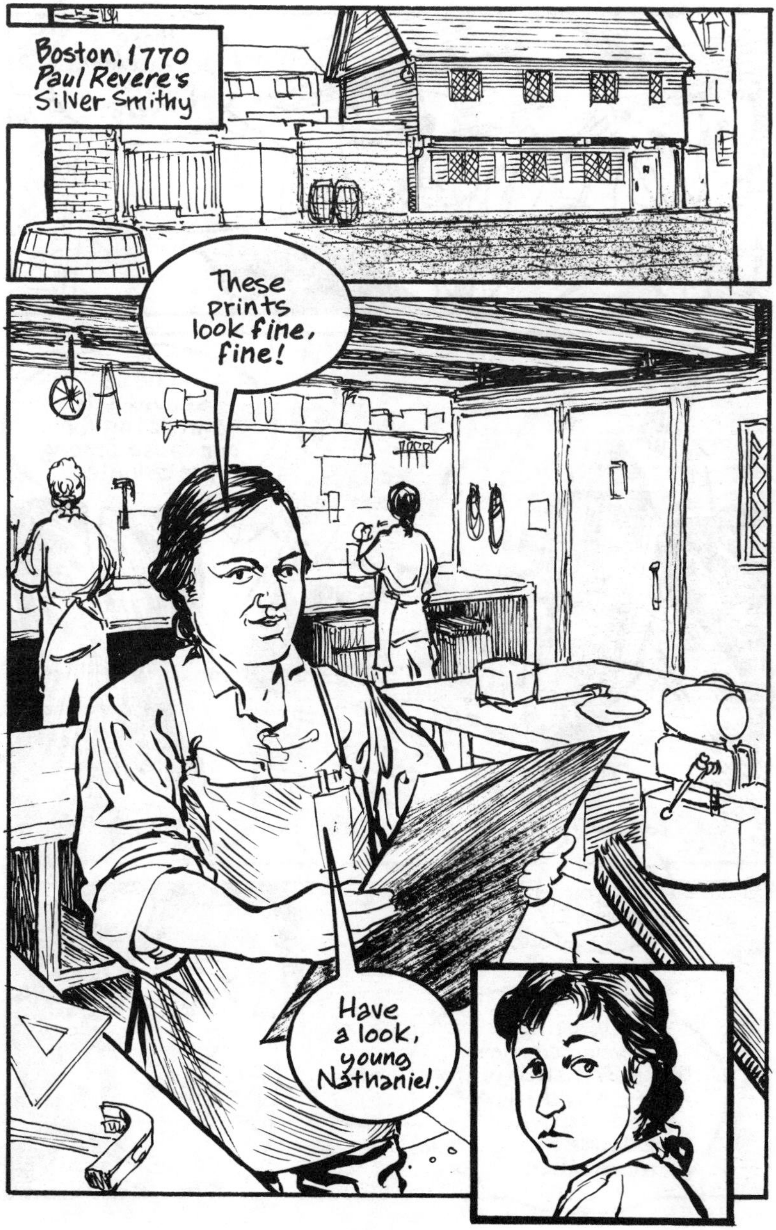
Boston, 1770
Paul Revere's
Silver Smithy
These prints look fine, fine!
Have a look, young Nathaniel.

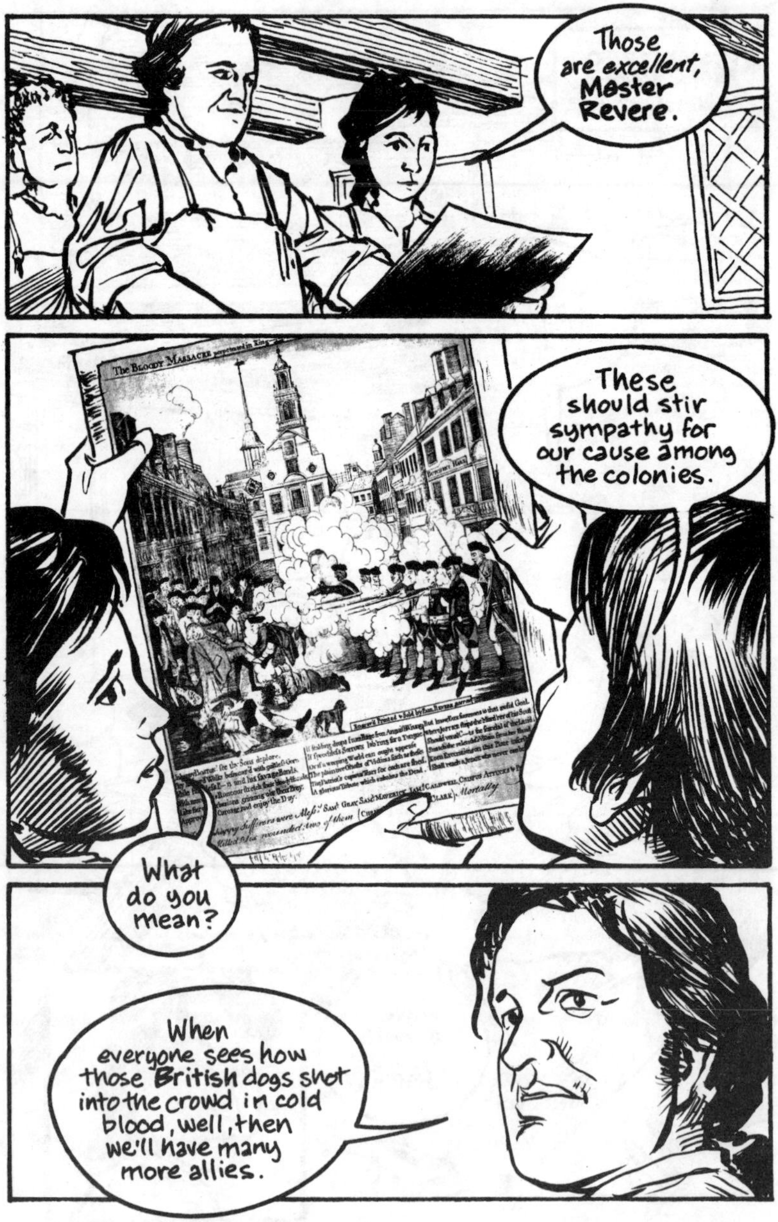
Those are excellent, Master Revere.
The Bloody Massacre
These should stir sympathy for our cause among the colonies.
What do you mean?
When everyone sees how those British dogs shot into the crowd in cold blood, well, then we'll have many more allies.

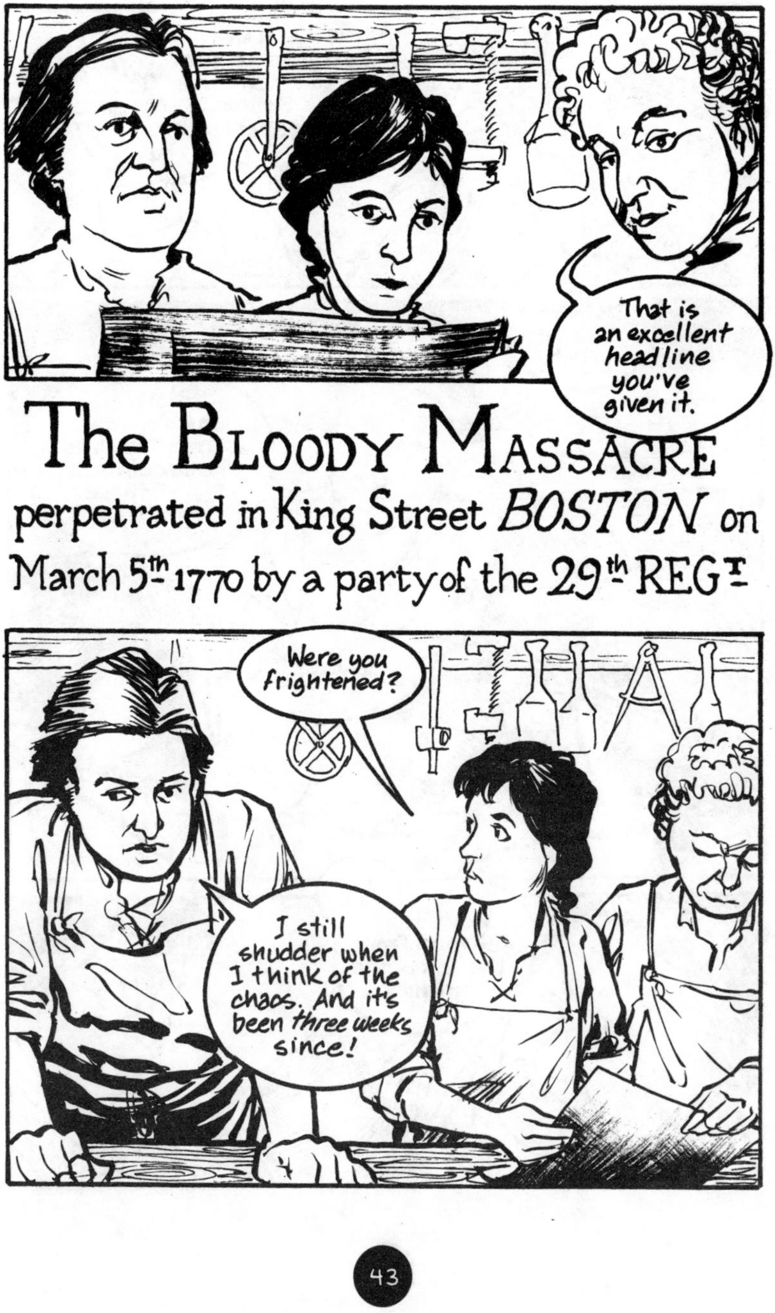
That is an excellent headline you've given it.
The Bloody Massacre
perpetrated in King Street BOSTON on
March 5th 1770 by a party of the 29th REGT
Were you frightened?
I still shudder when I think of the chaos. And it's been *three weeks* since!

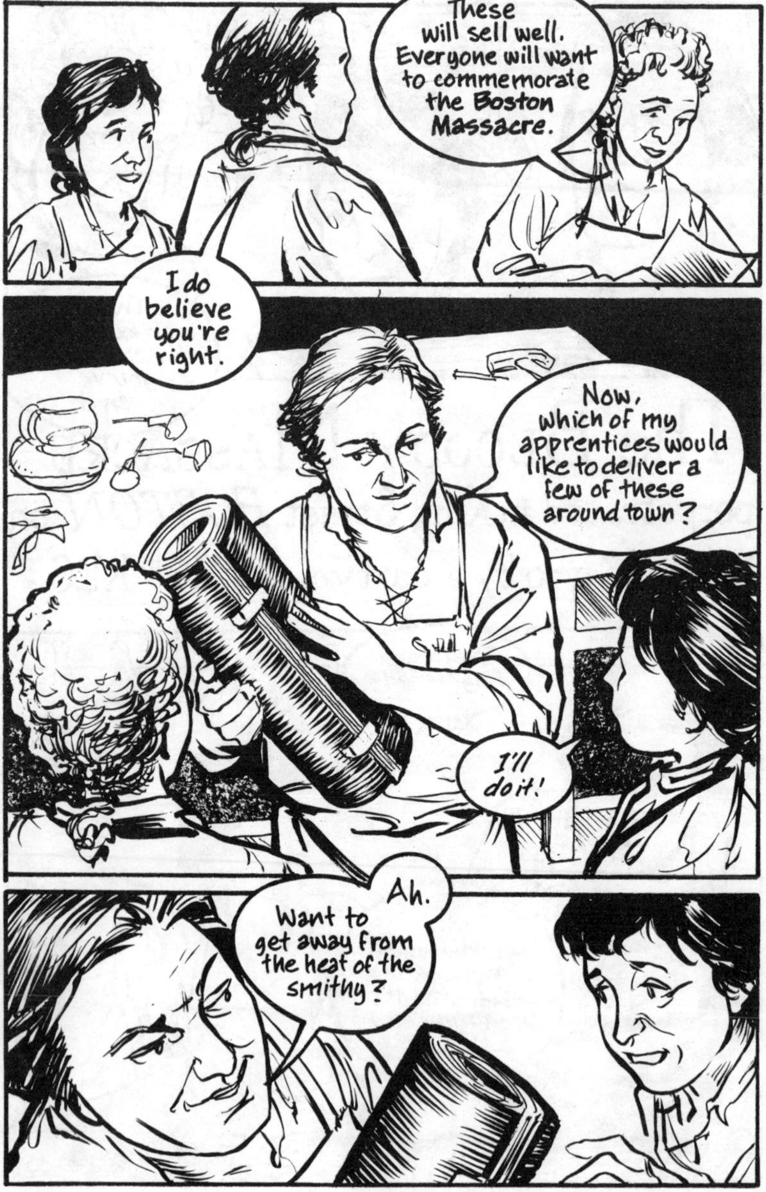
These will sell well. Everyone will want to commemorate the Boston Massacre.
I do believe you're right.
Now, which of my apprentices would like to deliver a few of these around town?
I'll do it!
Ah.
Want to get away from the heat of the smithy?

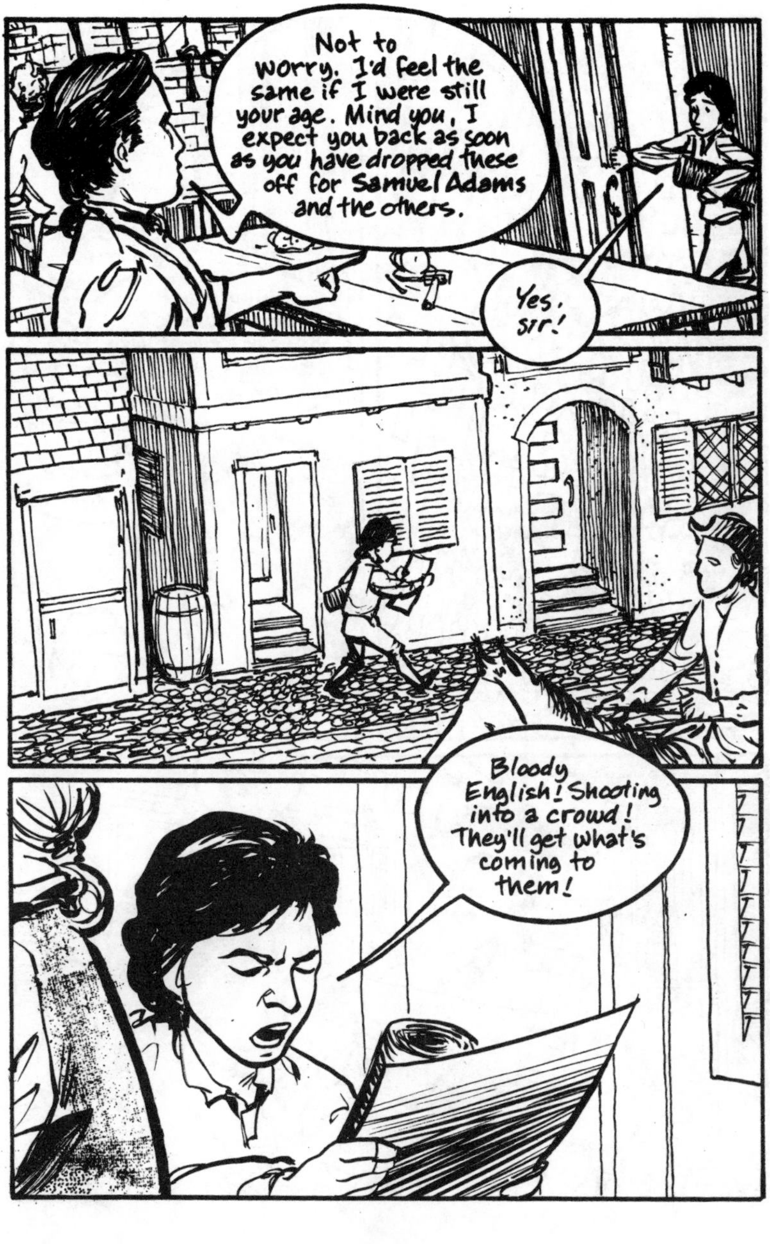
Not to worry. I'd feel the same if I were still your age. Mind you, I expect you back as soon as you have dropped these off for Samuel Adams and the others.
Yes, sir!
Bloody English! Shooting into a crowd! They'll get what's coming to them!

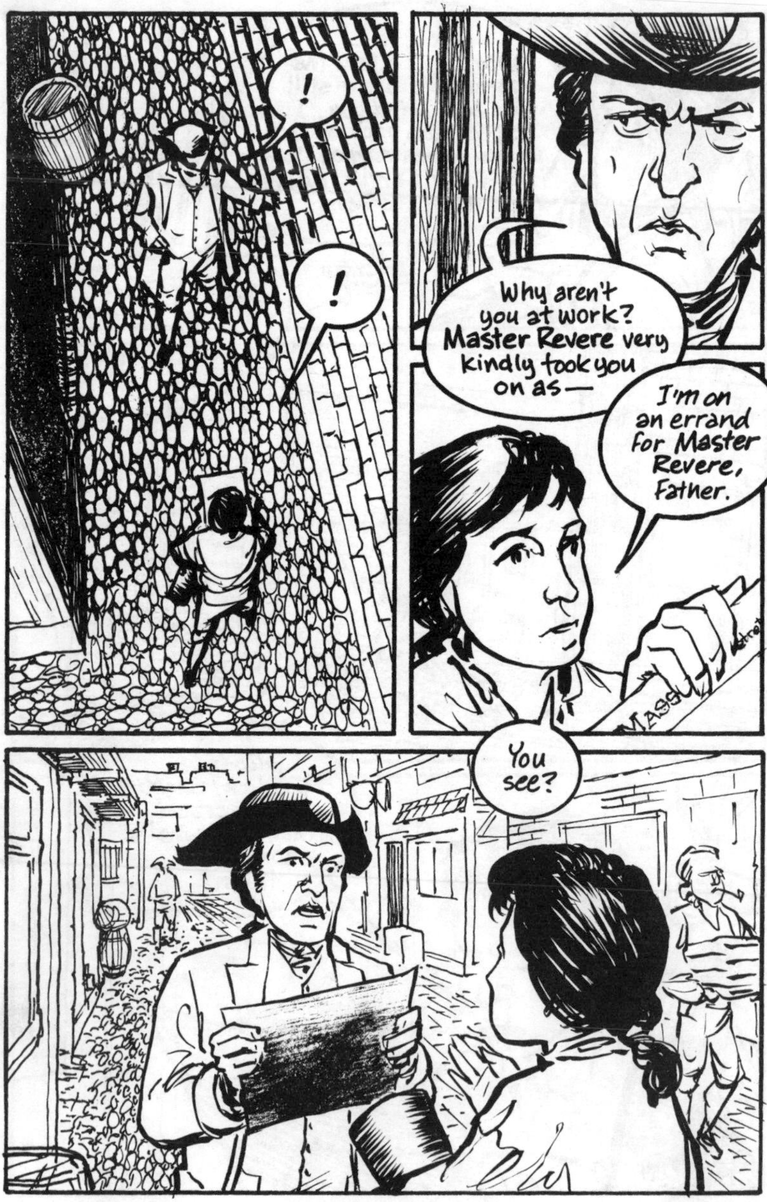
!
!
Why aren't you at work? Master Revere very kindly took you on as—
I'm on an errand for Master Revere, Father.
You see?

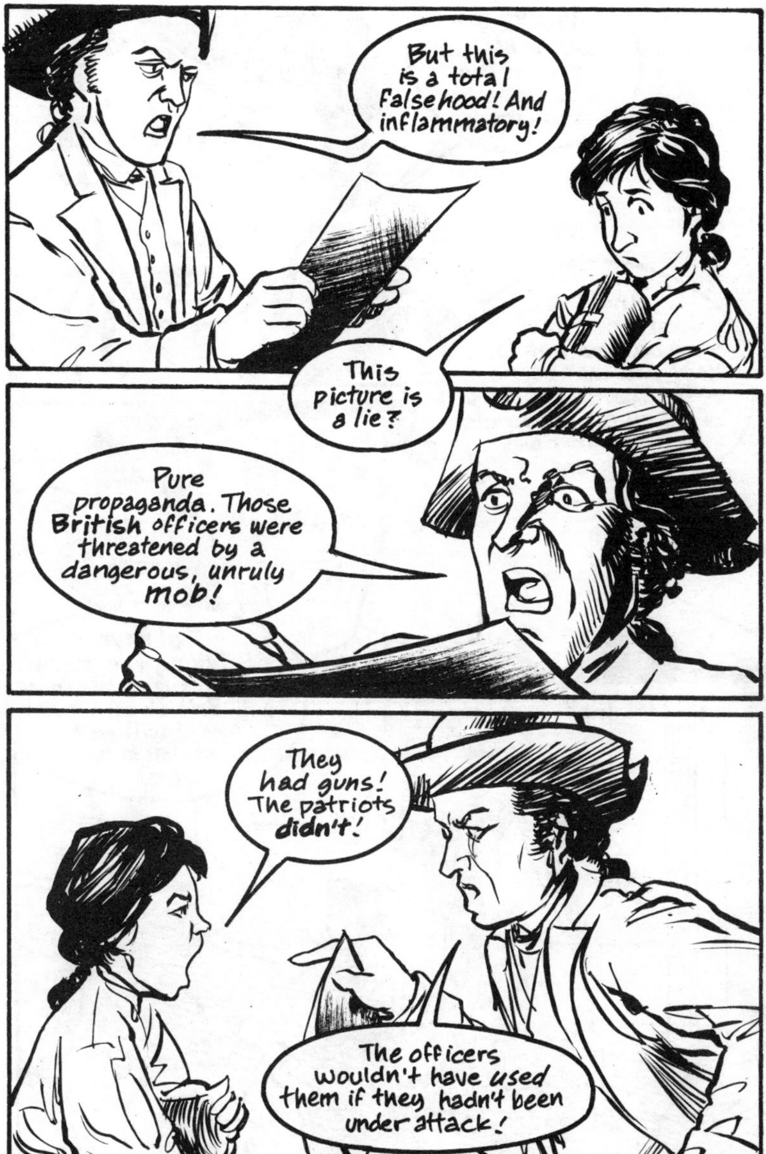
But this is a total falsehood! And inflammatory!
This picture is a lie?
Pure propaganda. Those British officers were threatened by a dangerous, unruly mob!
They had guns! The patriots didn't!
The officers wouldn't have used them if they hadn't been under attack!

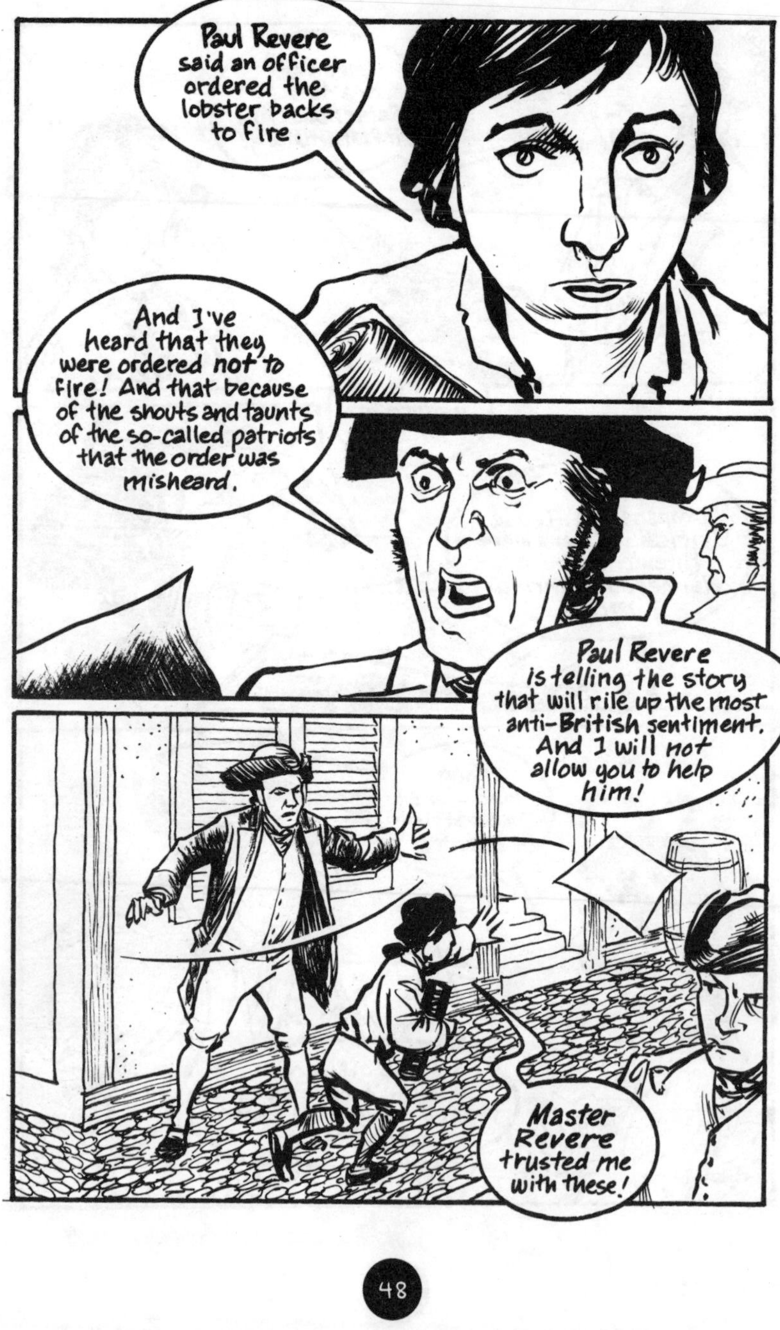
Paul Revere said an officer ordered the lobster backs to fire.
And I've heard that they were ordered not to fire! And that because of the shouts and taunts of the so-called patriots that the order was misheard.
Paul Revere is telling the story that will rile up the most anti-British sentiment. And I will not allow you to help him!
Master Revere trusted me with these!

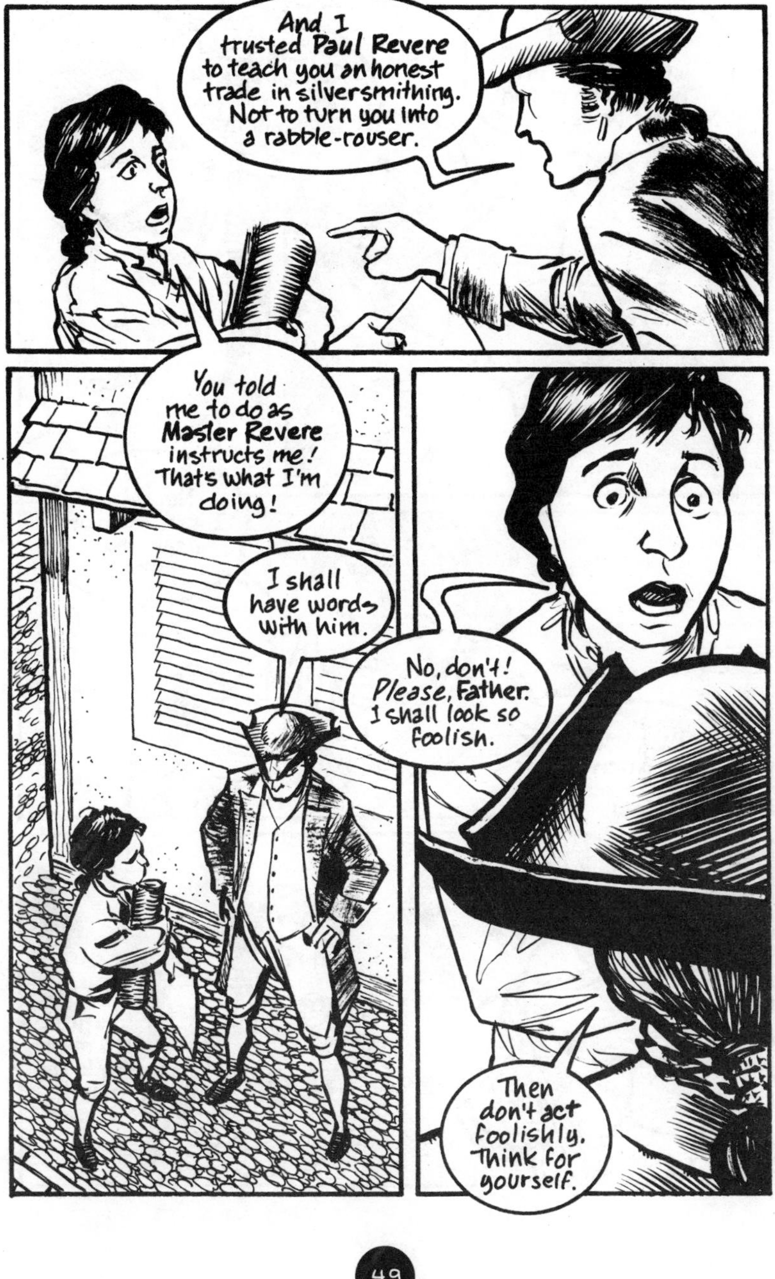
And I trusted Paul Revere to teach you an honest trade in silversmithing. Not to turn you into a rabble-rouser.
You told me to do as Master Revere instructs me! That's what I'm doing!
I shall have words with him.
No, don't! Please, Father. I shall look so foolish.
Then don't act foolishly. Think for yourself.

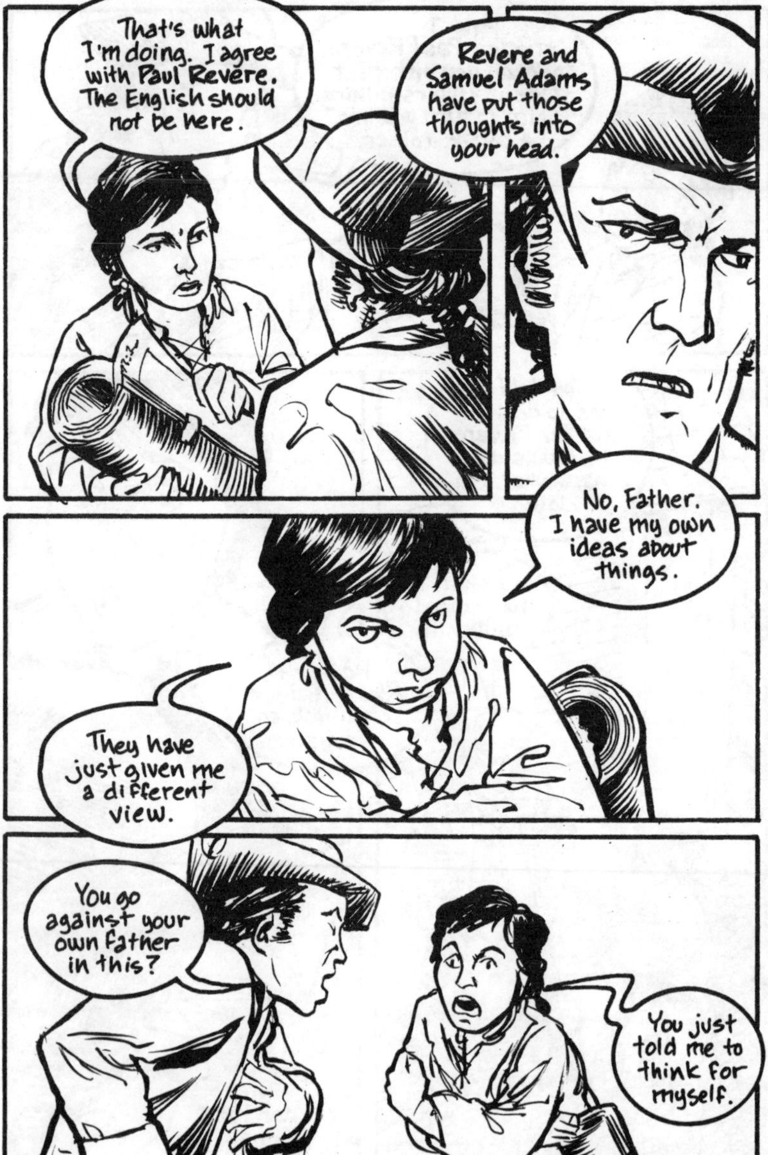
That's what I'm doing. I agree with Paul Revere. The English should not be here.
Revere and Samuel Adams have put those thoughts into your head.
No, Father. I have my own ideas about things.
They have just given me a different view.
You go against your own father in this?
You just told me to think for myself.

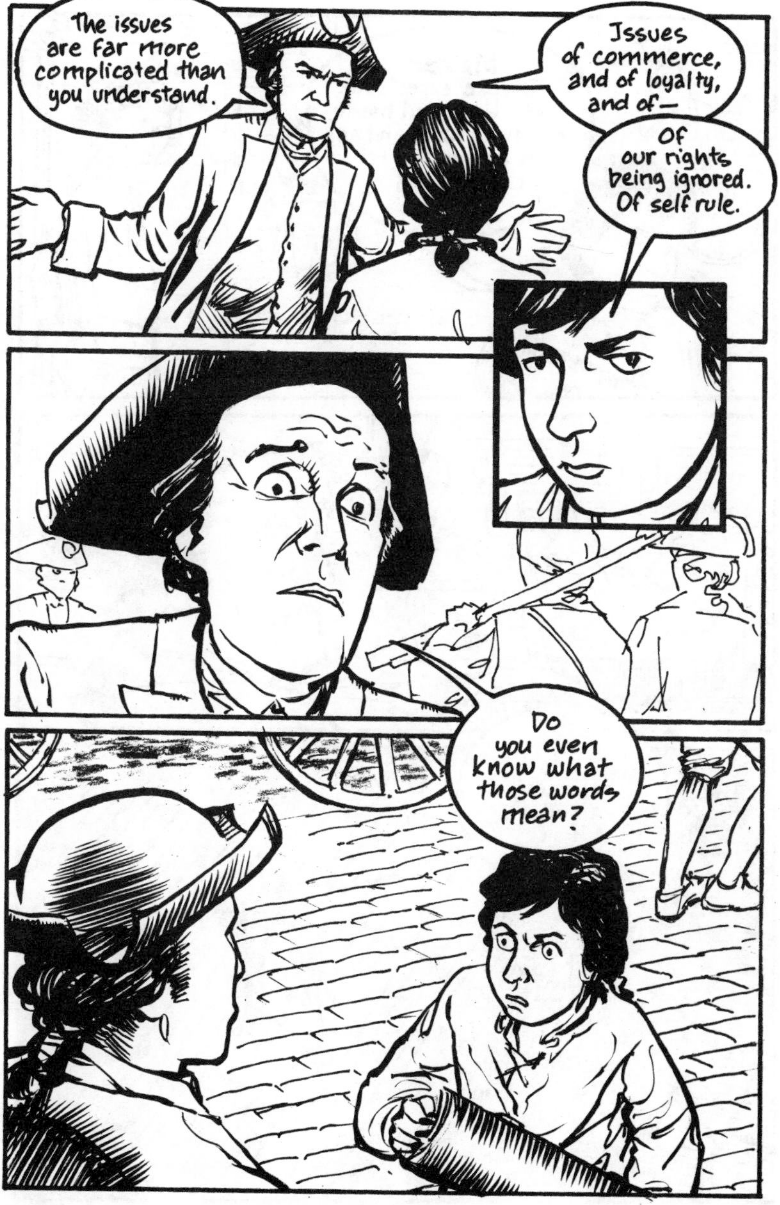
The issues are far more complicated than you understand.
Issues of commerce, and of loyalty, and of—
Of our rights being ignored. Of self rule.
Do you even know what those words mean?

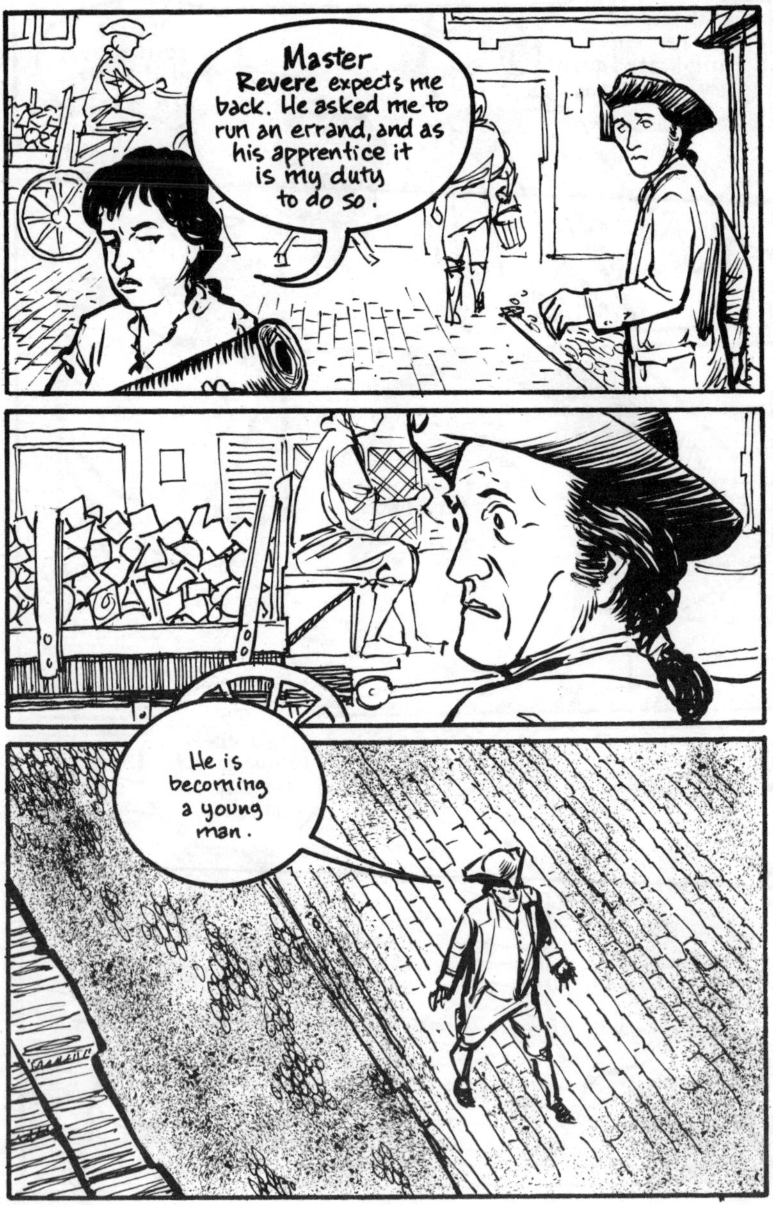
Master Revere expects me back. He asked me to run an errand, and as his apprentice it is my duty to do so.
He is becoming a young man.

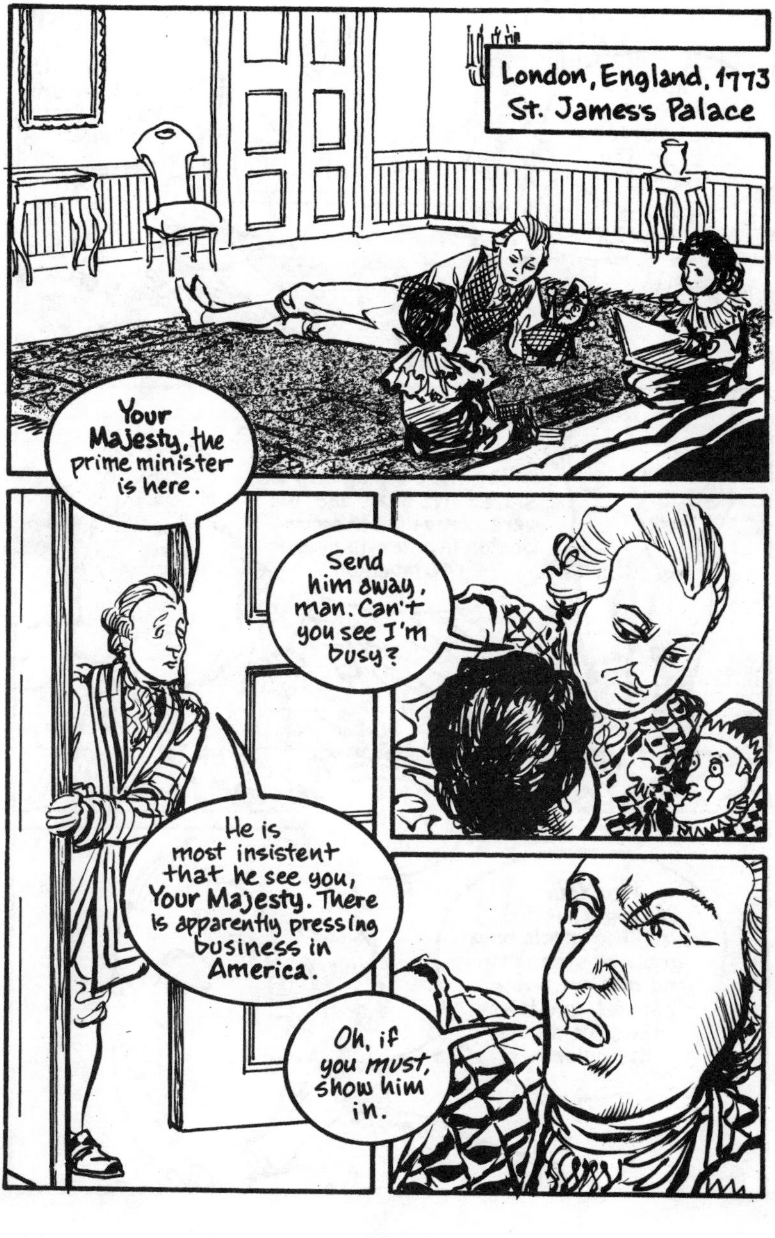
London, England, 1773
St. James's Palace
Your Majesty, the prime minister is here.
Send him away, man. Can't you see I'm busy?
He is most insistent that he see you, Your Majesty. There is apparently pressing business in America.
Oh, if you *must*, show him in.

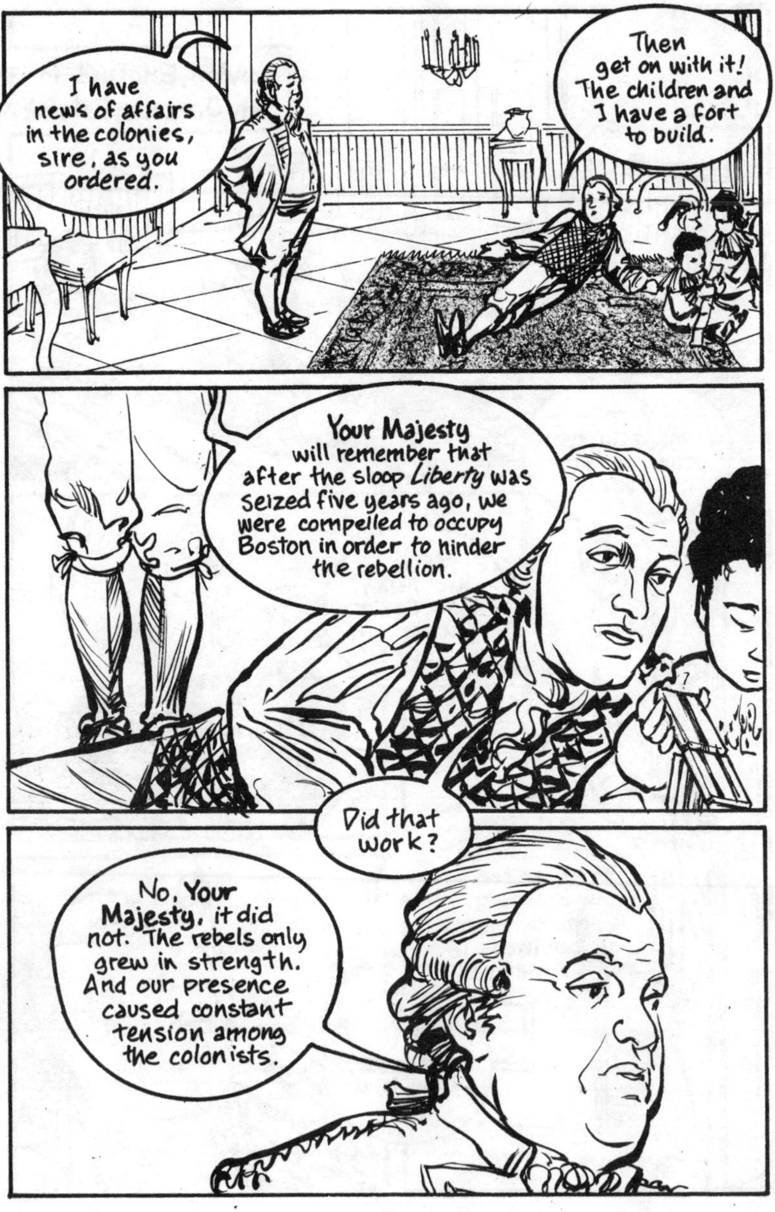
I have news of affairs in the colonies, sire, as you ordered.
Then get on with it! The children and I have a fort to build.
Your Majesty will remember that after the sloop *Liberty* was seized five years ago, we were compelled to occupy Boston in order to hinder the rebellion.
Did that work?
No, Your Majesty, it did not. The rebels only grew in strength. And our presence caused constant tension among the colonists.

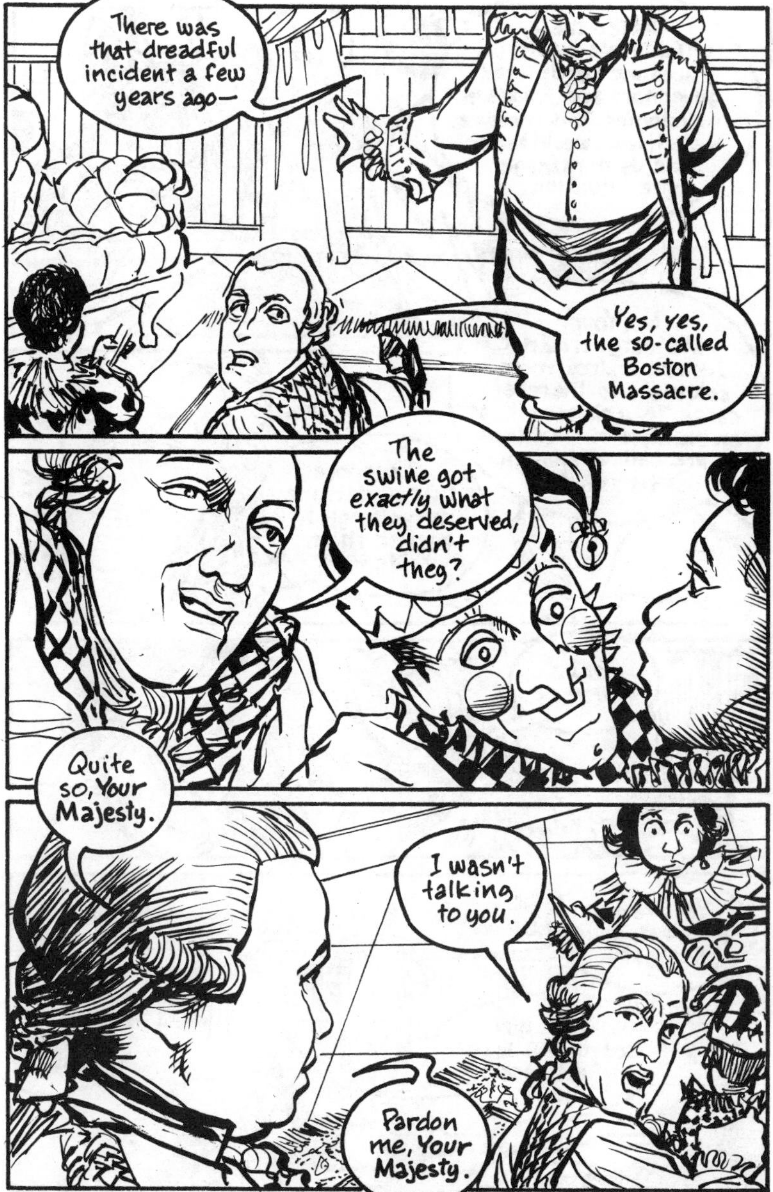
There was that dreadful incident a few years ago—
Yes, yes, the so-called Boston Massacre.
The swine got *exactly* what they deserved, didn't they?
Quite so, Your Majesty.
I wasn't talking to you.
Pardon me, Your Majesty.

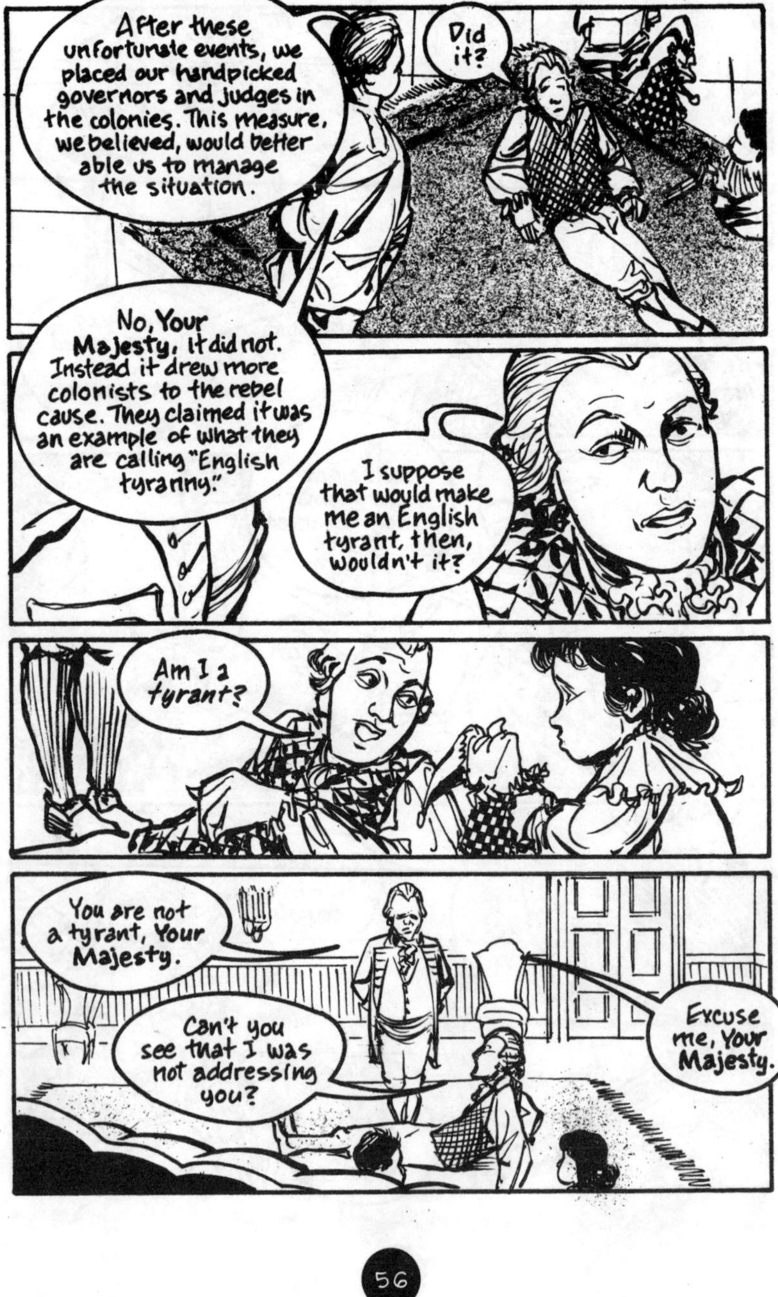
After these unfortunate events, we placed our handpicked governors and judges in the colonies. This measure, we believed, would better able us to manage the situation.
Did it?
No, Your Majesty. It did not. Instead it drew more colonists to the rebel cause. They claimed it was an example of what they are calling "English tyranny."
I suppose that would make me an English tyrant, then, wouldn't it?
Am I a *tyrant*?
You are not a tyrant, Your Majesty.
Can't you see that I was not addressing you?
Excuse me, Your Majesty.

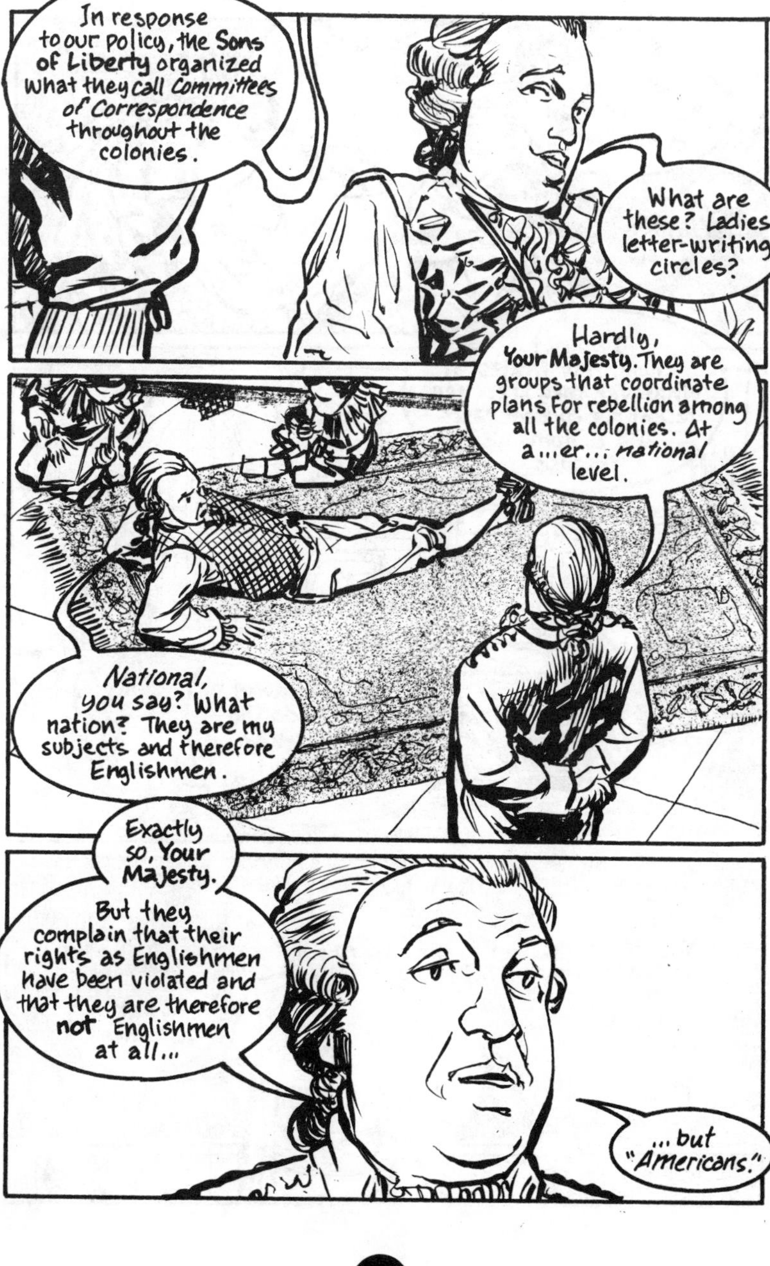
In response to our policy, the Sons of Liberty organized what they call Committees of Correspondence throughout the colonies.
What are these? Ladies' letter-writing circles?
Hardly, Your Majesty. They are groups that coordinate plans for rebellion among all the colonies. At a...er... national level.
National, you say? What nation? They are my subjects and therefore Englishmen.
Exactly so, Your Majesty.
But they complain that their rights as Englishmen have been violated and that they are therefore not Englishmen at all...
...but "Americans."

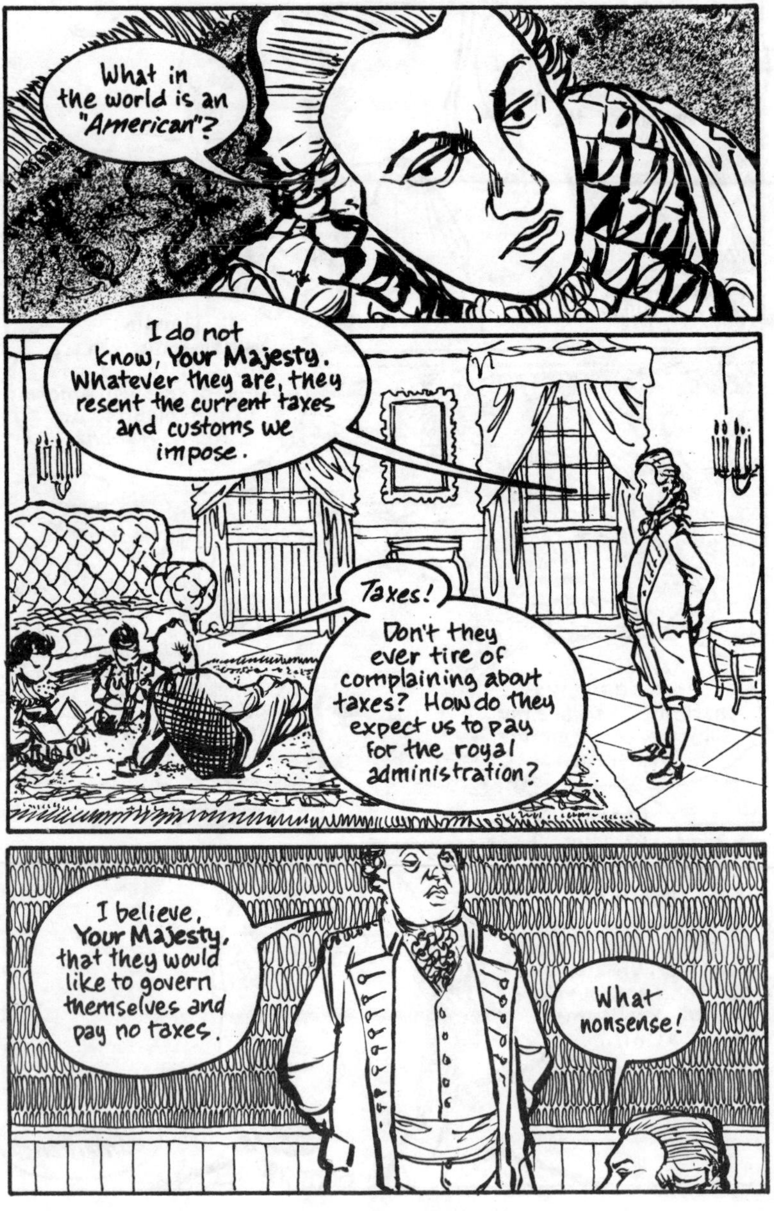
What in the world is an "American"?
I do not know, Your Majesty. Whatever they are, they resent the current taxes and customs we impose.
Taxes!
Don't they ever tire of complaining about taxes? How do they expect us to pay for the royal administration?
I believe, Your Majesty, that they would like to govern themselves and pay no taxes.
What nonsense!

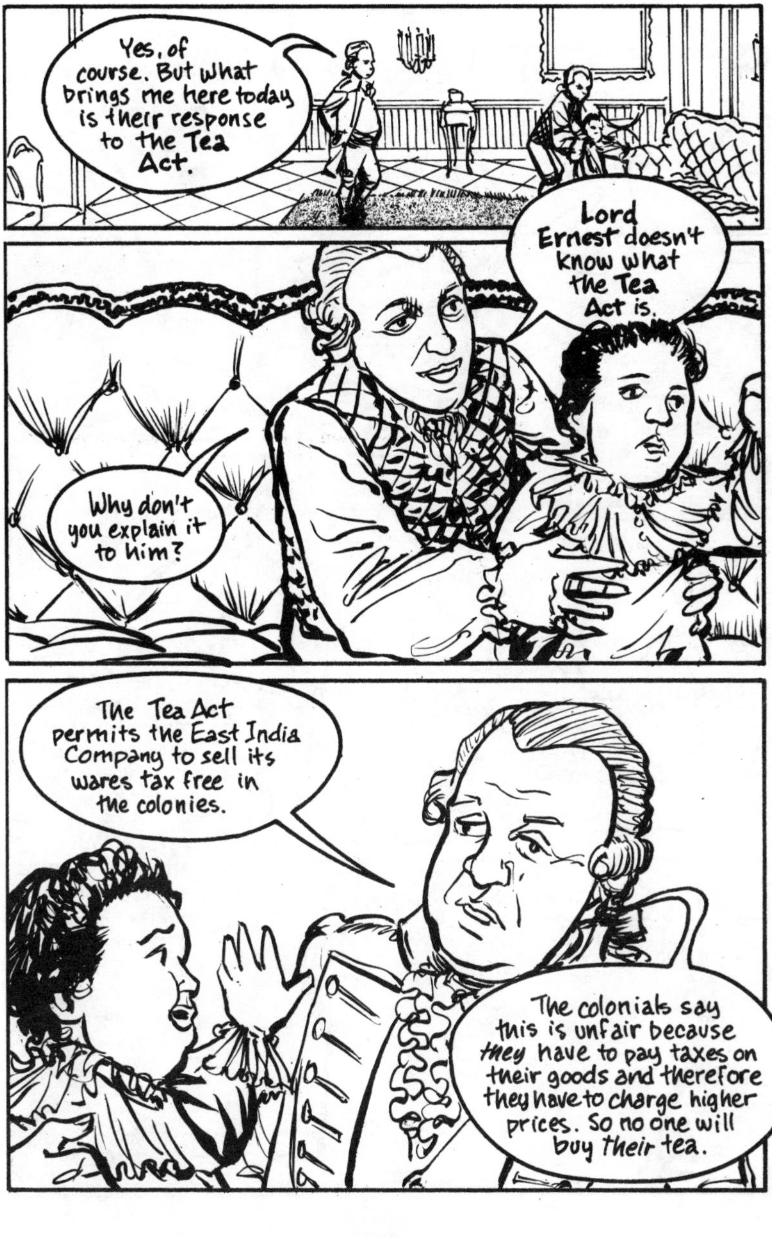
Yes, of course. But what brings me here today is their response to the Tea Act.
Lord Ernest doesn't know what the Tea Act is.
Why don't you explain it to him?
The Tea Act permits the East India Company to sell its wares tax free in the colonies.
The colonials say this is unfair because *they* have to pay taxes on their goods and therefore they have to charge higher prices. So no one will buy *their* tea.

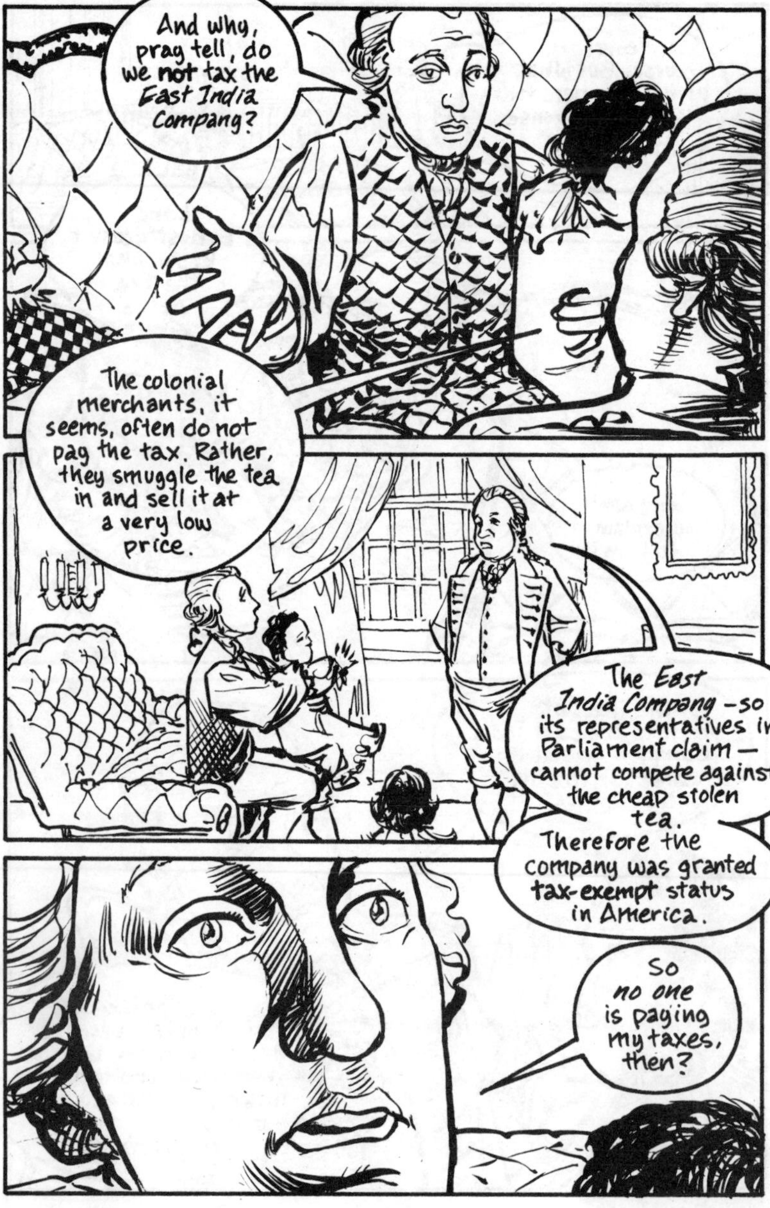
And why, pray tell, do we not tax the East India Company?
The colonial merchants, it seems, often do not pay the tax. Rather, they smuggle the tea in and sell it at a very low price.
The East India Company—so its representatives in Parliament claim—cannot compete against the cheap stolen tea.
Therefore the company was granted tax-exempt status in America.
So no one is paying my taxes, then?

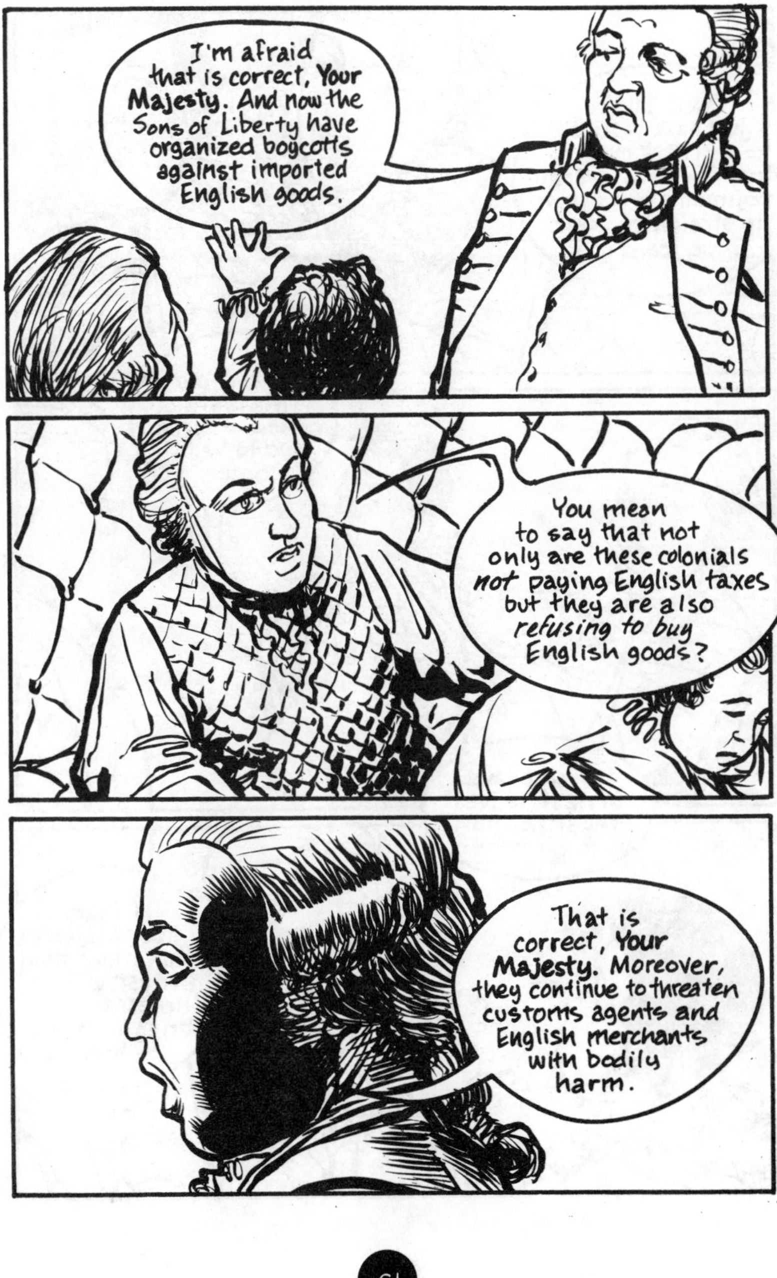
I'm afraid that is correct, Your Majesty. And now the Sons of Liberty have organized boycotts against imported English goods.
You mean to say that not only are these colonials *not* paying English taxes but they are also *refusing to buy* English goods?
That is correct, Your Majesty. Moreover, they continue to threaten customs agents and English merchants with bodily harm.

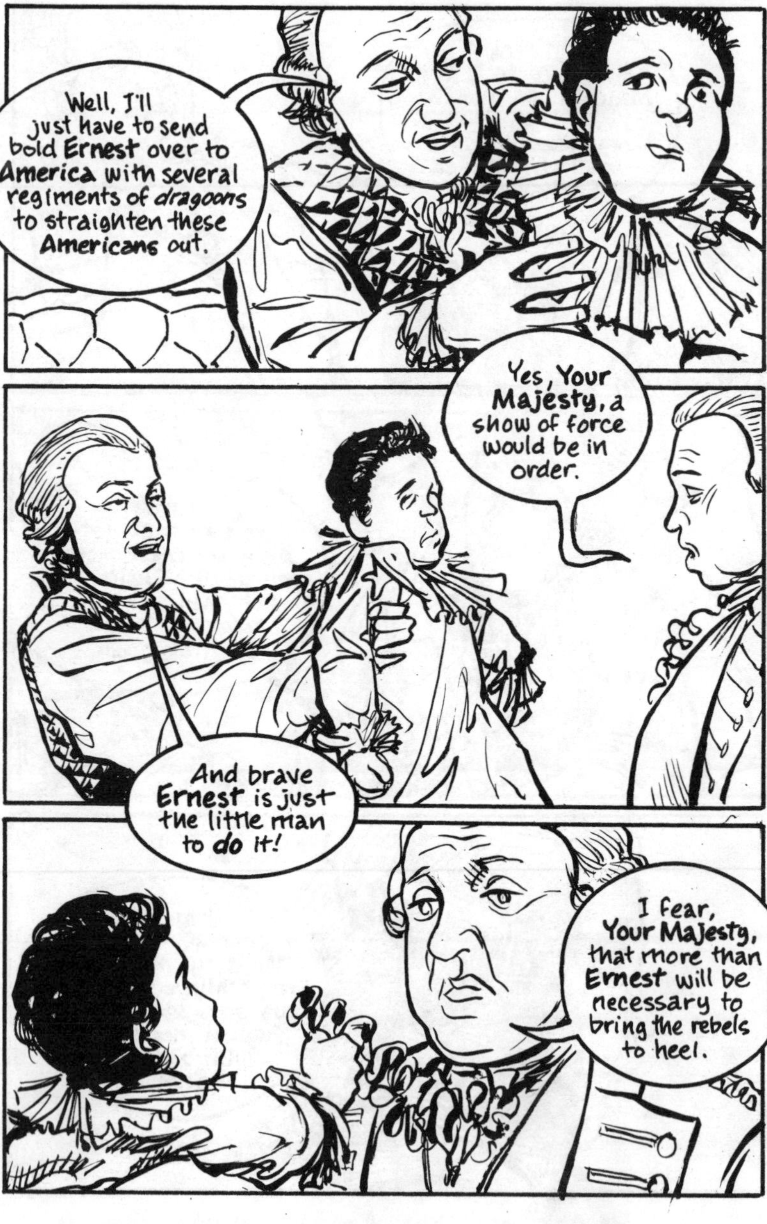
Well, I'll just have to send bold Ernest over to America with several regiments of dragoons to straighten these Americans out.
Yes, Your Majesty, a show of force would be in order.
And brave Ernest is just the little man to do it!
I fear, Your Majesty, that more than Ernest will be necessary to bring the rebels to heel.

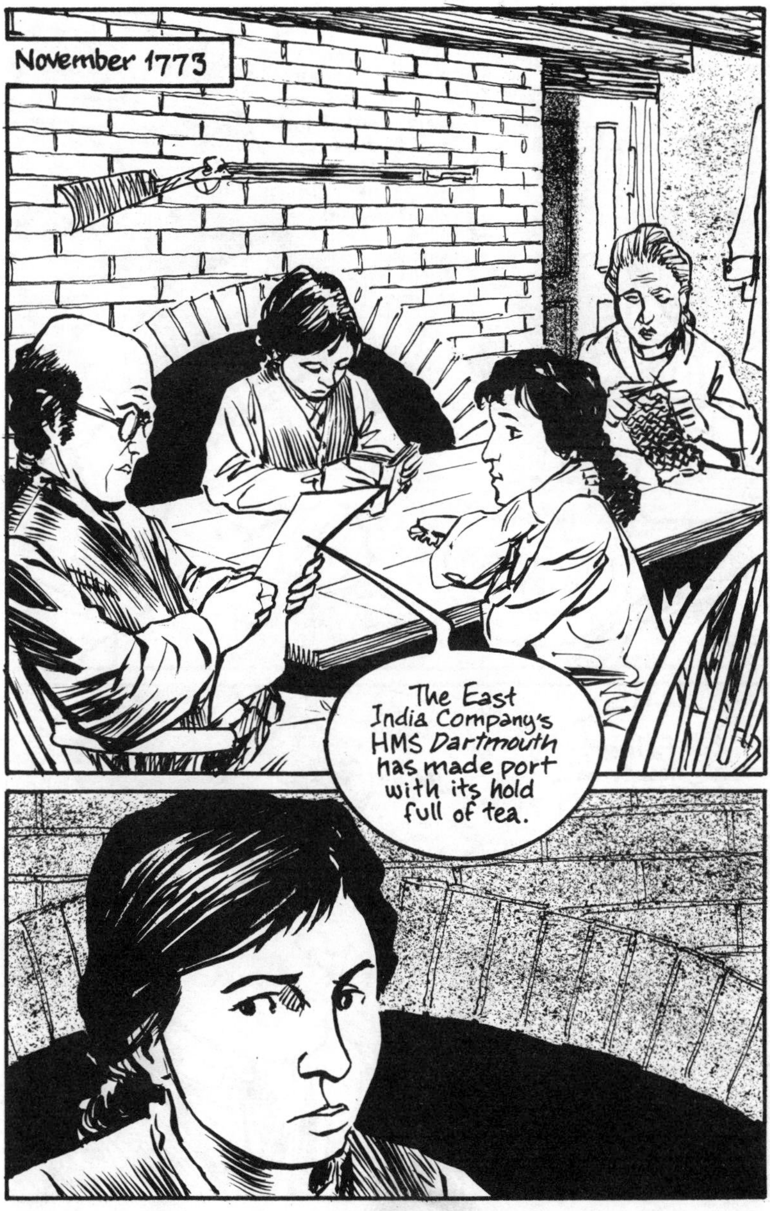
November 1773
The East India Company's HMS *Dartmouth* has made port with its hold full of tea.

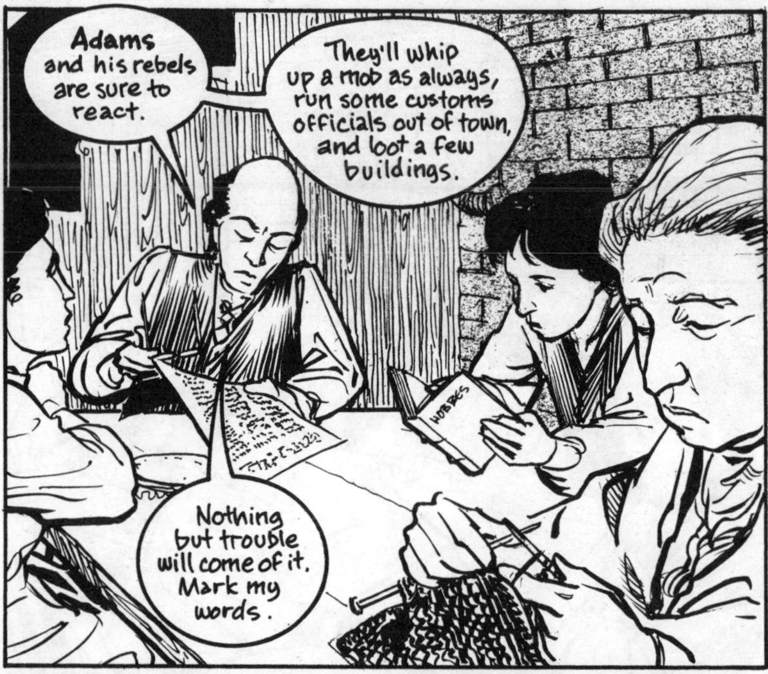
Adams and his rebels are sure to react.
They'll whip up a mob as always, run some customs officials out of town, and loot a few buildings.
HOBBES
Nothing but trouble will come of it. Mark my words.

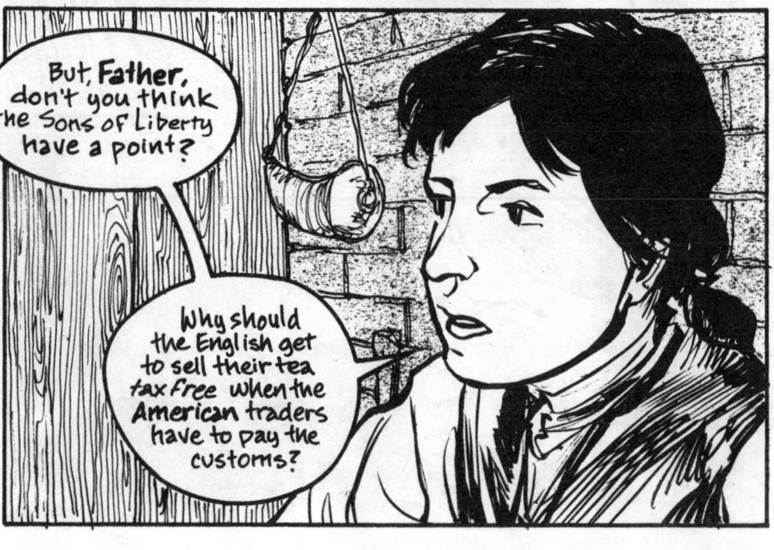
But, Father, don't you think the Sons of Liberty have a point?
Why should the English get to sell their tea tax free when the American traders have to pay the customs?

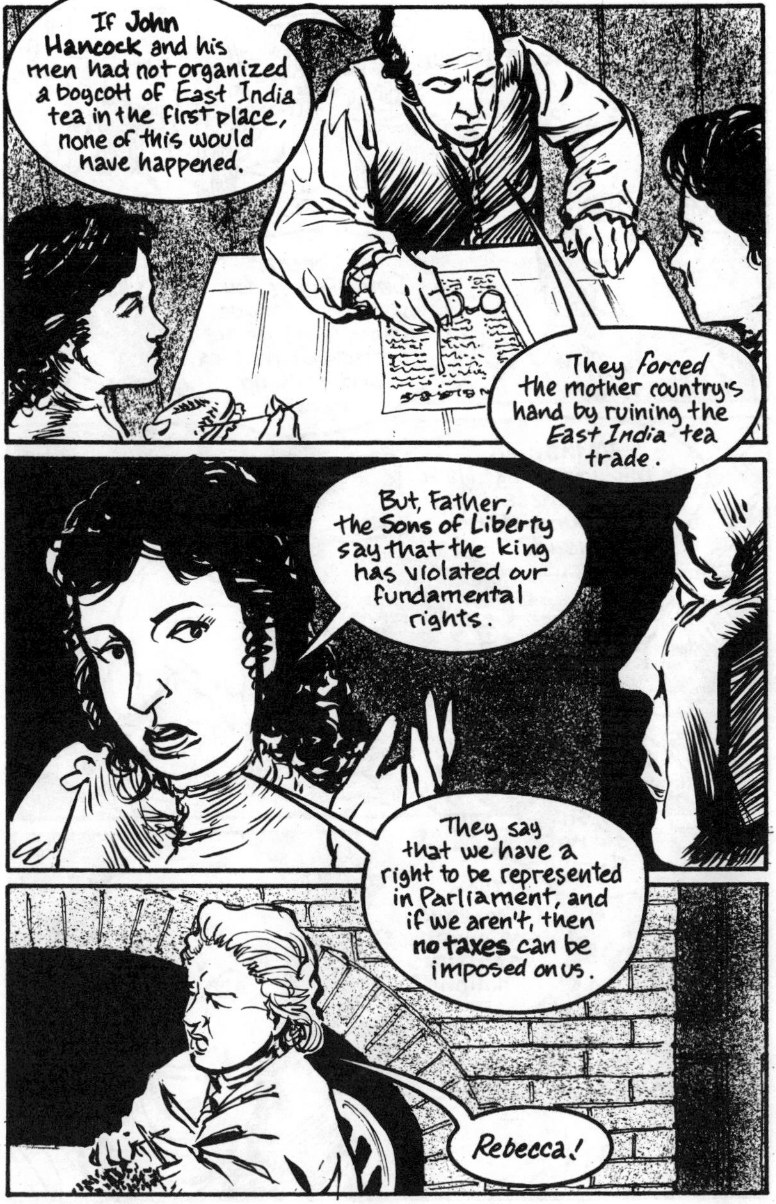
If John Hancock and his men had not organized a boycott of East India tea in the first place, none of this would have happened.
They *forced* the mother country's hand by ruining the *East India* tea trade.
But, Father, the Sons of Liberty say that the king has violated our fundamental rights.
They say that we have a right to be represented in Parliament, and if we aren't, then **no taxes** can be imposed on us.
Rebecca!

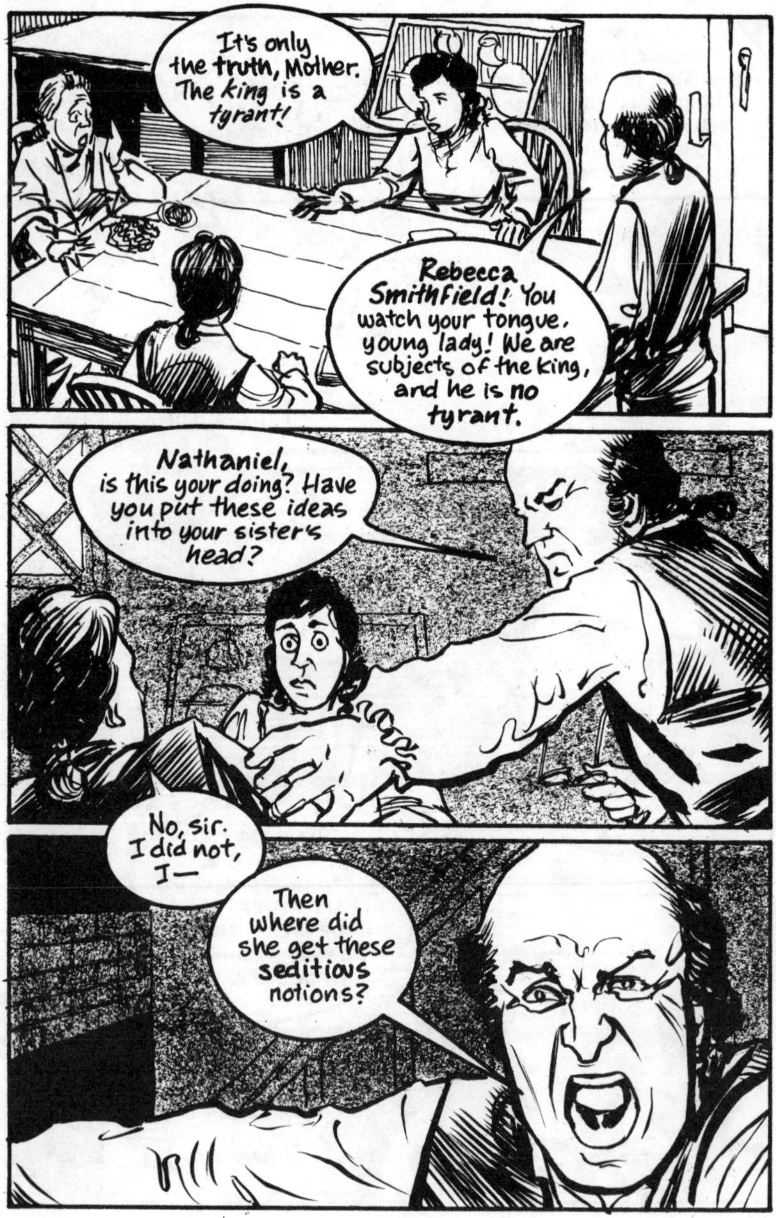
It's only the truth, Mother. The *king* is a *tyrant!*
Rebecca Smithfield! You watch your tongue, young lady! We are subjects of the king, and he is no *tyrant.*
Nathaniel, is this your doing? Have you put these ideas into your sister's head?
No, sir. I did not, I—
Then where did she get these seditious notions?

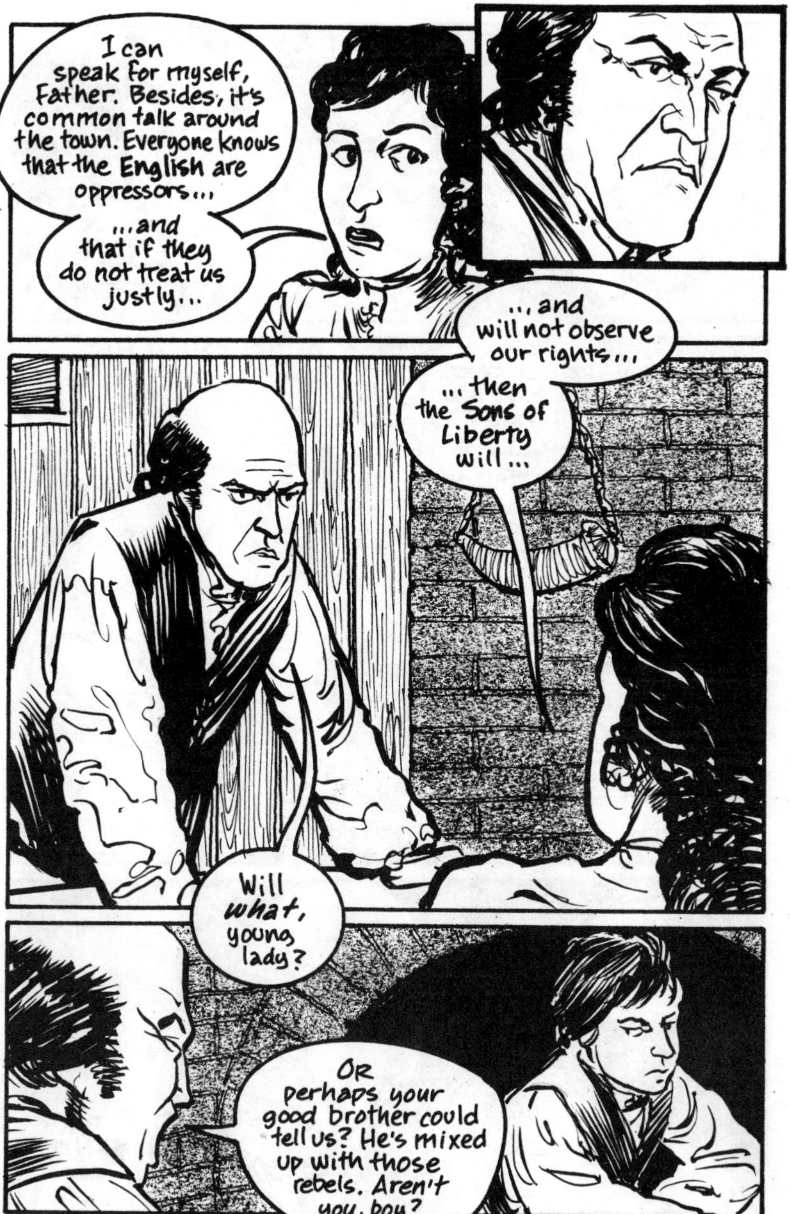
I can speak for myself, Father. Besides, it's common talk around the town. Everyone knows that the English are oppressors...
...and that if they do not treat us justly...
..., and will not observe our rights...,
... then the Sons of Liberty will...
Will *what*, young lady?
Or perhaps your good brother could tell us? He's mixed up with those rebels. Aren't you, boy?

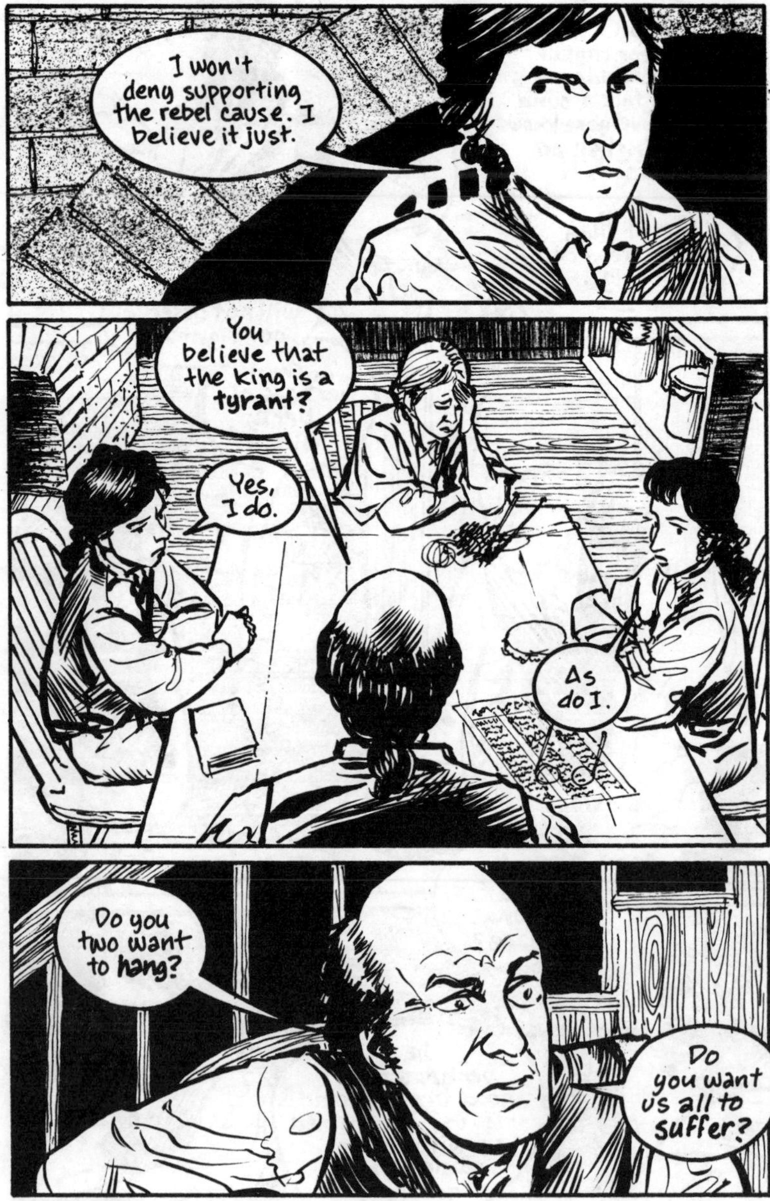

I won't deny supporting the rebel cause. I believe it just.
You believe that the King is a tyrant?
Yes, I do.
As do I.
Do you two want to hang?
Do you want us all to suffer?

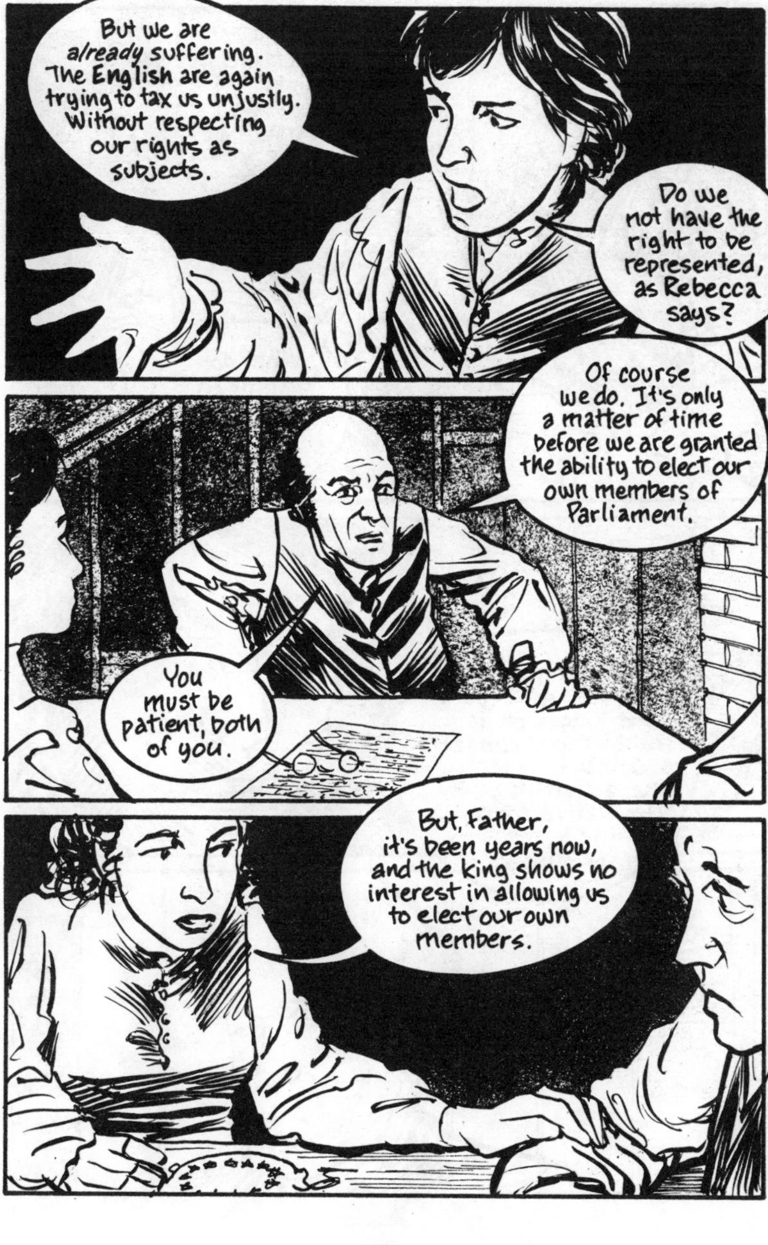
But we are *already* suffering. The English are again trying to tax us unjustly. Without respecting our rights as subjects.
Do we not have the right to be represented, as Rebecca says?
Of course we do. It's only a matter of time before we are granted the ability to elect our own members of Parliament.
You must be patient, both of you.
But, Father, it's been years now, and the king shows no interest in allowing us to elect our own members.

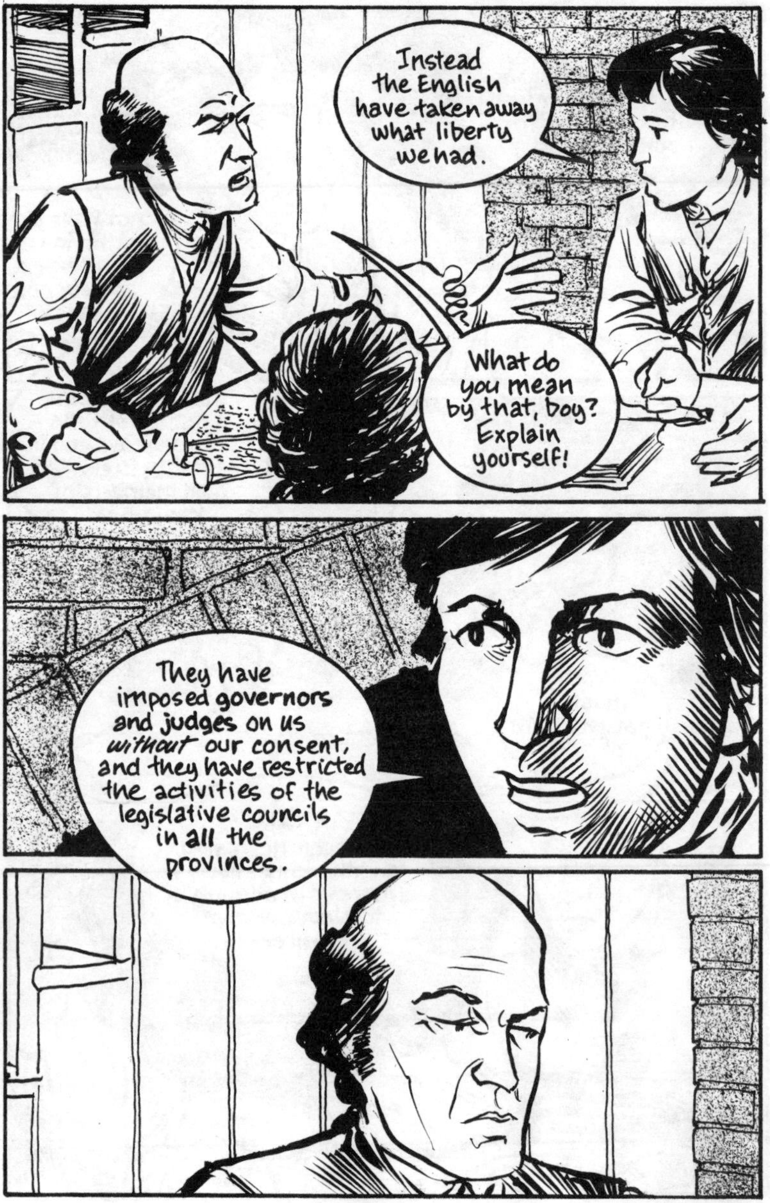
Instead the English have taken away what liberty we had.
What do you mean by that, boy? Explain yourself!
They have imposed governors and judges on us *without* our consent, and they have restricted the activities of the legislative councils in all the provinces.

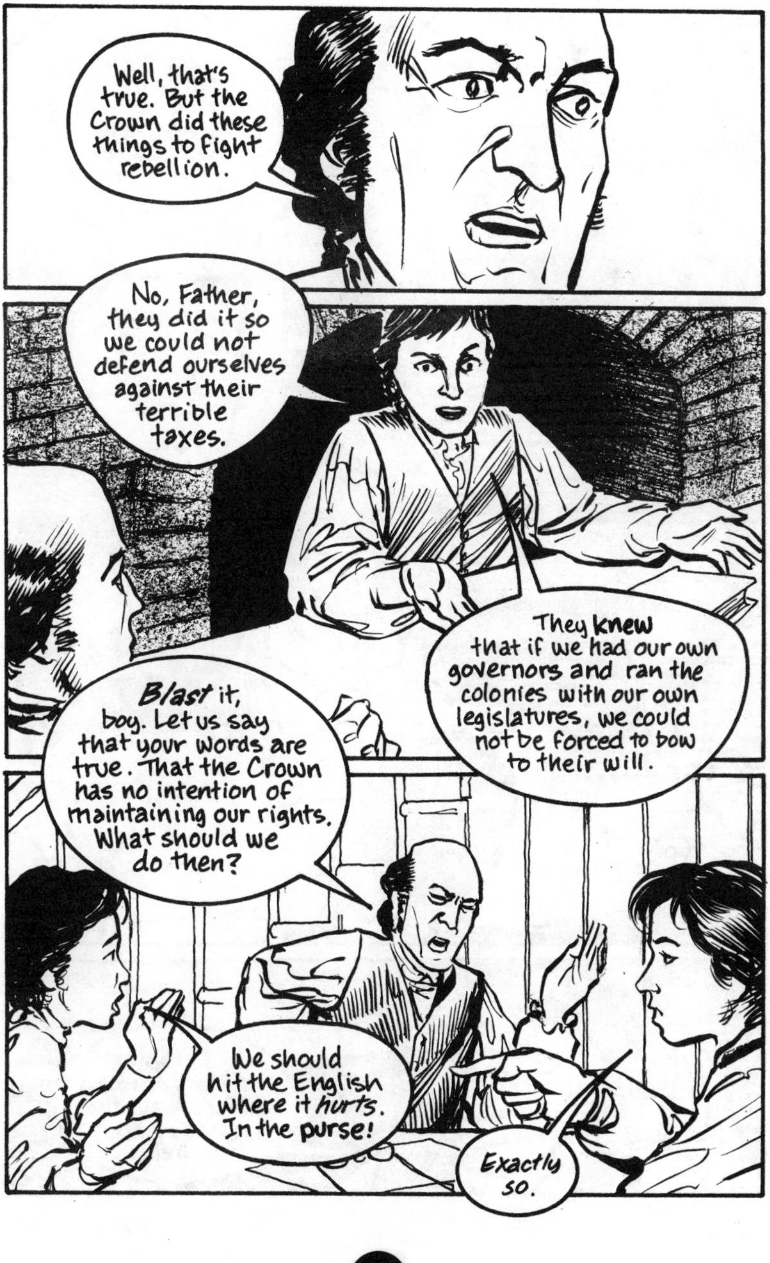
Well, that's true. But the Crown did these things to fight rebellion.
No, Father, they did it so we could not defend ourselves against their terrible taxes.
They knew that if we had our own governors and ran the colonies with our own legislatures, we could not be forced to bow to their will.
Blast it, boy. Let us say that your words are true. That the Crown has no intention of maintaining our rights. What should we do then?
We should hit the English where it hurts. In the purse!
Exactly so.

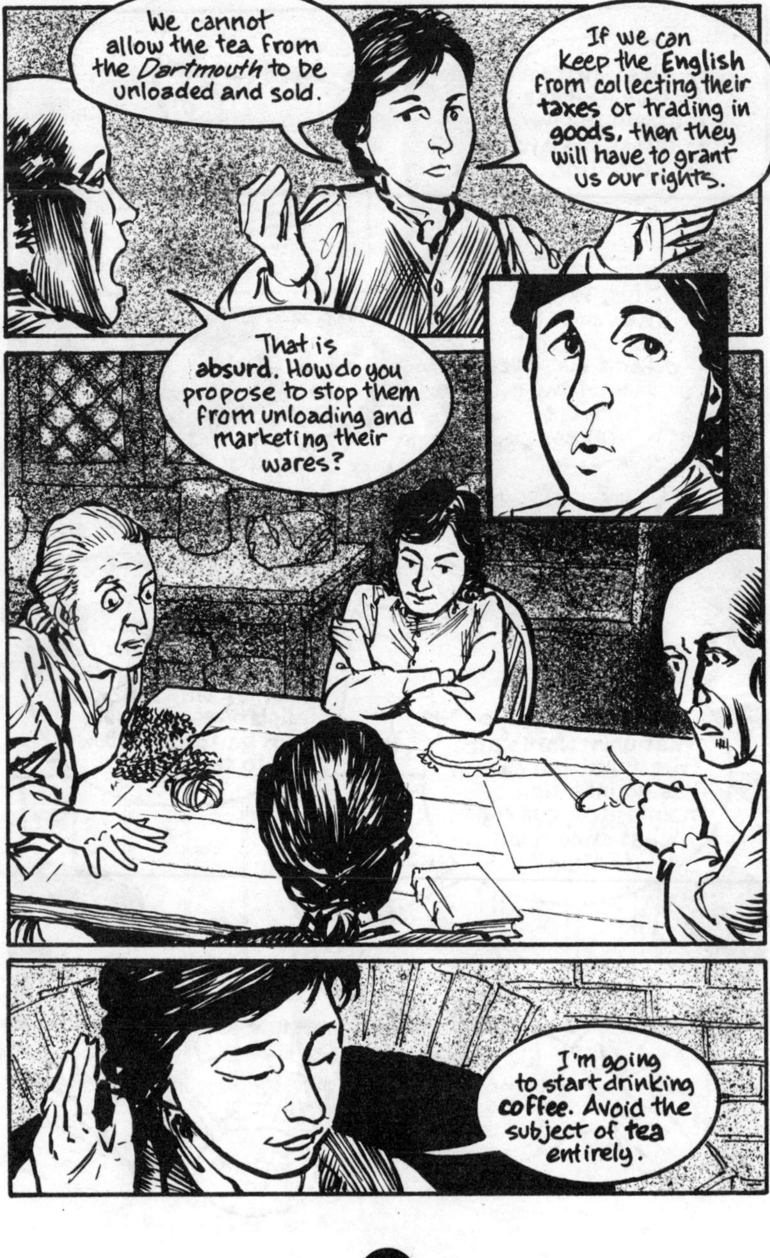
We cannot allow the tea from the *Dartmouth* to be unloaded and sold.
If we can keep the English from collecting their taxes or trading in goods, then they will have to grant us our rights.
That is **absurd**. How do you propose to stop them from unloading and marketing their wares?
I'm going to start drinking coffee. Avoid the subject of tea entirely.

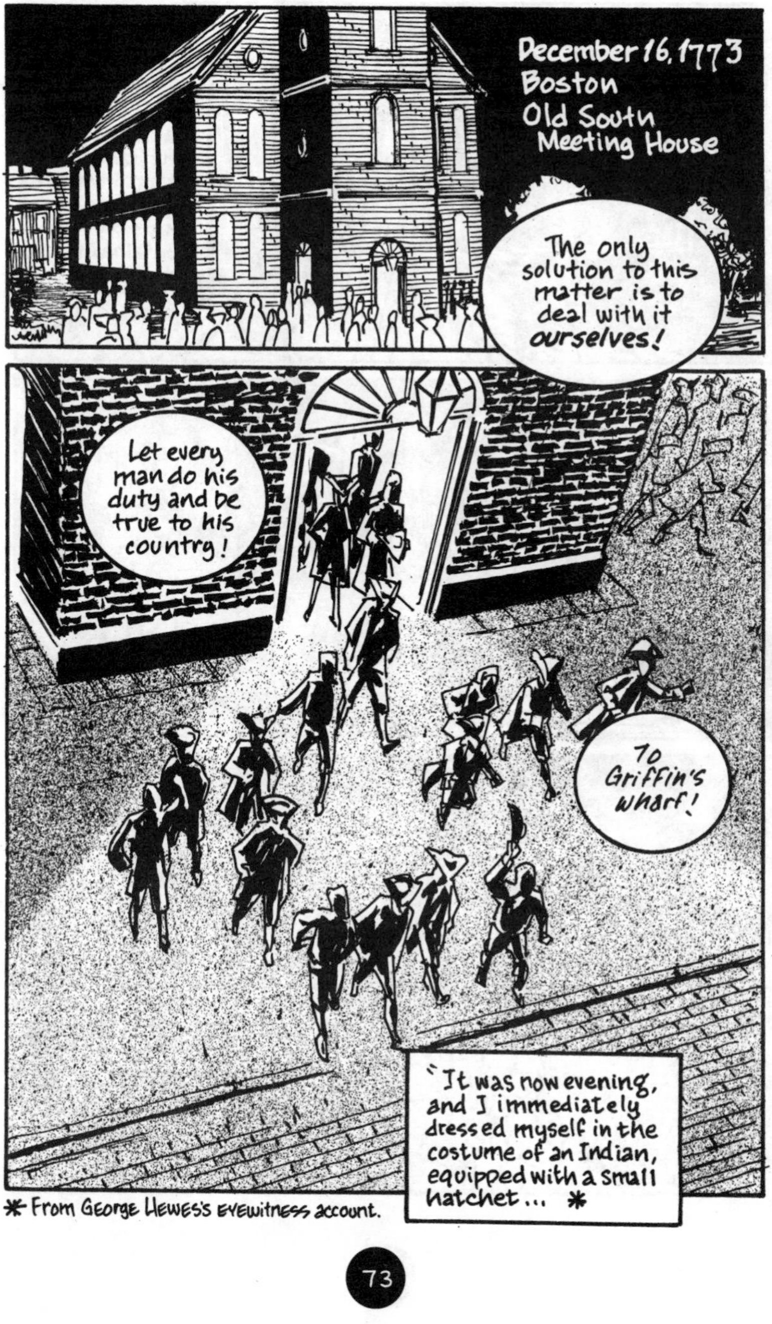
December 16, 1773
Boston
Old South Meeting House
The only solution to this matter is to deal with it ourselves!
Let every man do his duty and be true to his countrg!
To Griffin's wharf!
"It was now evening, and I immediately dressed myself in the costume of an Indian, equipped with a small hatchet... *

* From George Hewes's eyewitness account.

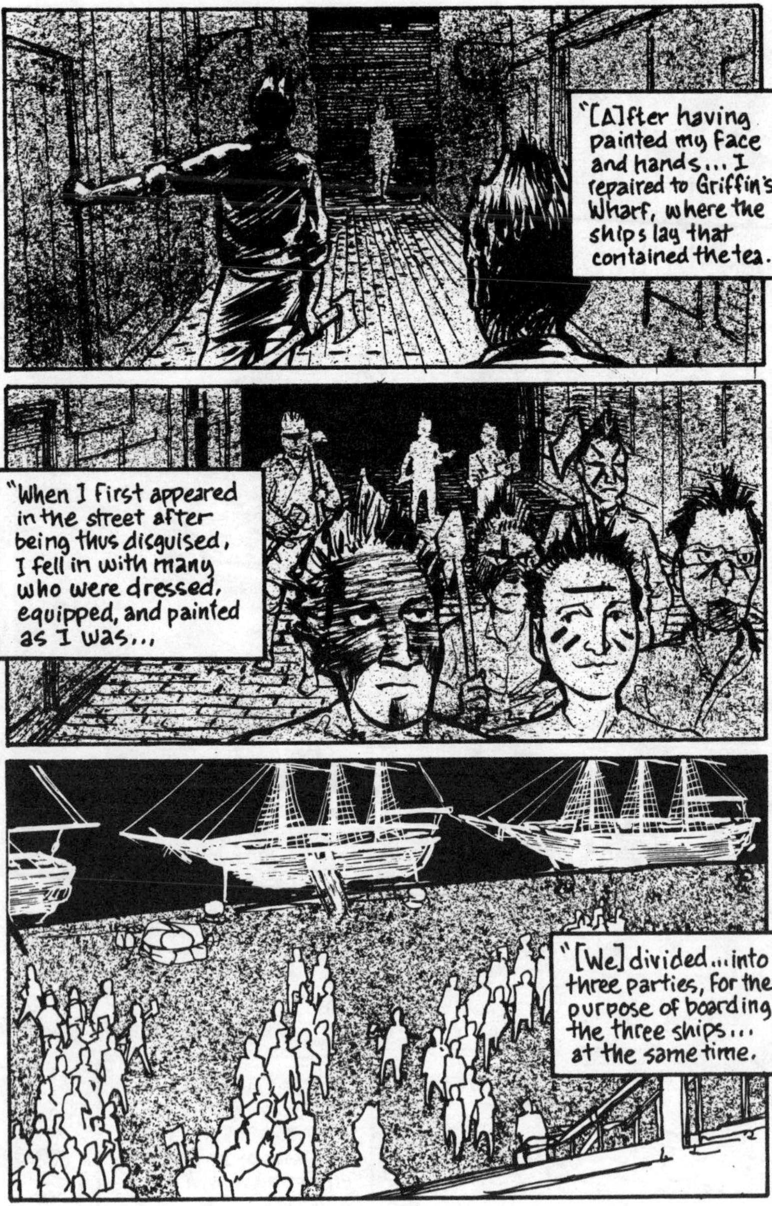
"[A]fter having painted my face and hands... I repaired to Griffin's Wharf, where the ships lay that contained the tea.
"When I first appeared in the street after being thus disguised, I fell in with many who were dressed, equipped, and painted as I was...
"[We] divided...into three parties, for the purpose of boarding the three ships... at the same time.

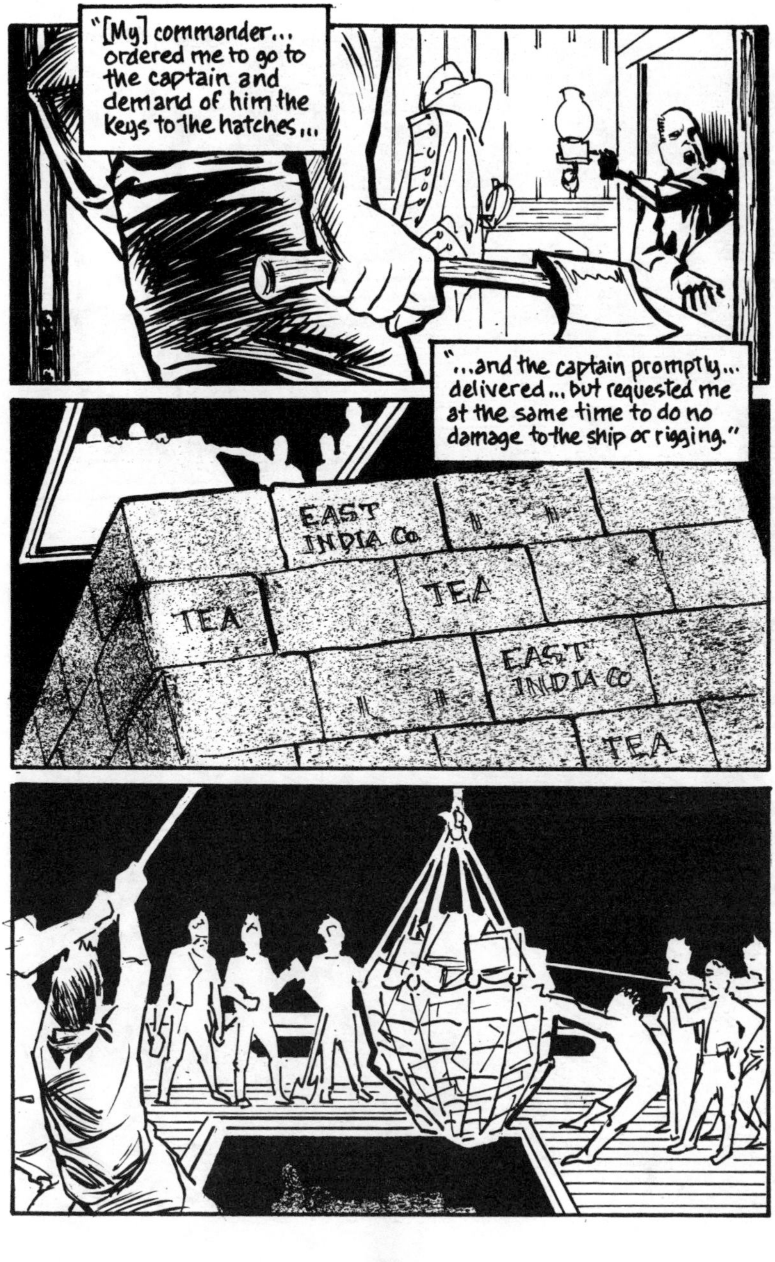
"[My] commander... ordered me to go to the captain and demand of him the keys to the hatches...
"...and the captain promptly... delivered... but requested me at the same time to do no damage to the ship or rigging."
EAST INDIA Co
TEA
TEA
TEA
EAST INDIA Co
TEA

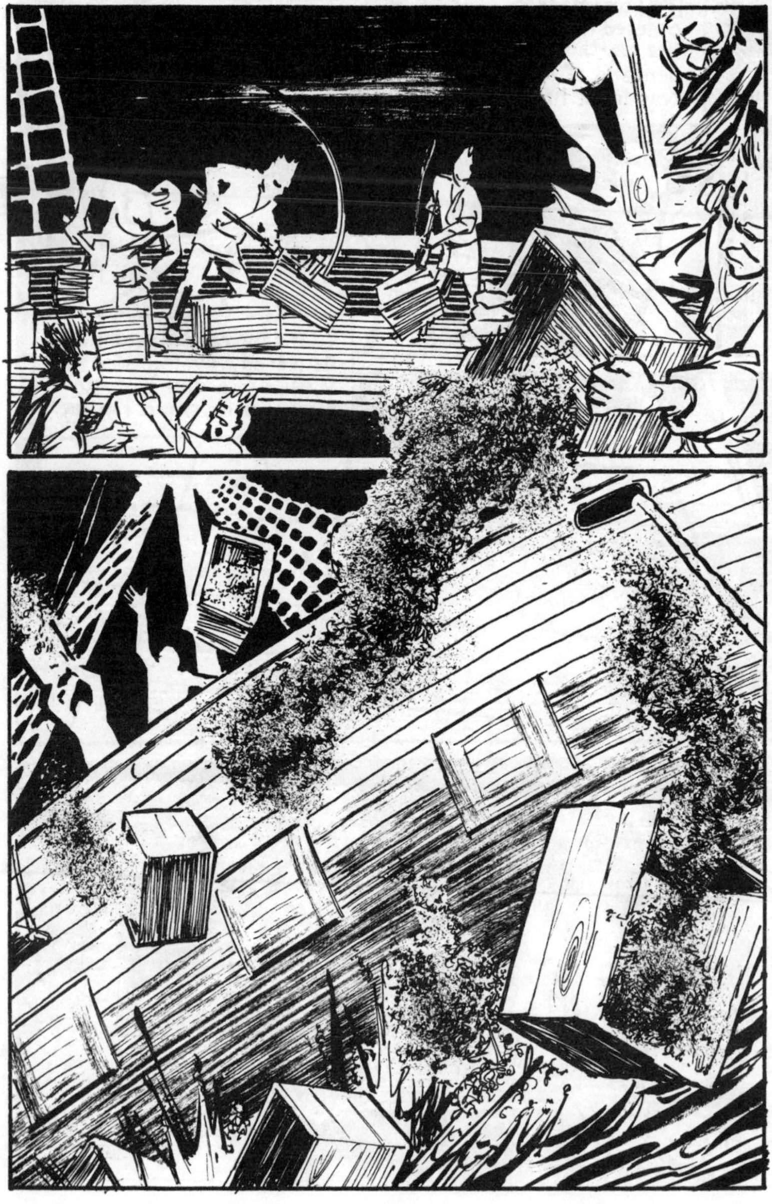

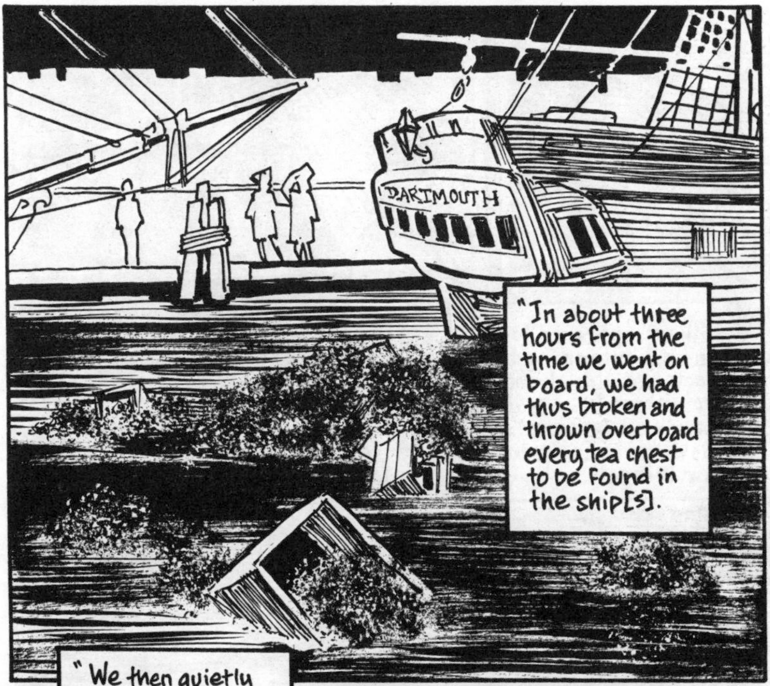
DARTMOUTH
"In about three hours from the time we went on board, we had thus broken and thrown overboard every tea chest to be found in the ship[s].

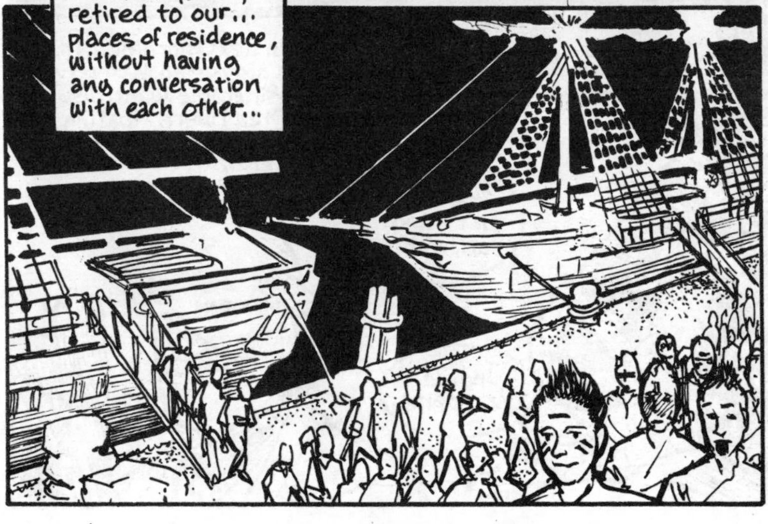
"We then quietly retired to our... places of residence, without having any conversation with each other...

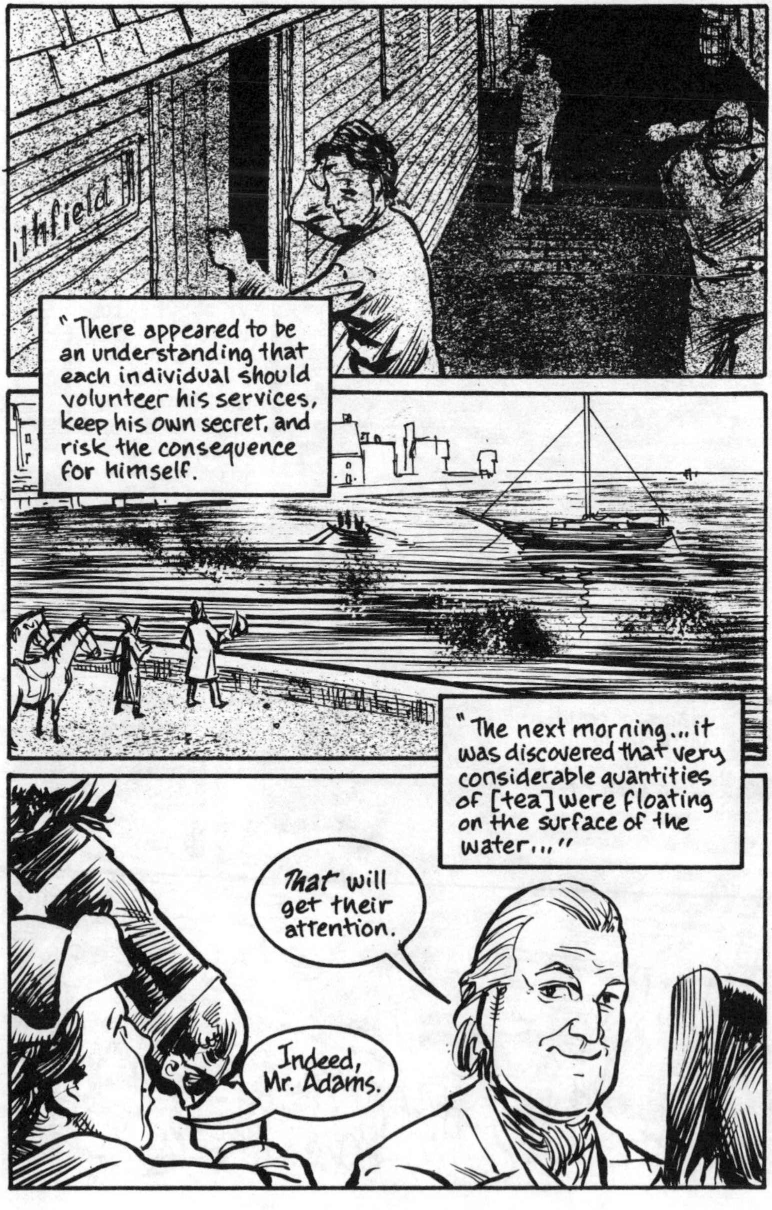

ithfield
"There appeared to be an understanding that each individual should volunteer his services, keep his own secret, and risk the consequence for himself.
"The next morning... it was discovered that very considerable quantities of [tea] were floating on the surface of the water..."
That will get their attention.
Indeed, Mr. Adams.

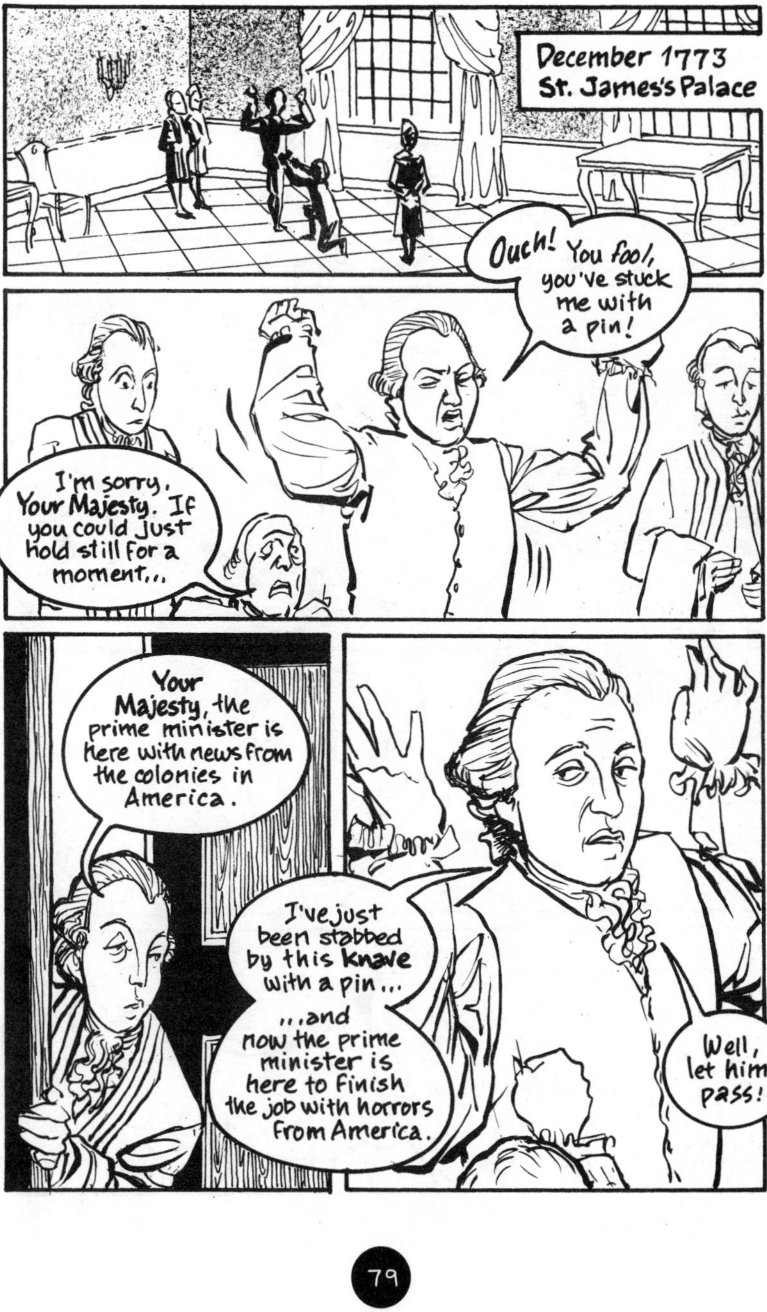
December 1773
St. James's Palace
Ouch! You fool, you've stuck me with a pin!
I'm sorry, Your Majesty. If you could just hold still for a moment...
Your Majesty, the prime minister is here with news from the colonies in America.
I've just been stabbed by this knave with a pin...
...and now the prime minister is here to finish the job with horrors from America.
Well, let him pass!

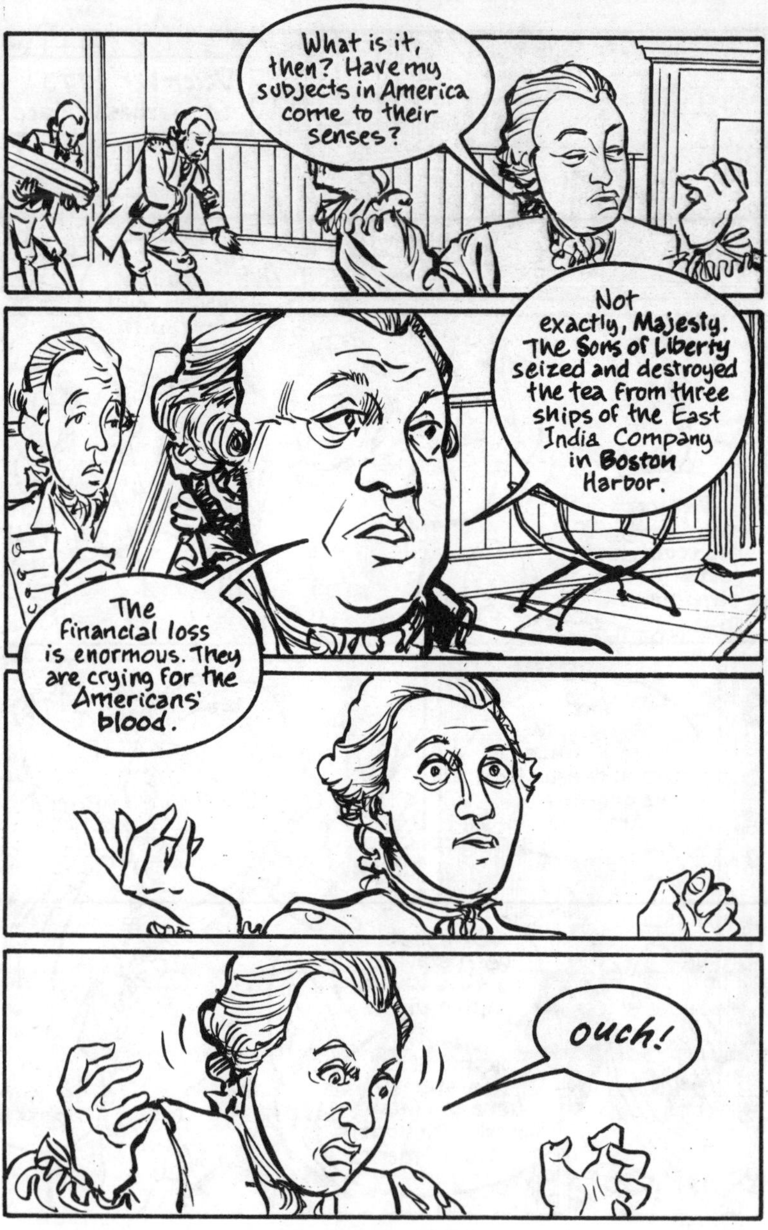
What is it, then? Have my subjects in America come to their senses?
Not exactly, Majesty. The Sons of Liberty seized and destroyed the tea from three ships of the East India Company in Boston Harbor.
The financial loss is enormous. They are crying for the Americans' blood.
ouch!

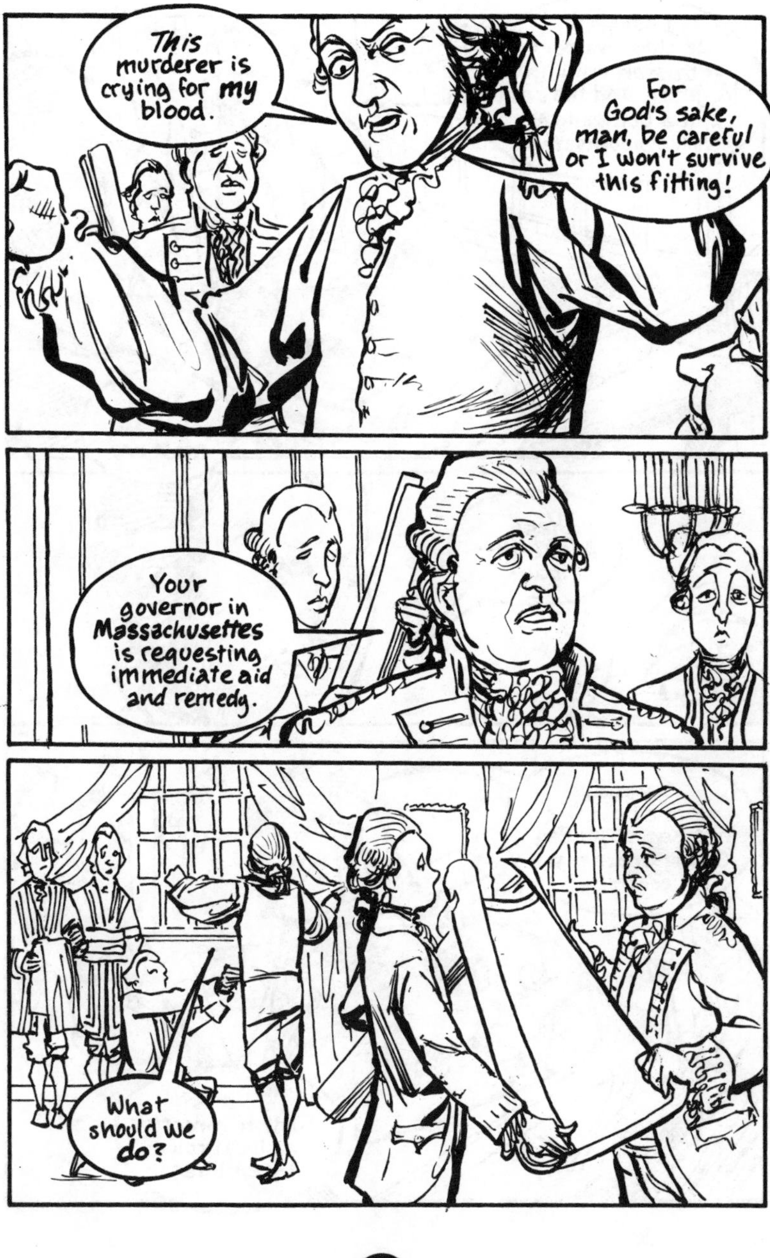
This murderer is crying for my blood.
For God's sake, man, be careful or I won't survive this fitting!
Your governor in Massachusettes is requesting immediate aid and remedy.
What should we do?

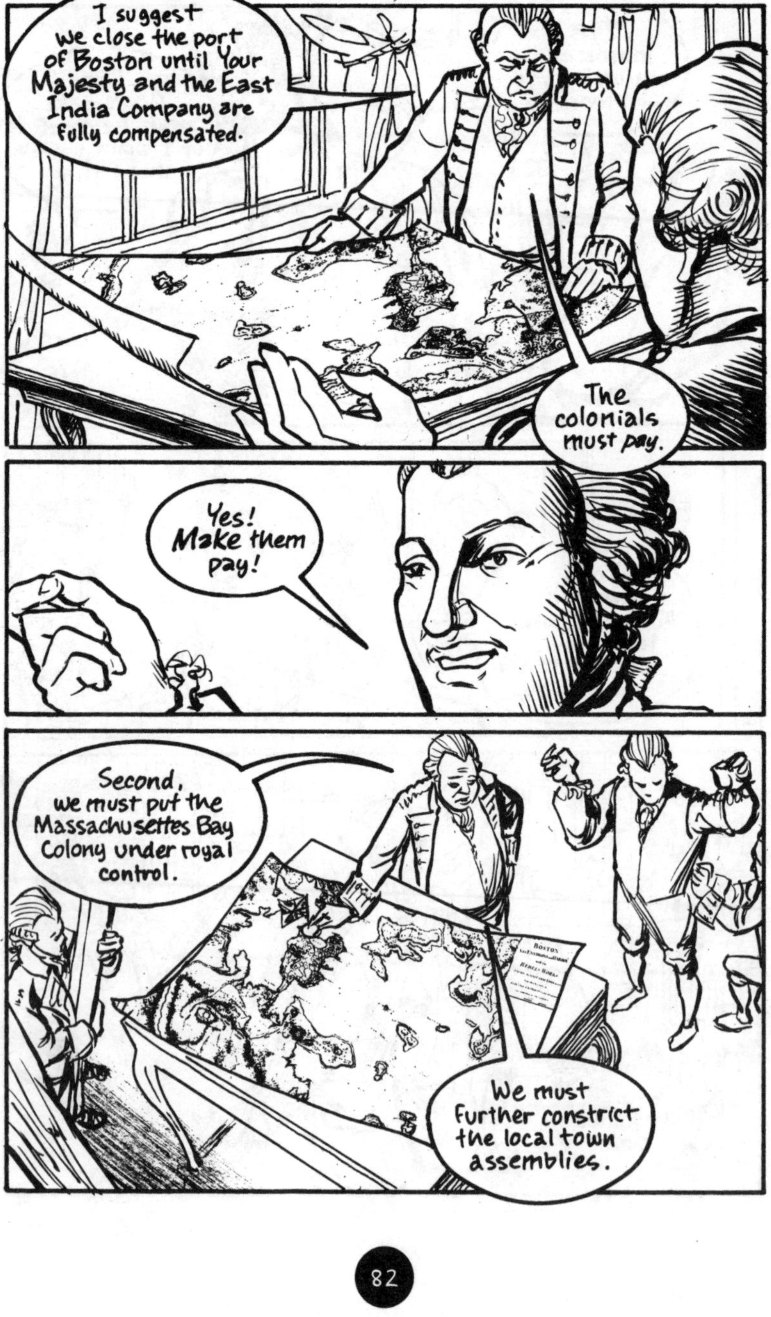

I suggest we close the port of Boston until Your Majesty and the East India Company are fully compensated.
The colonials must *pay*.
Yes! Make them pay!
Second, we must put the Massachusettes Bay Colony under royal control.
We must further constrict the local town assemblies.

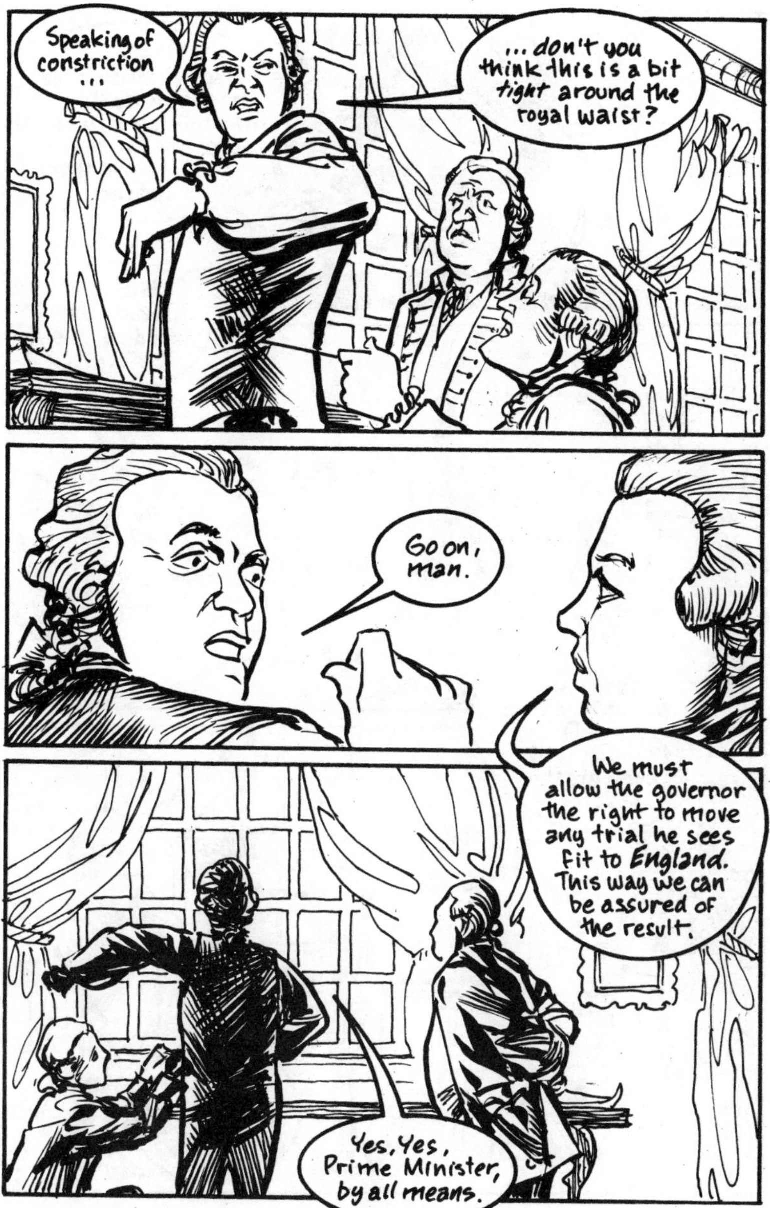
Speaking of constriction ...
... don't you think this is a bit *tight* around the royal waist?
Go on, man.
We must allow the governor the right to move any trial he sees fit to *England*. This way we can be assured of the result.
Yes, Yes, Prime Minister, by all means.

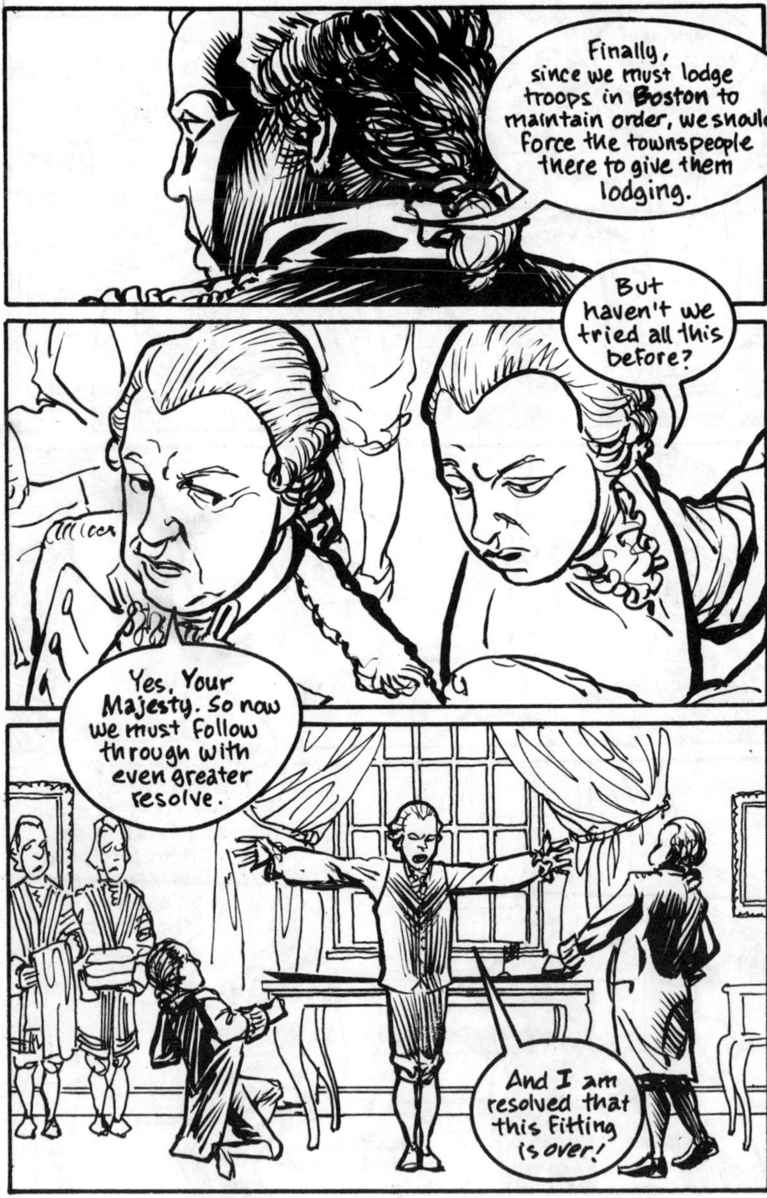
Finally, since we must lodge troops in Boston to maintain order, we should force the townspeople there to give them lodging.
But haven't we tried all this before?
Yes, Your Majesty. So now we must follow through with even greater resolve.
And I am resolved that this fitting is over!

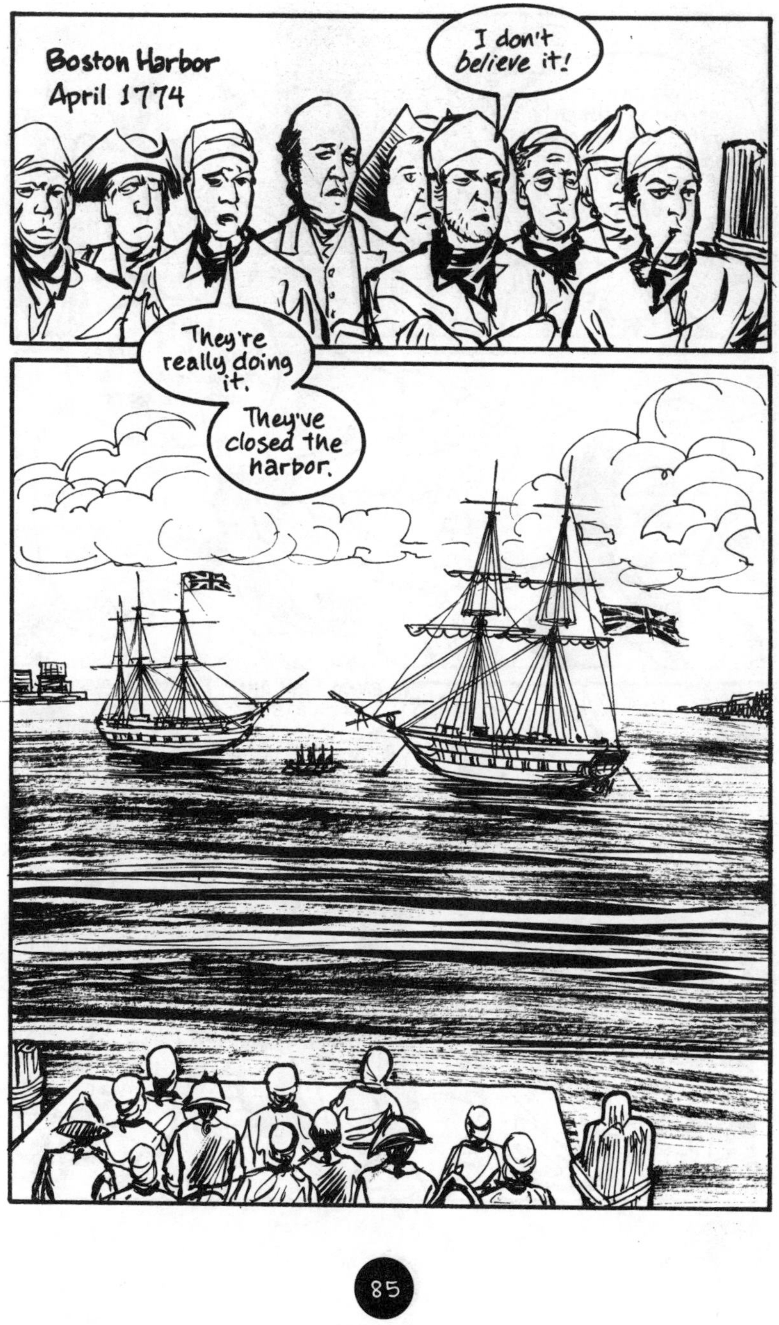
Boston Harbor
April 1774
I don't believe it!
They're really doing it.
They've closed the harbor.

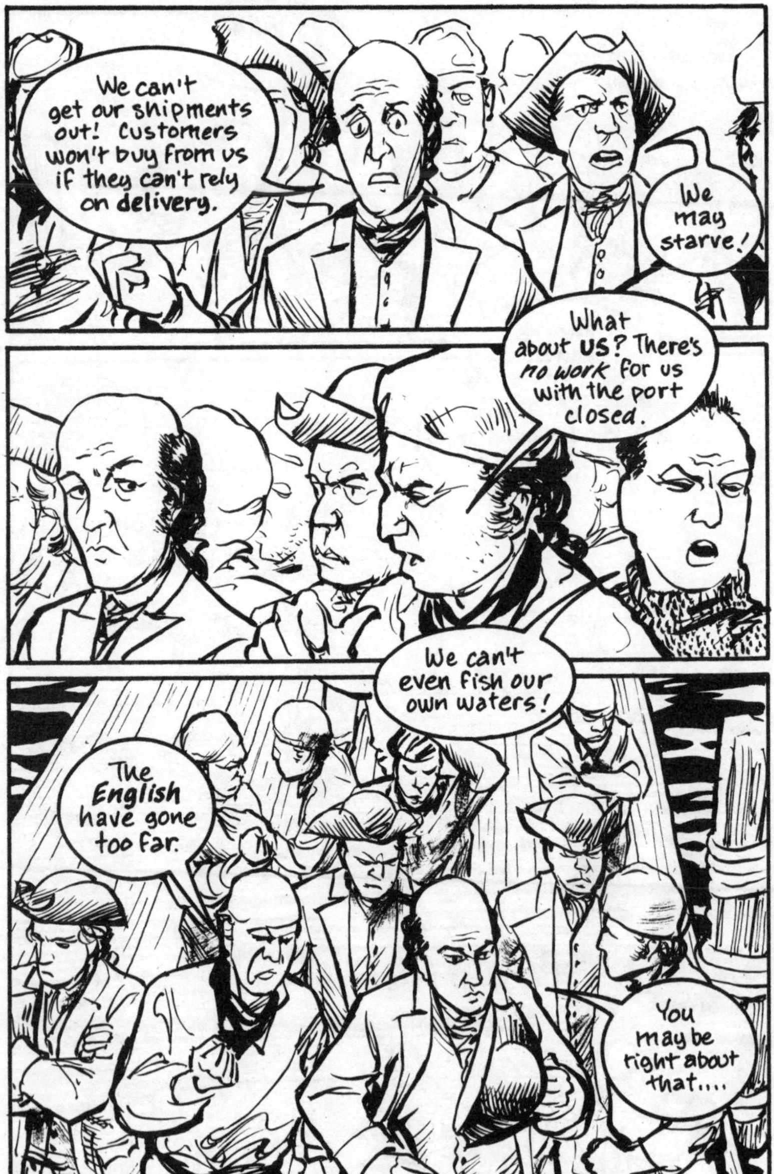
We can't get our shipments out! Customers won't buy from us if they can't rely on delivery.
We may starve!
What about US? There's no work for us with the port closed.
We can't even fish our own waters!
The English have gone too far.
You may be right about that....

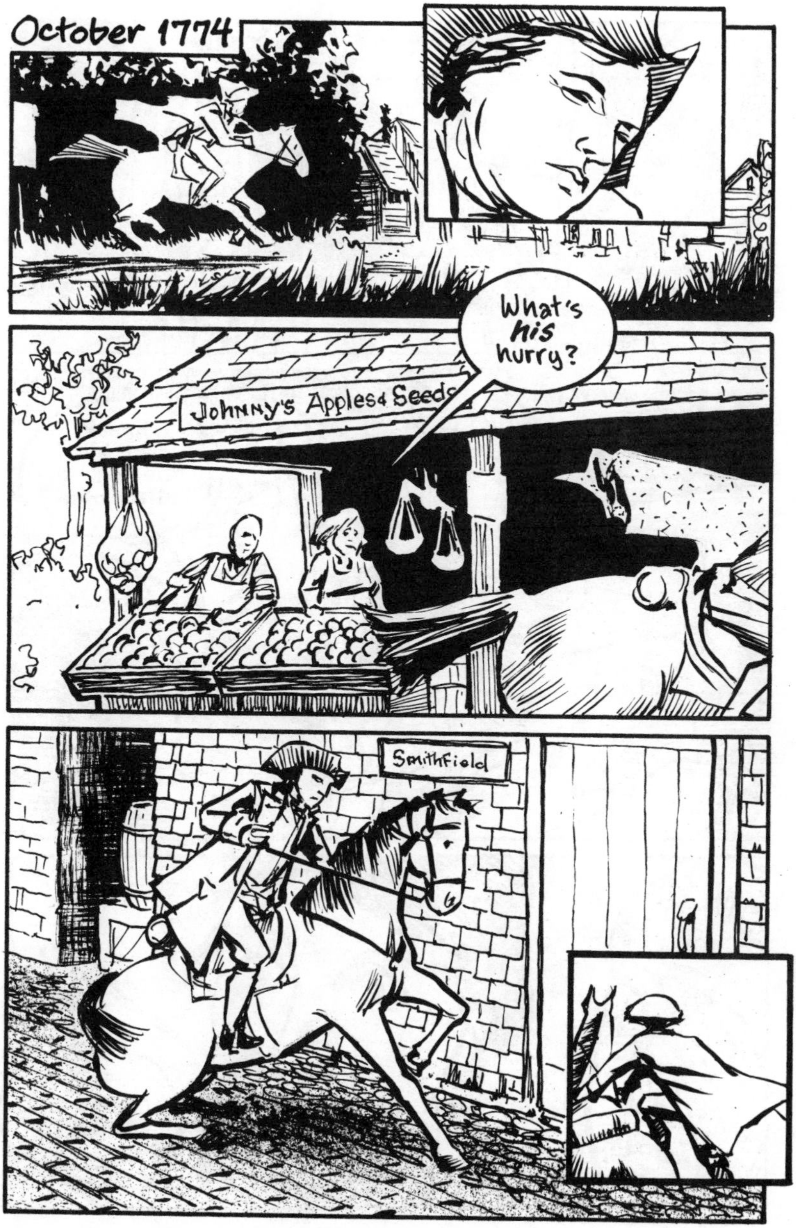
October 1774
What's his hurry?
Johnny's Apples & Seeds
Smithfield

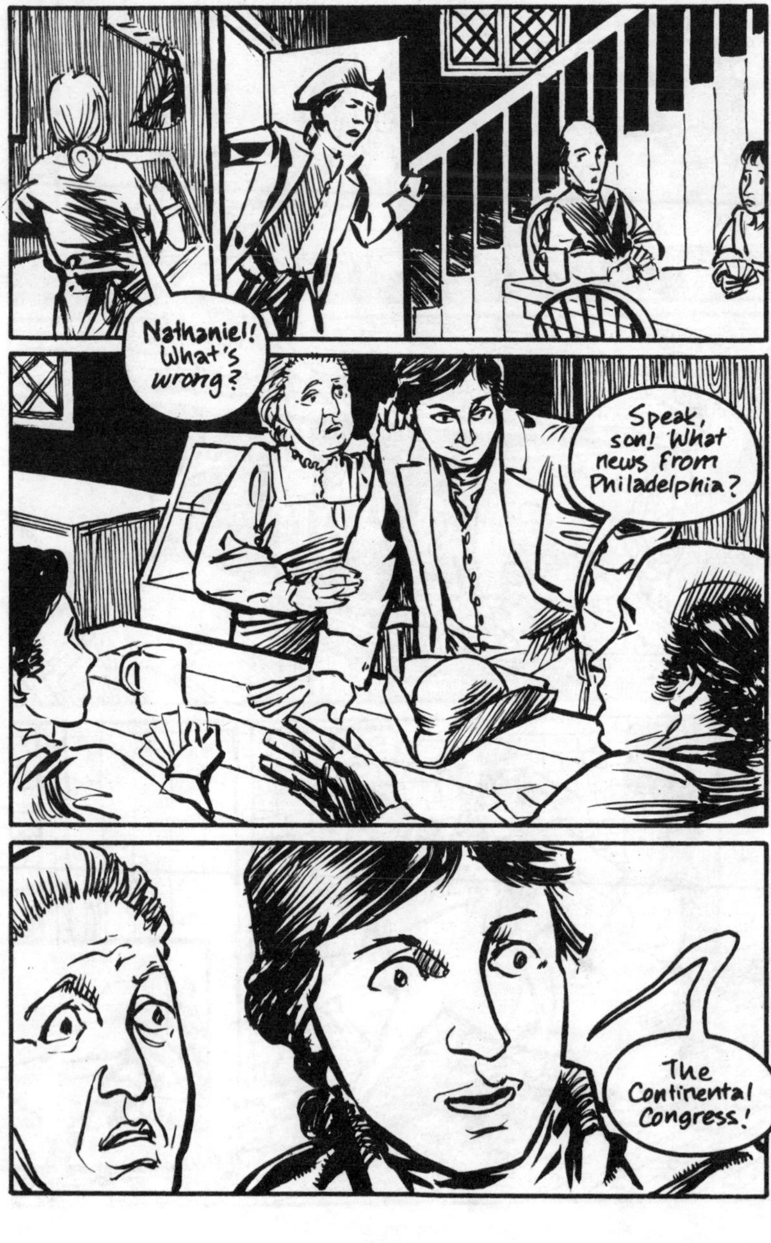
Nathaniel! What's wrong?
Speak, son! What news from Philadelphia?
The Continental Congress!

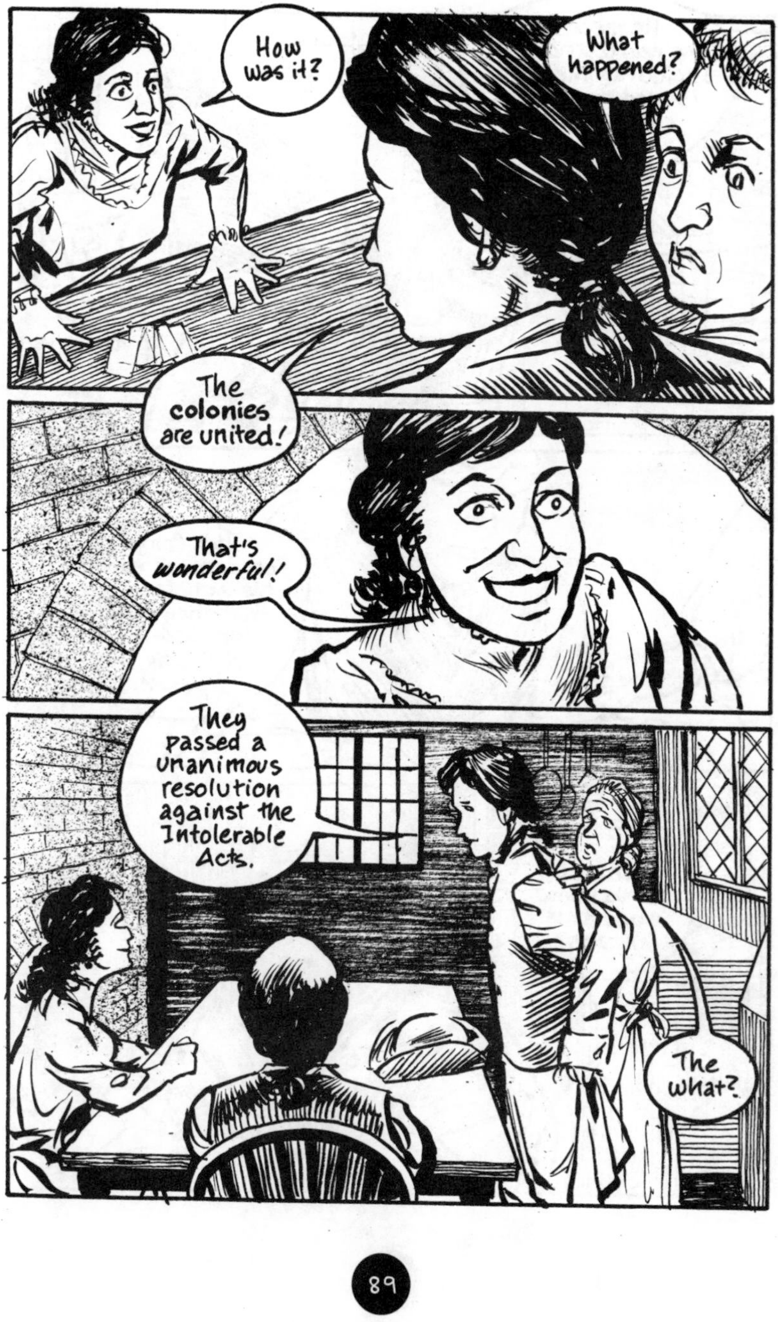
How was it?
What happened?
The colonies are united!
That's *wonderful*!
They passed a unanimous resolution against the Intolerable Acts.
The what?

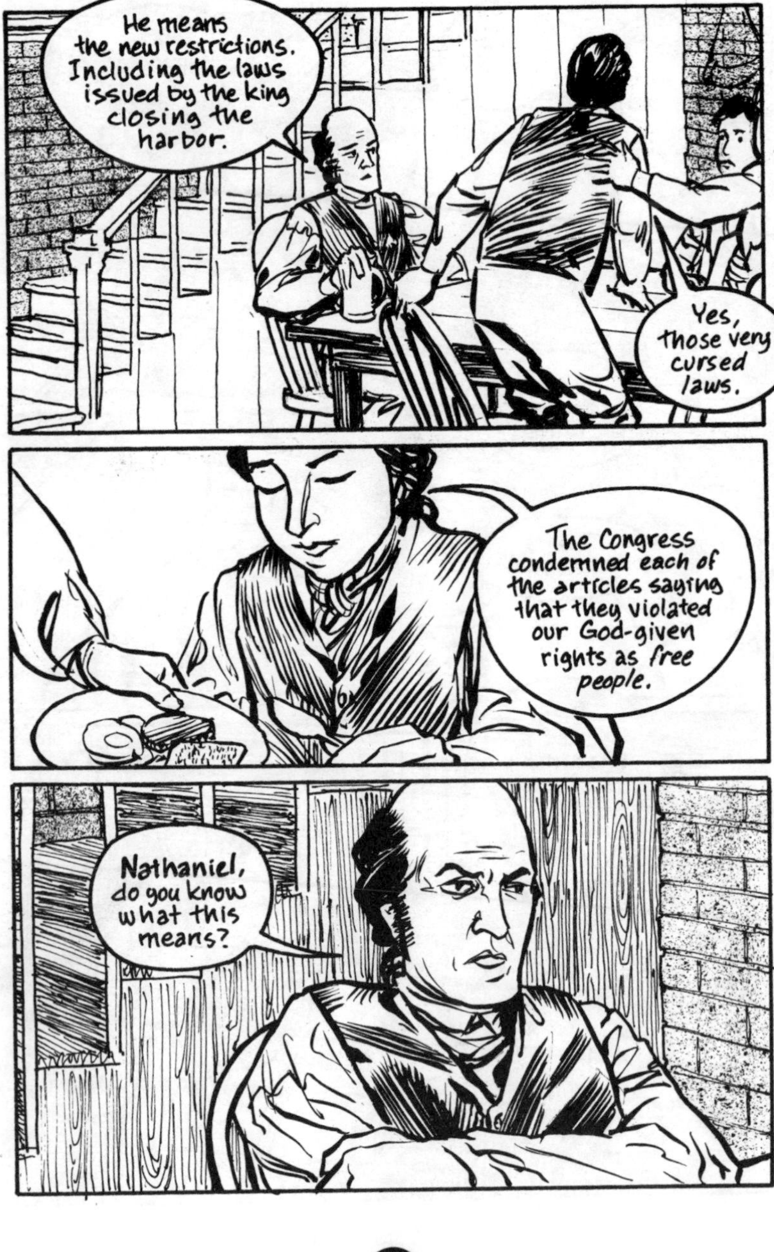
He means the new restrictions. Including the laws issued by the king closing the harbor.
Yes, those very cursed laws.
The Congress condemned each of the articles saying that they violated our God-given rights as *free people*.
Nathaniel, do you know what this means?

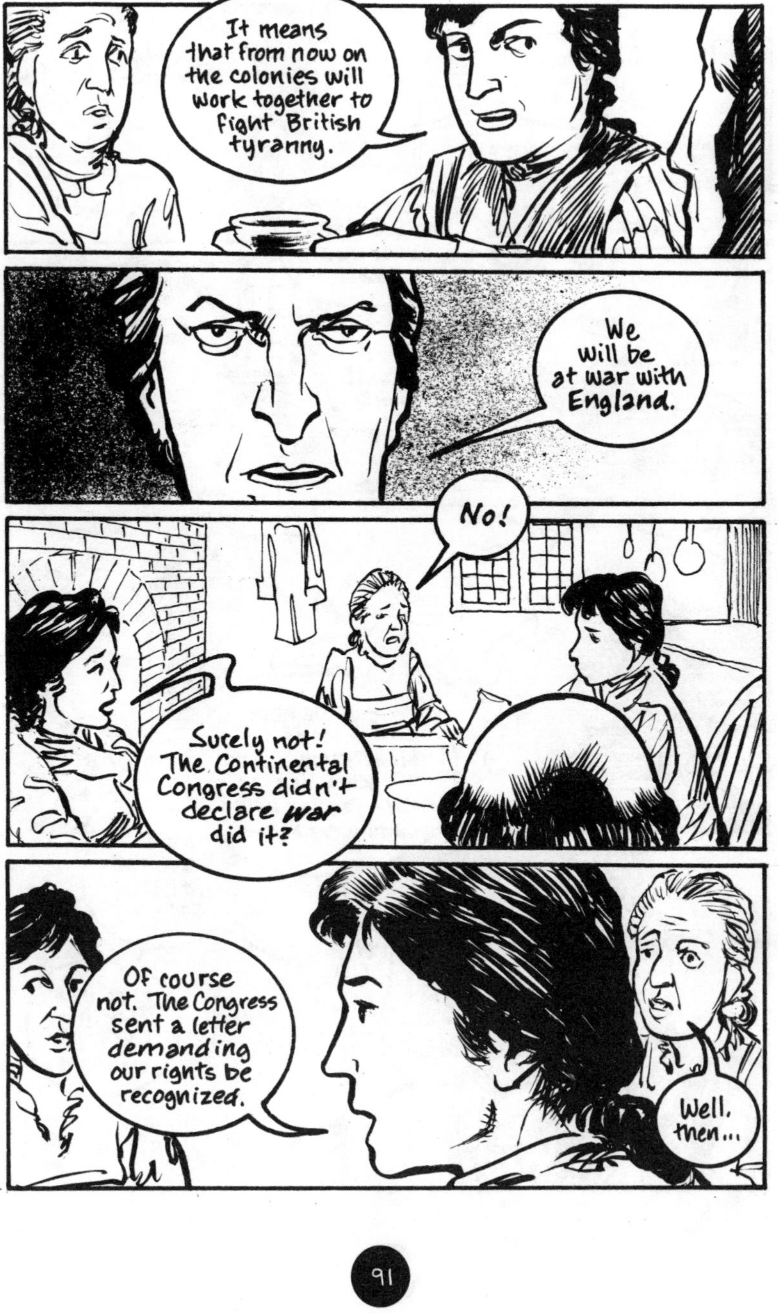
It means that from now on the colonies will work together to fight British tyranny.
We will be at war with England.
No!
Surely not! The Continental Congress didn't declare *war* did it?
Of course not. The Congress sent a letter demanding our rights be recognized.
Well, then...

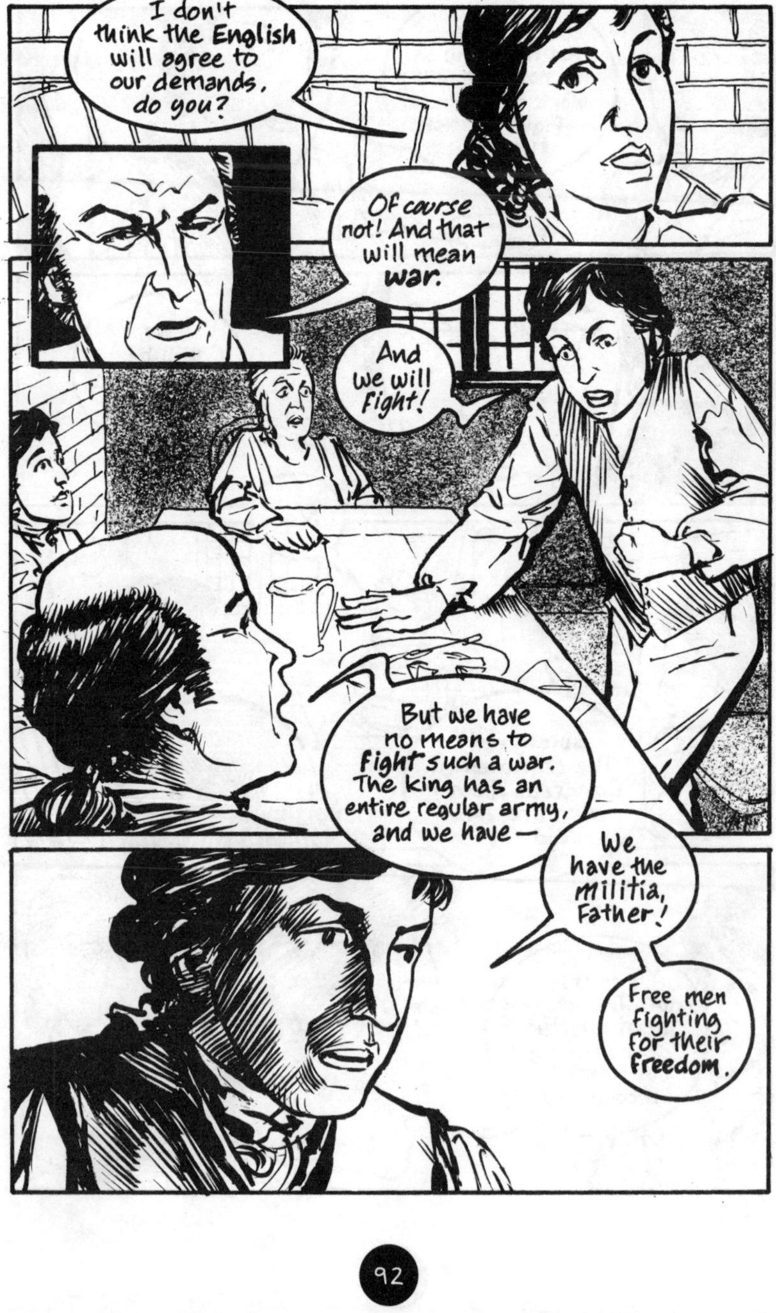
I don't think the English will agree to our demands, do you?
Of course not! And that will mean war.
And we will fight!
But we have no means to fight such a war. The king has an entire regular army, and we have—
We have the militia, Father!
Free men fighting for their freedom.

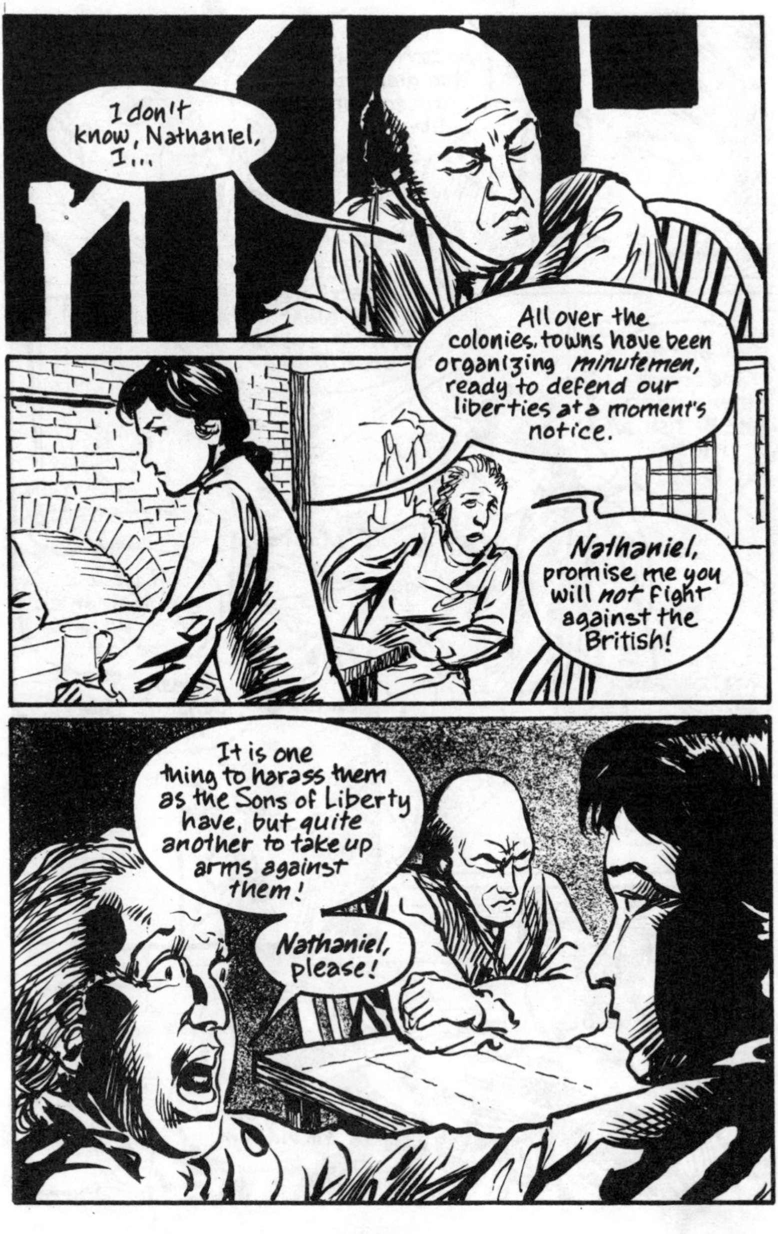
I don't know, Nathaniel, I...
All over the colonies, towns have been organizing *minutemen*, ready to defend our liberties at a moment's notice.
Nathaniel, promise me you will *not* fight against the British!
It is one thing to harass them as the Sons of Liberty have, but quite another to take up arms against them!
Nathaniel, please!

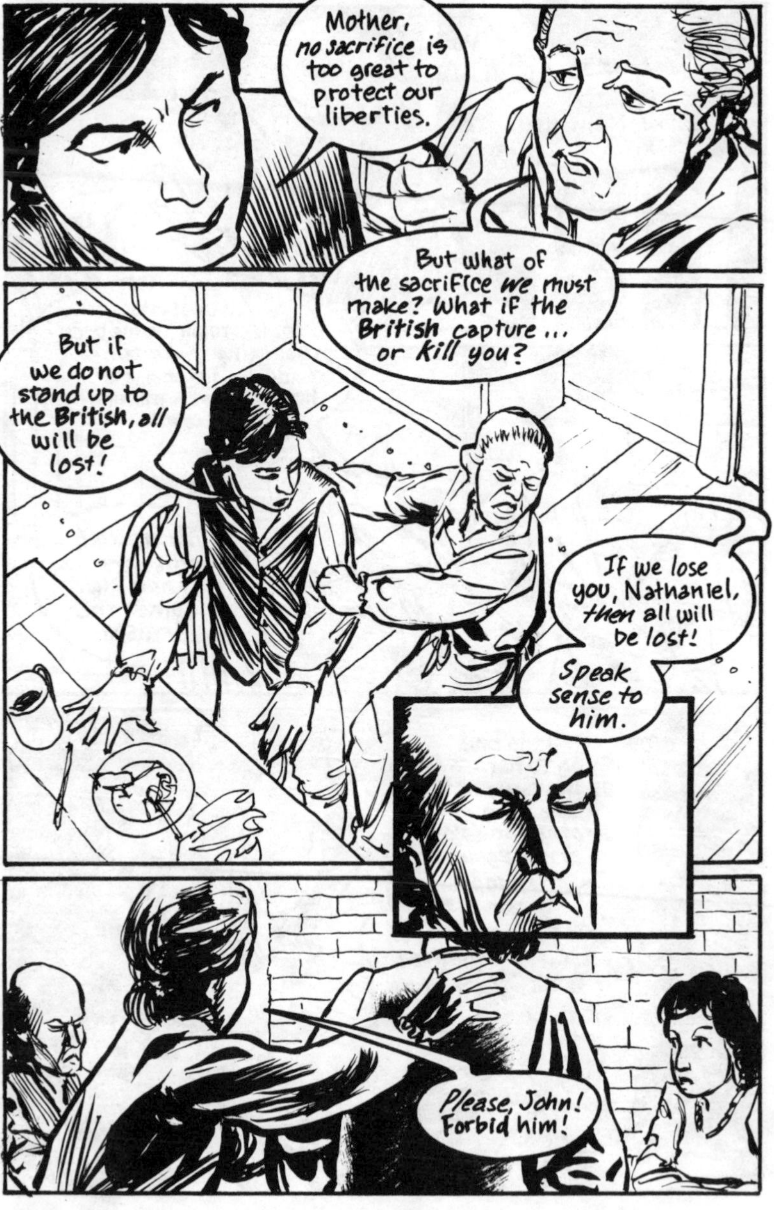
Mother, no sacrifice is too great to protect our liberties.
But what of the sacrifice we must make? What if the British capture ... or kill you?
But if we do not stand up to the British, all will be lost!
If we lose you, Nathaniel, then all will be lost!
Speak sense to him.
Please, John! Forbid him!

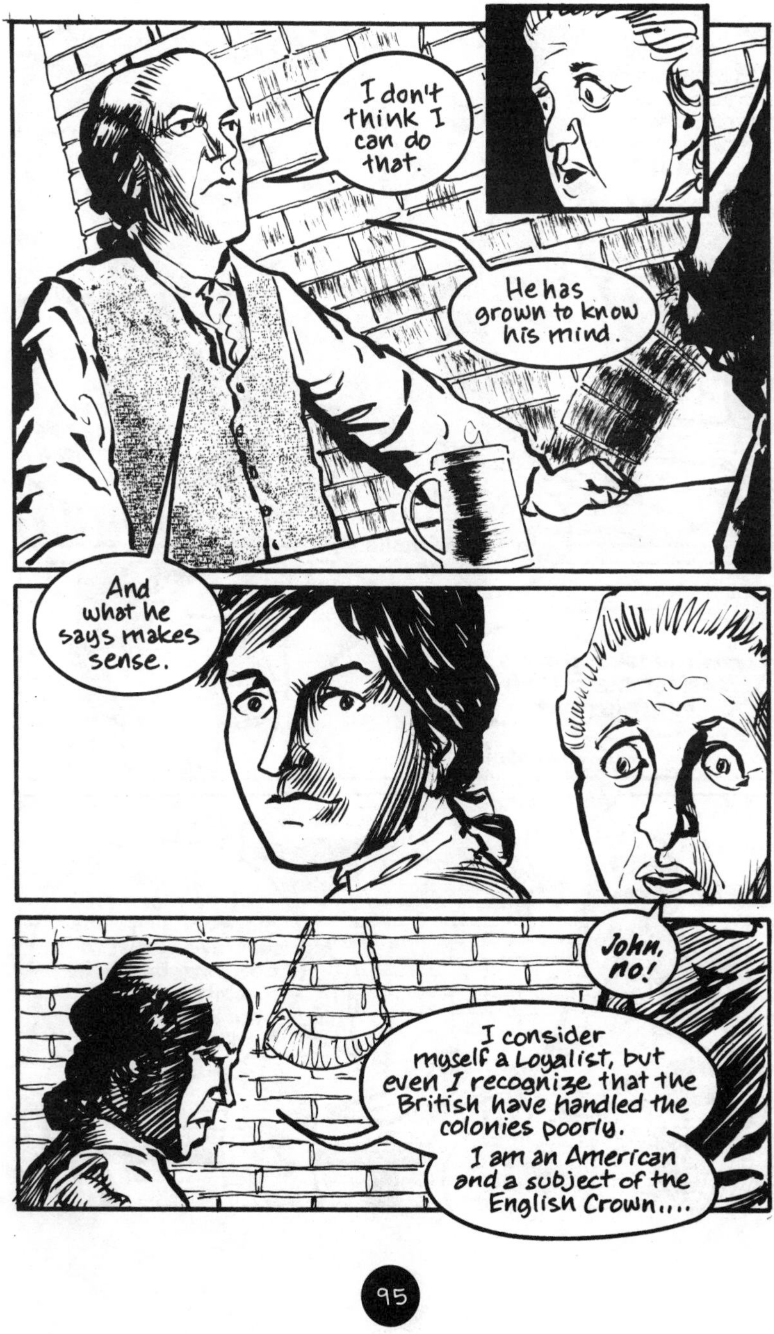
I don't think I can do that.
He has grown to know his mind.
And what he says makes sense.
John, no!
I consider myself a Loyalist, but even *I* recognize that the British have handled the colonies poorly.
I am an American and a subject of the English Crown....

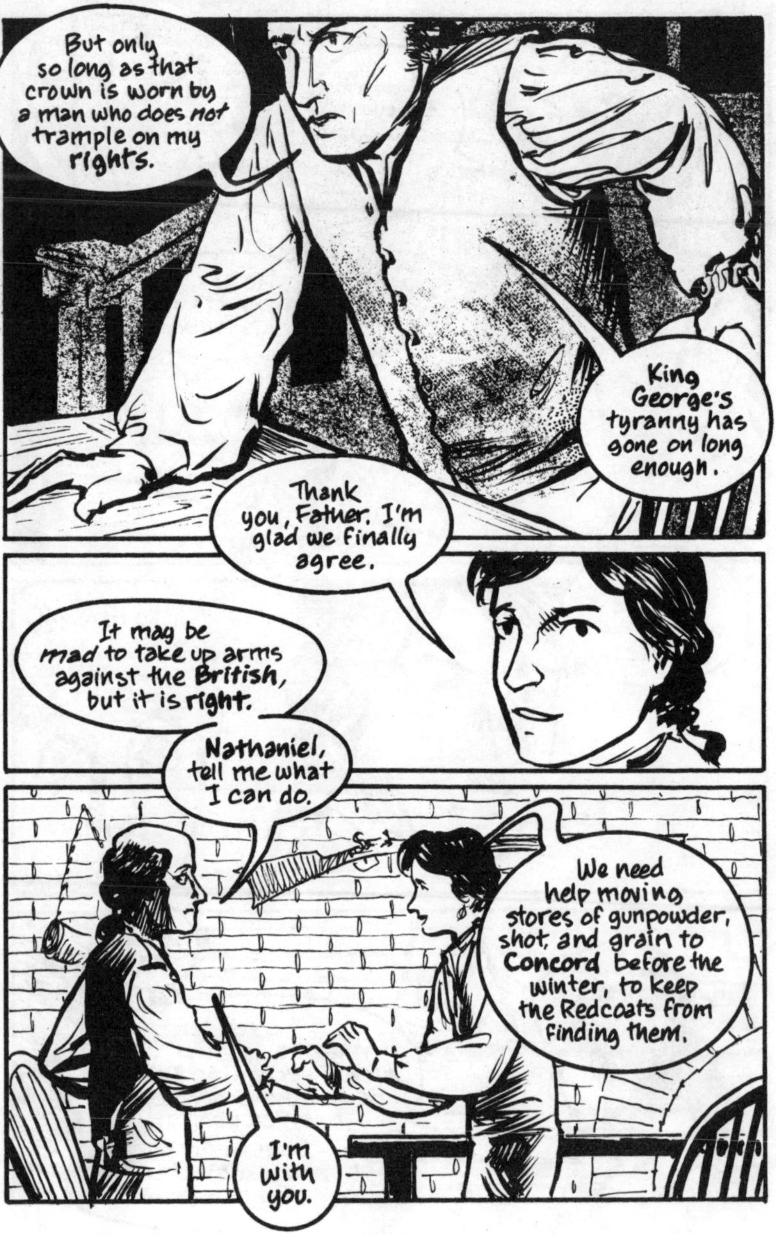
But only so long as that crown is worn by a man who does *not* trample on my **rights.**
King George's tyranny has gone on long enough.
Thank you, Father. I'm glad we finally agree.
It may be *mad* to take up arms against the **British**, but it is **right.**
Nathaniel, tell me what I can do.
We need help moving stores of gunpowder, shot, and grain to **Concord** before the winter, to keep the Redcoats from finding them.
I'm with you.

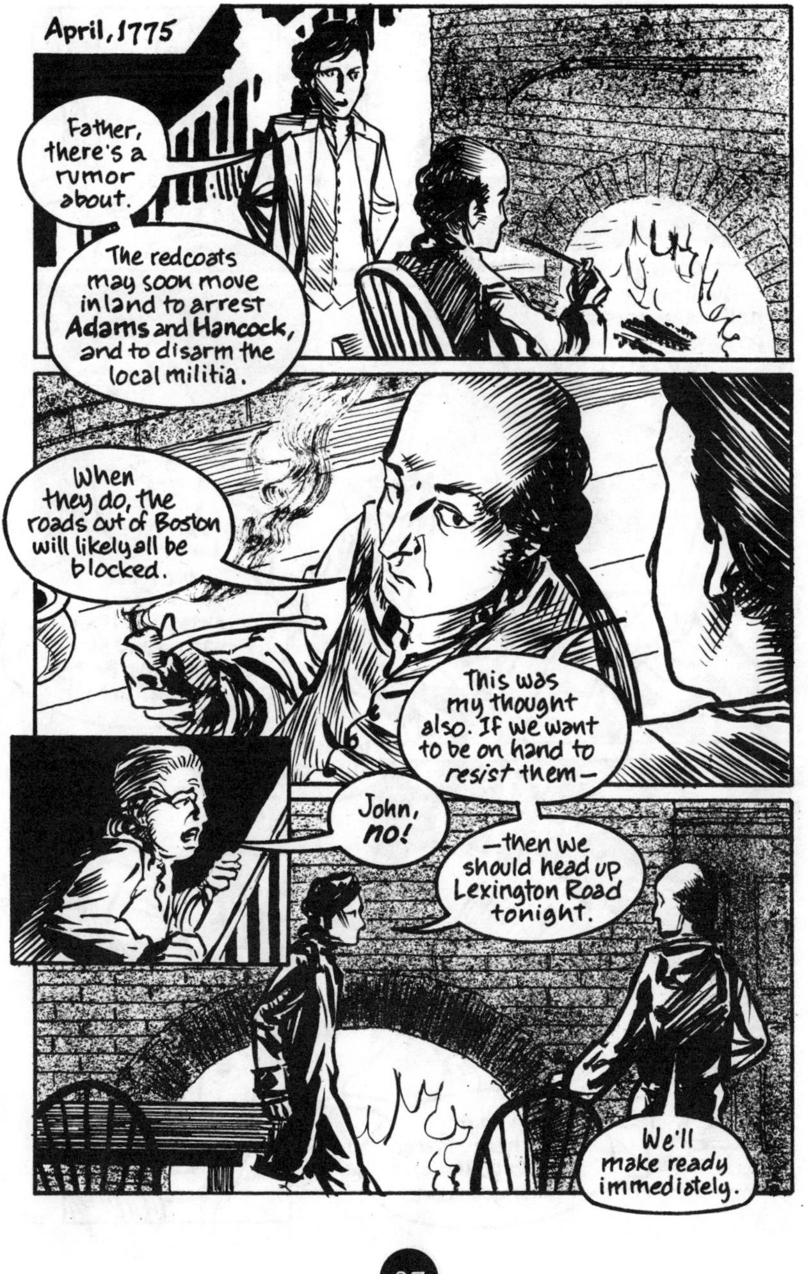
April, 1775
Father, there's a rumor about.
The redcoats may soon move inland to arrest **Adams and Hancock**, and to disarm the local militia.
When they do, the roads out of Boston will likely all be blocked.
This was my thought also. If we want to be on hand to *resist* them—
John, ***no!***
—then we should head up Lexington Road tonight.
We'll make ready immediately.

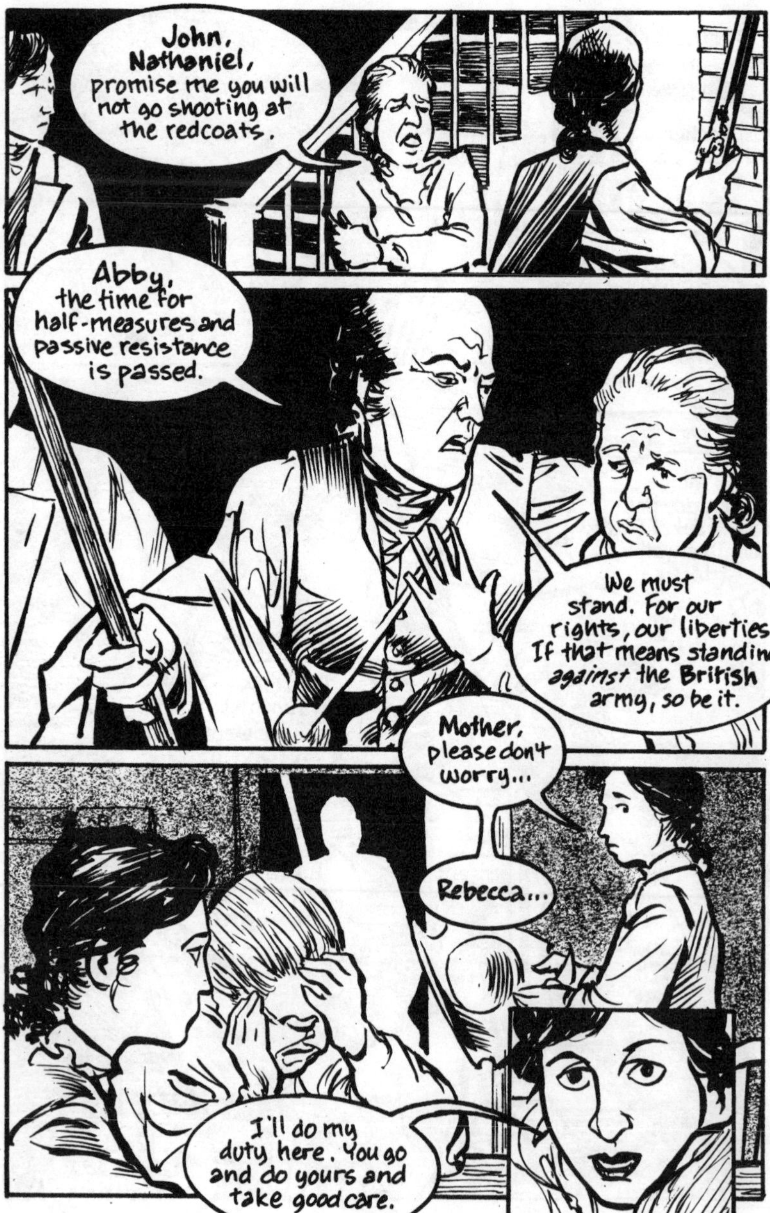
John, Nathaniel, promise me you will not go shooting at the redcoats.
Abby, the time for half-measures and passive resistance is passed.
We must stand. For our rights, our liberties. If that means standing *against* the British army, so be it.
Mother, please don't worry...
Rebecca...
I'll do my duty here. You go and do yours and take good care.

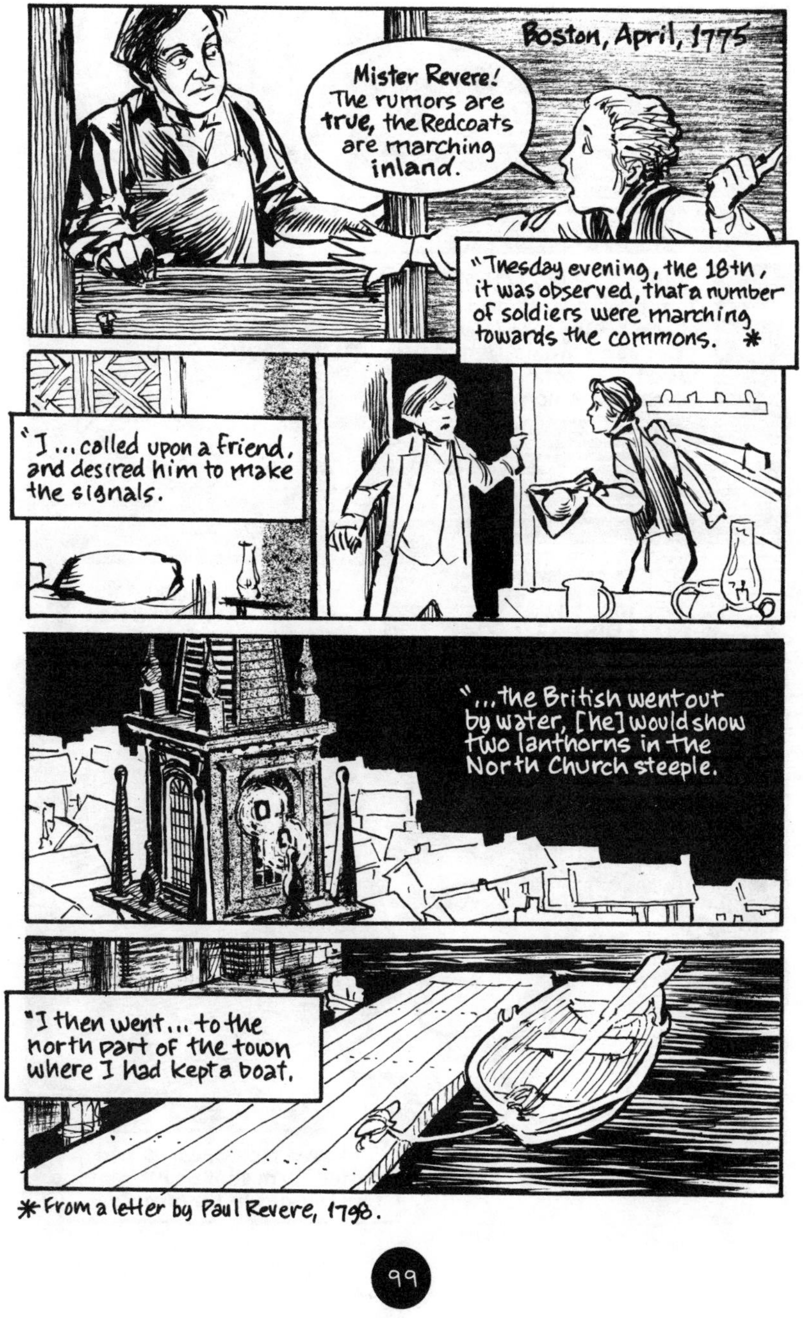
Boston, April, 1775
Mister Revere! The rumors are true, the Redcoats are marching inland.
"Tuesday evening, the 18th, it was observed, that a number of soldiers were marching towards the commons. *
"I ... called upon a friend, and desired him to make the signals.
"... the British went out by water, [he] would show two lanthorns in the North Church steeple.
"I then went ... to the north part of the town where I had kept a boat.

* From a letter by Paul Revere, 1798.

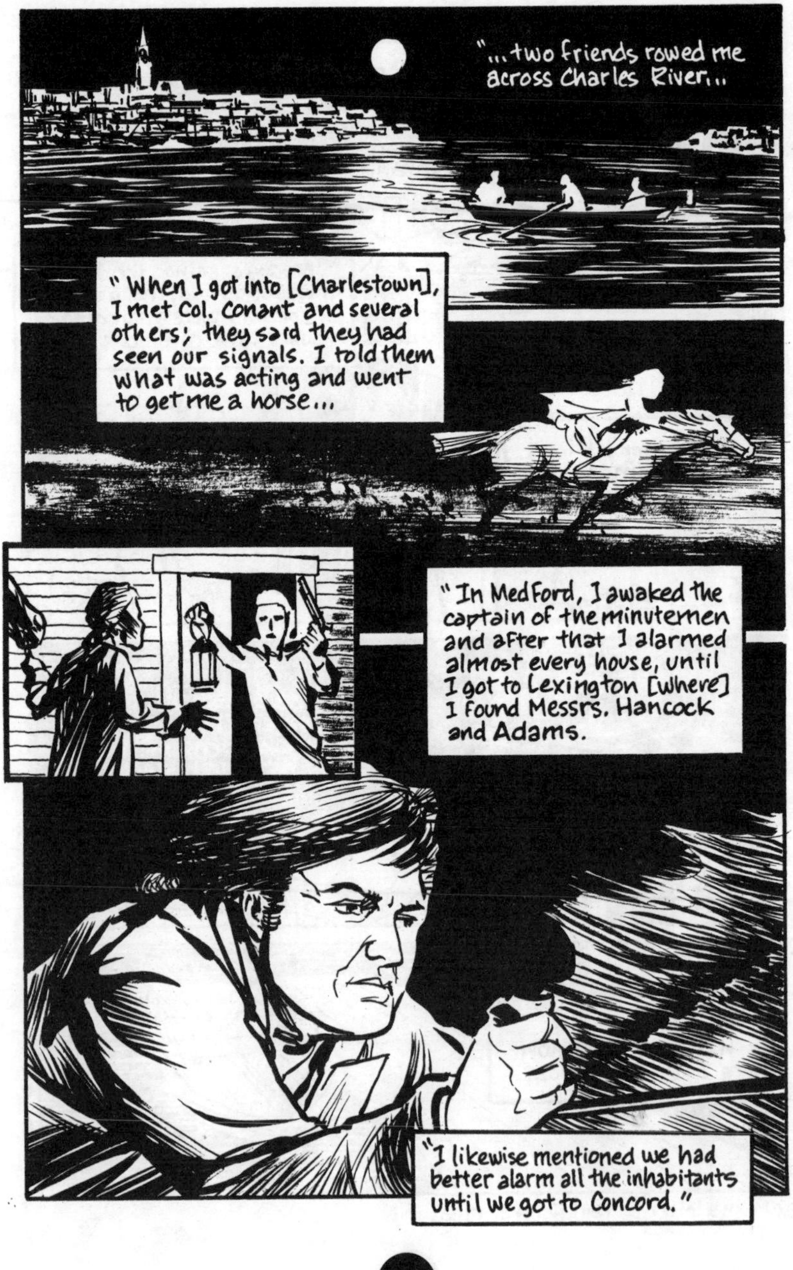
"...two friends rowed me across Charles River...
" When I got into [Charlestown], I met Col. Conant and several others; they said they had seen our signals. I told them what was acting and went to get me a horse...
" In Medford, I awaked the captain of the minutemen and after that I alarmed almost every house, until I got to Lexington [where] I found Messrs. Hancock and Adams.
"I likewise mentioned we had better alarm all the inhabitants until we got to Concord."

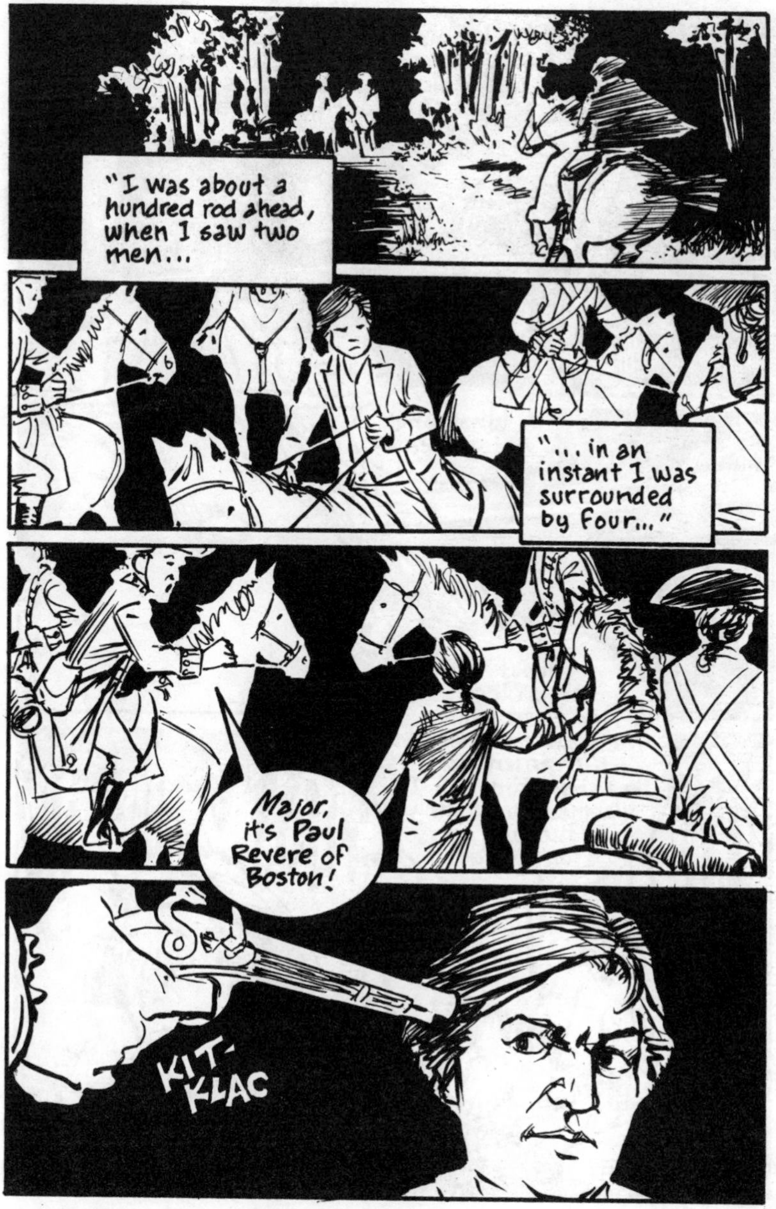
"I was about a hundred rod ahead, when I saw two men...
"...in an instant I was surrounded by four..."
Major, it's Paul Revere of Boston!
KIT-KLAC

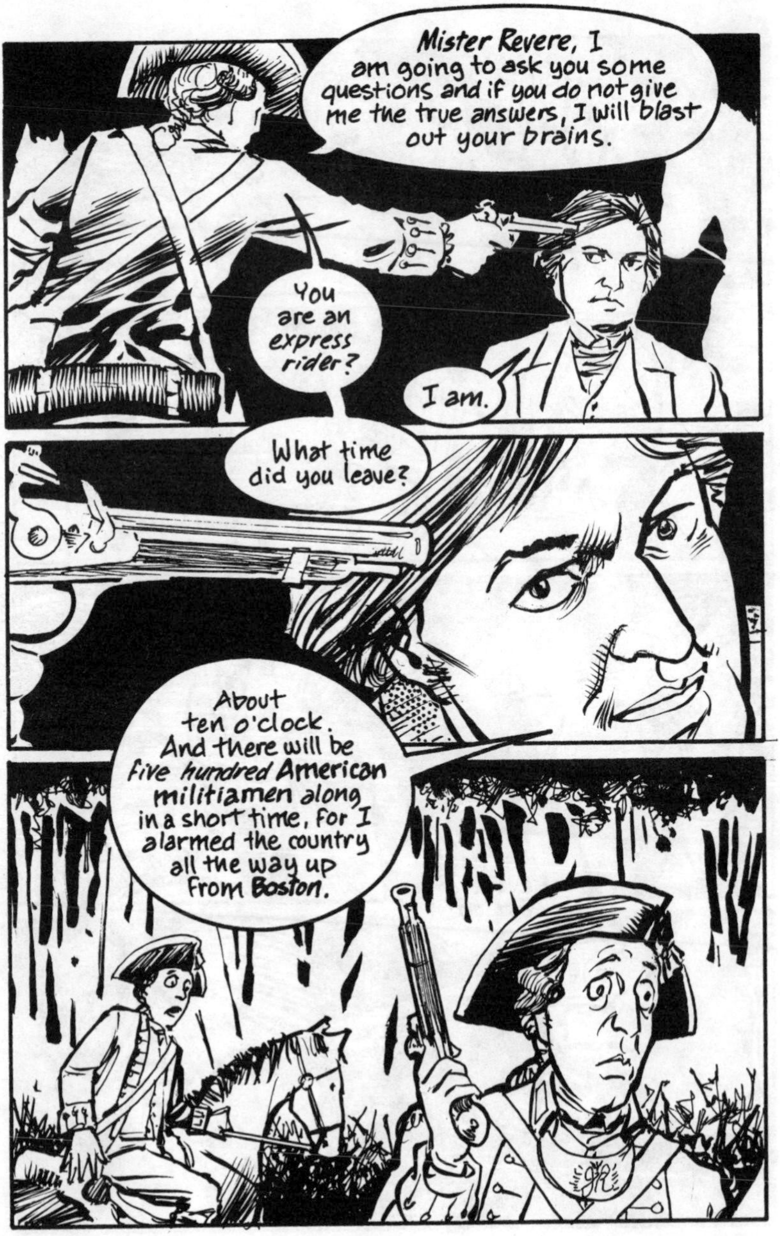
Mister Revere, I am going to ask you some questions and if you do not give me the true answers, I will blast out your brains.
You are an express rider?
I am.
What time did you leave?
About ten o'clock. And there will be five hundred American militiamen along in a short time, for I alarmed the country all the way up from Boston.

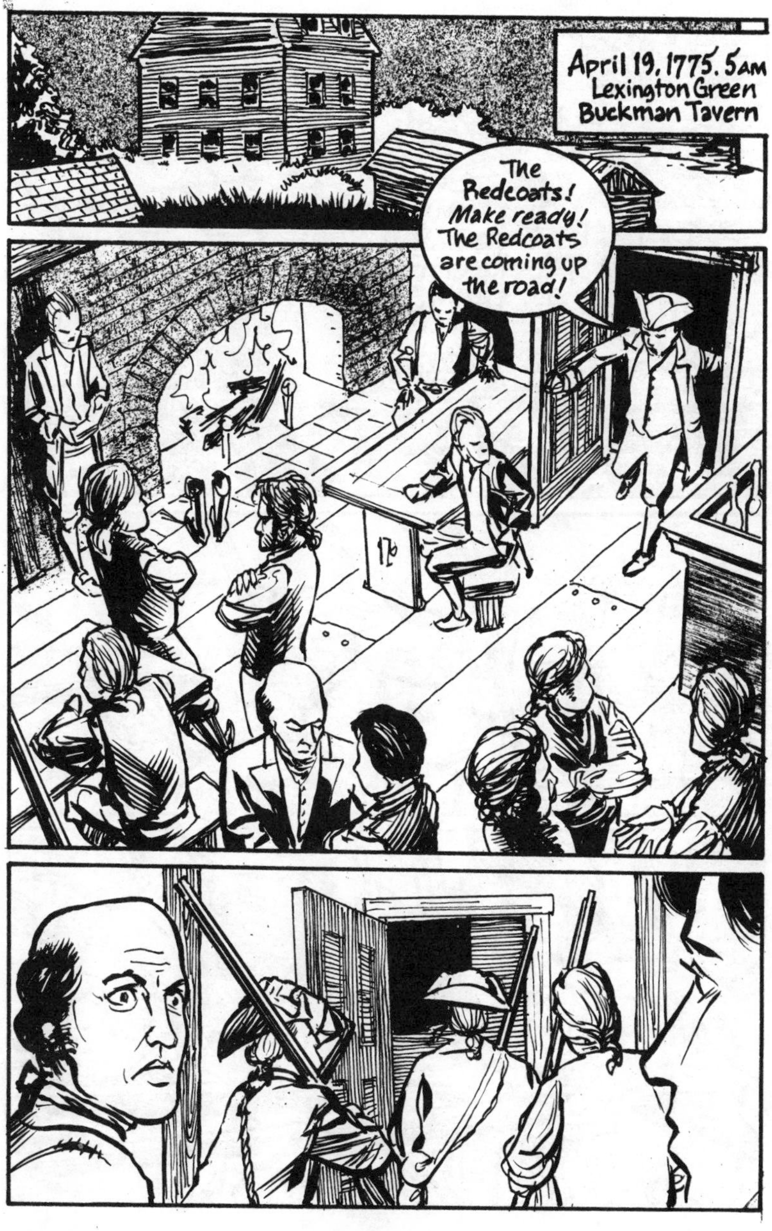
April 19, 1775. 5AM
Lexington Green
Buckman Tavern
The Redcoats! Make ready! The Redcoats are coming up the road!

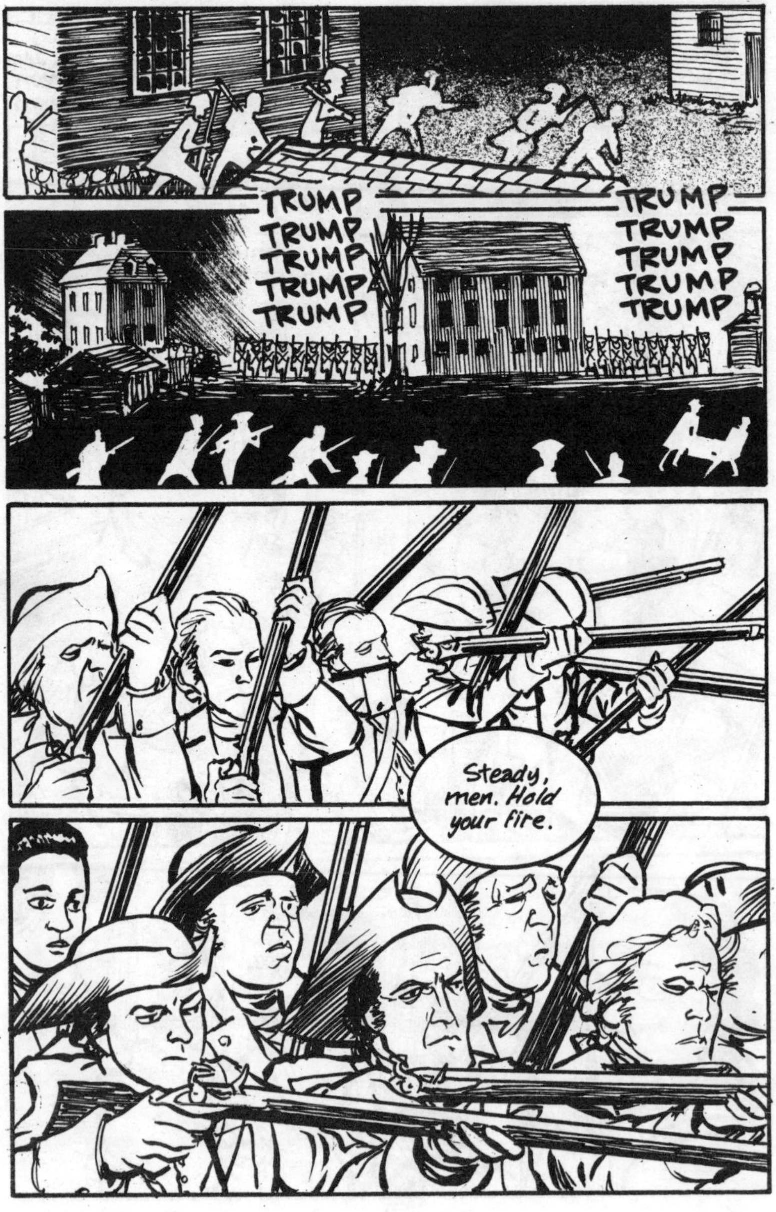
TRUMP
TRUMP
TRUMP
TRUMP
TRUMP
TRUMP
TRUMP
TRUMP
TRUMP
TRUMP
Steady, men. Hold your fire.

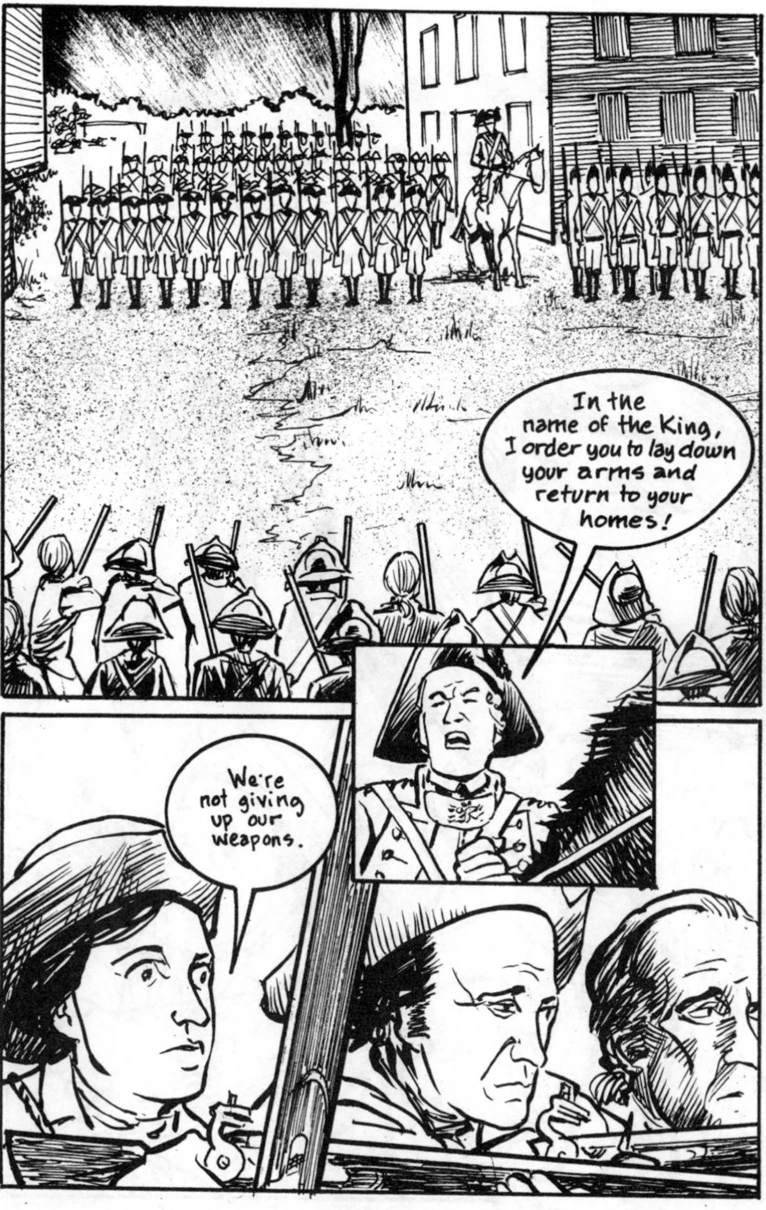
In the name of the King, I order you to lay down your arms and return to your homes!
We're not giving up our weapons.

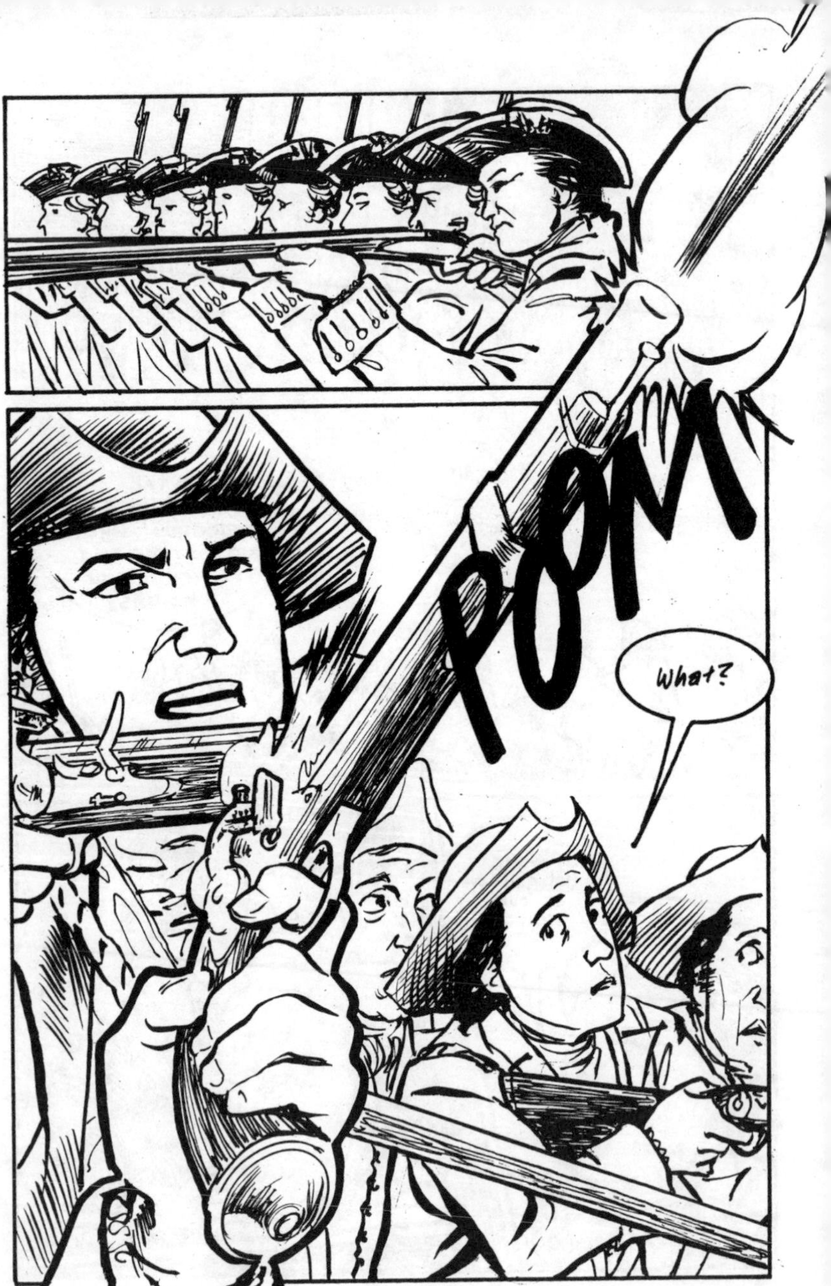
POOM
What?

BRATT
BRATT
BRATT
BRATT
BRATT
BRATT
BRATTTT
BRATT
BRATT
BRATT
BRATTT
BRATTT
ZZIPPP
TZIP

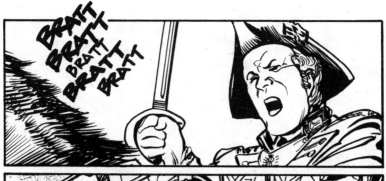

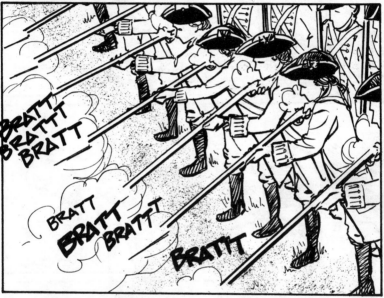

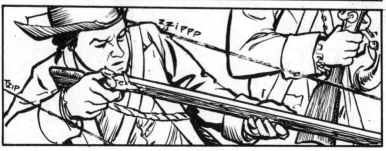

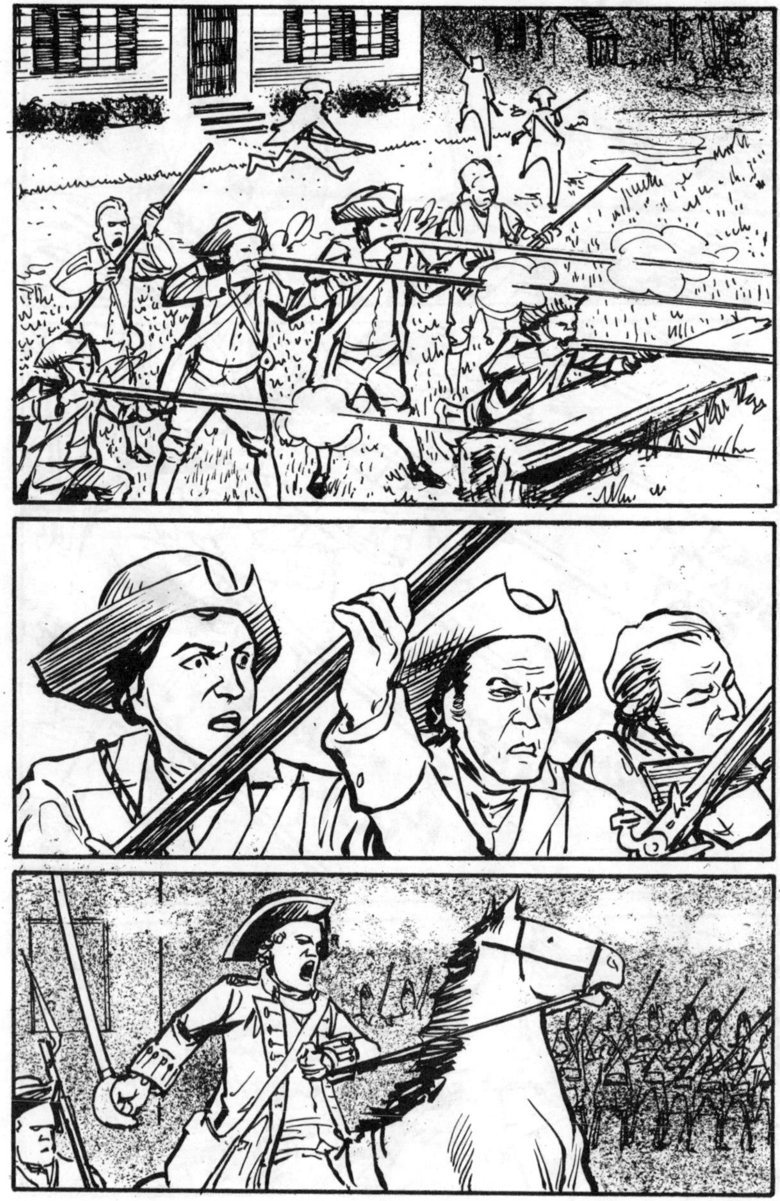

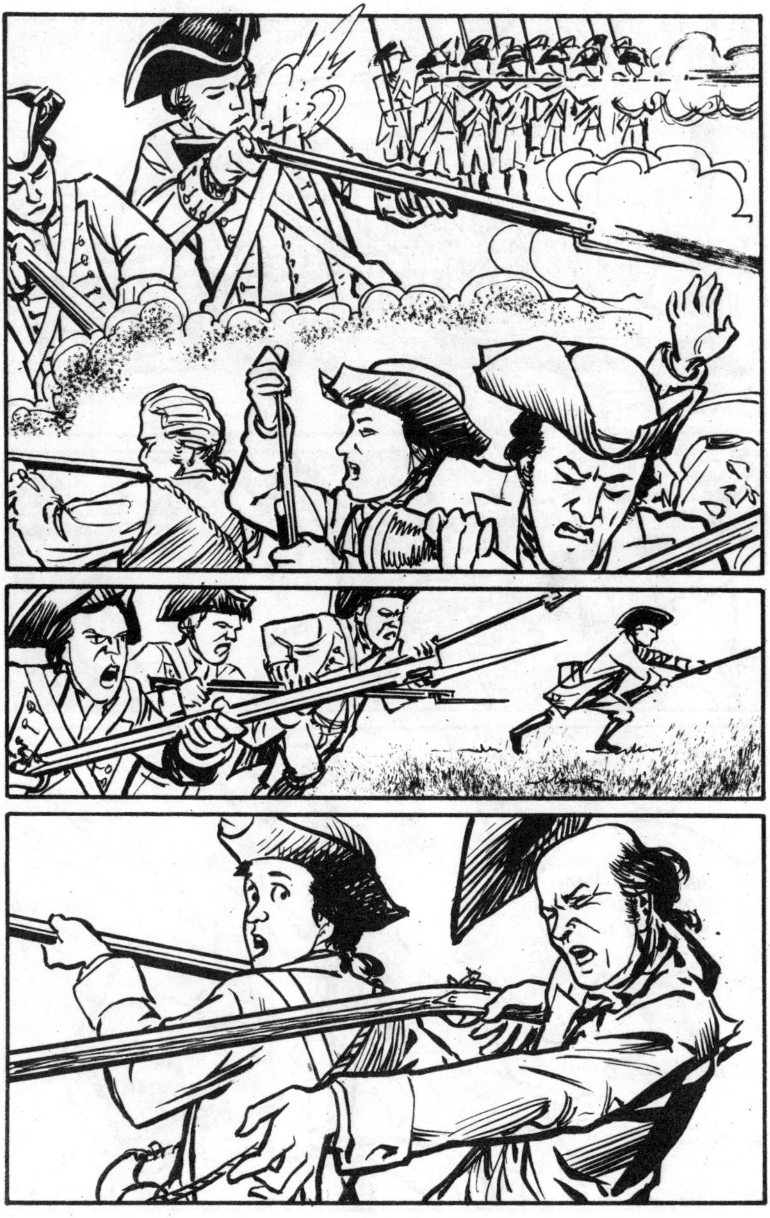

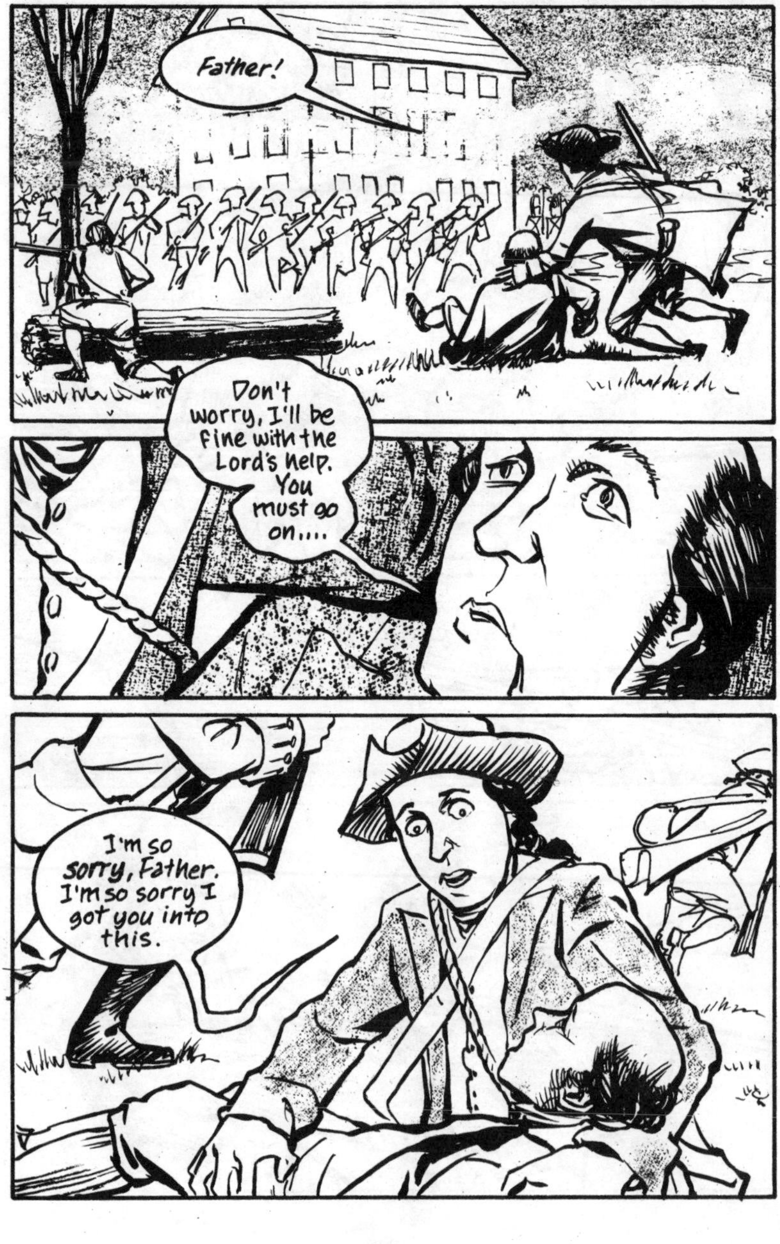
Father!
Don't worry, I'll be fine with the Lord's help. You must go on....
I'm so sorry, Father. I'm so sorry I got you into this.

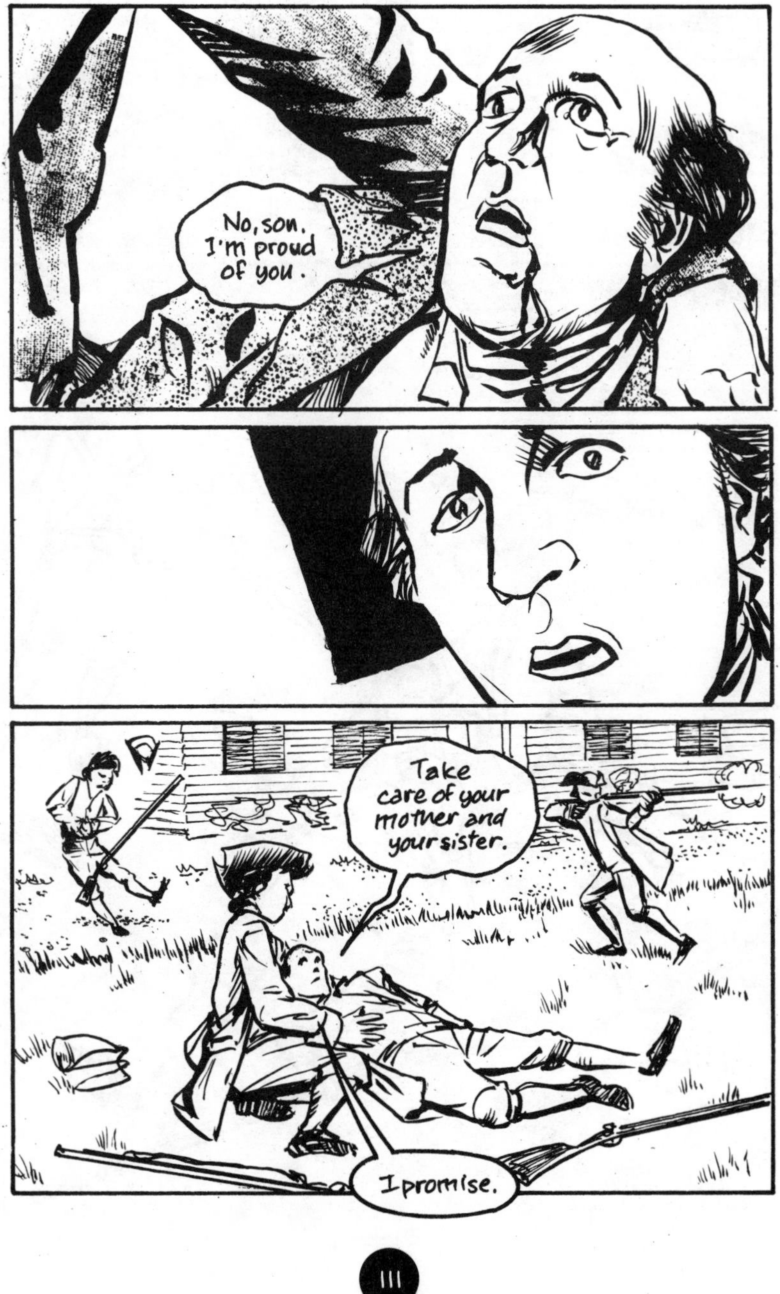
No, son. I'm proud of you.
Take care of your mother and your sister.
I promise.

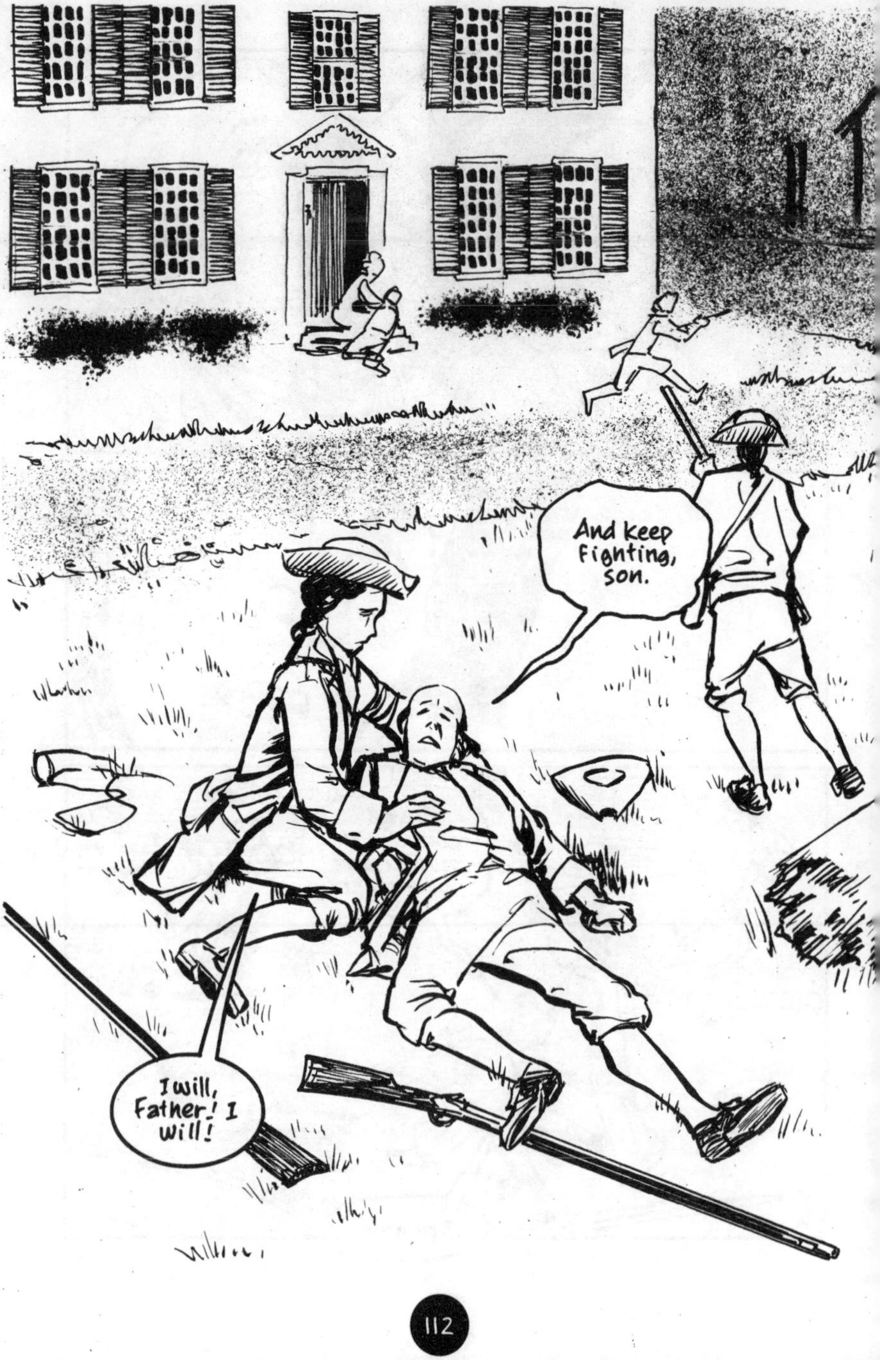
And keep fighting, son.
I will, Father! I will!

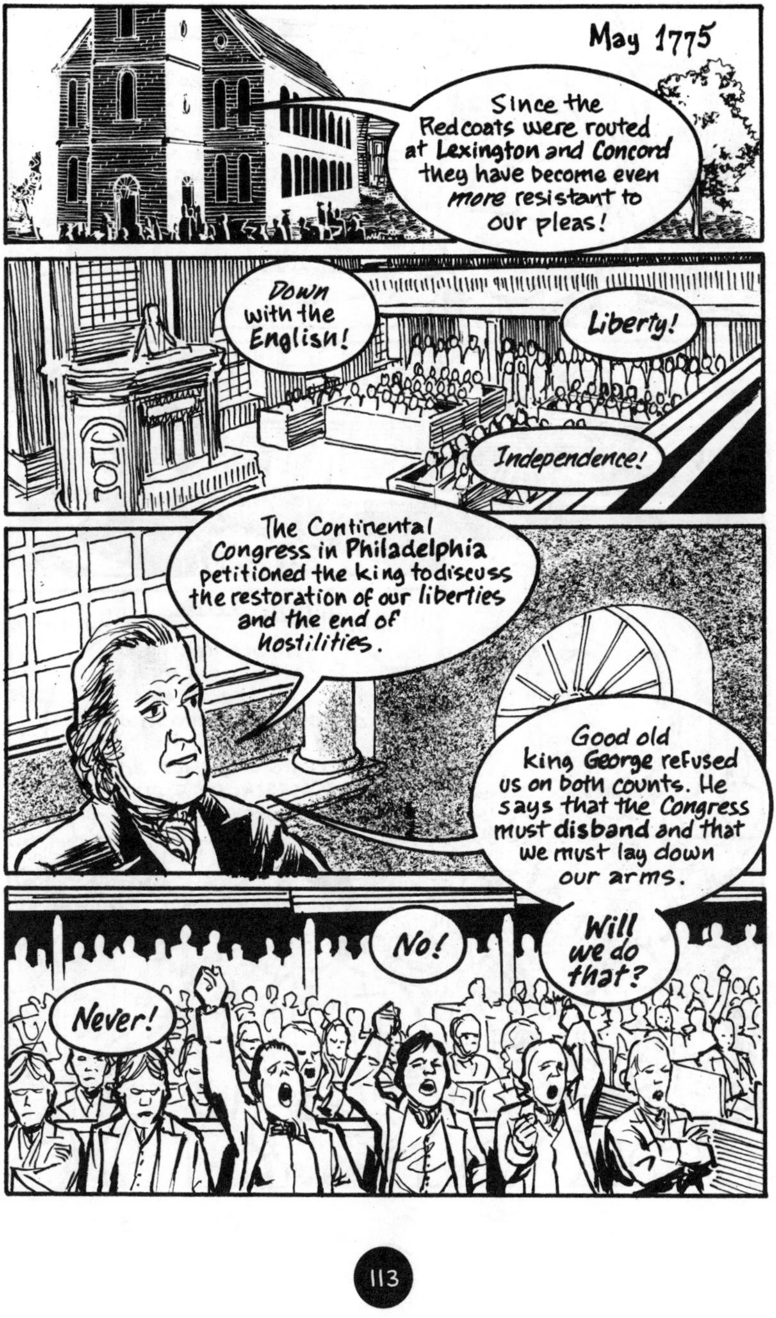
May 1775
Since the Redcoats were routed at Lexington and Concord they have become even *more* resistant to our pleas!
Down with the English!
Liberty!
Independence!
The Continental Congress in Philadelphia petitioned the king to discuss the restoration of our liberties and the end of hostilities.
Good old king George refused us on both counts. He says that the Congress must disband and that we must lay down our arms.
Will we do that?
No!
Never!

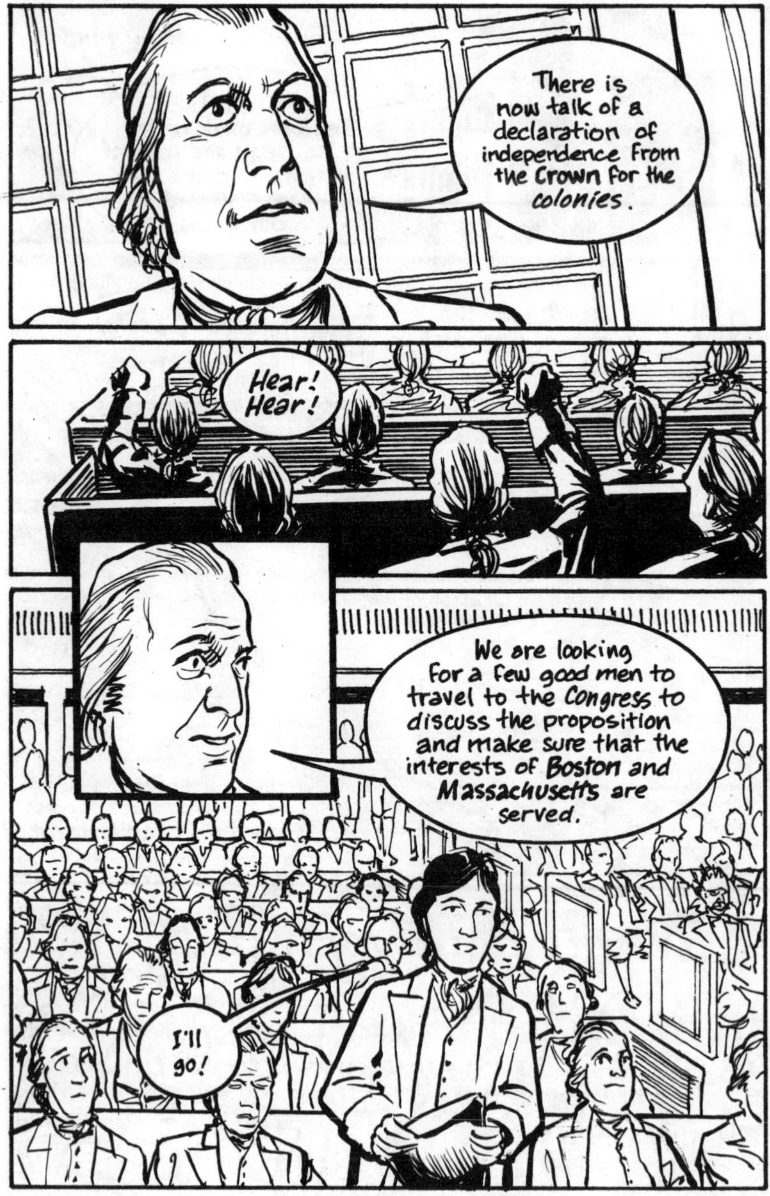
There is now talk of a declaration of independence from the Crown for the colonies.
Hear! Hear!
We are looking for a few good men to travel to the Congress to discuss the proposition and make sure that the interests of Boston and Massachusetts are served.
I'll go!

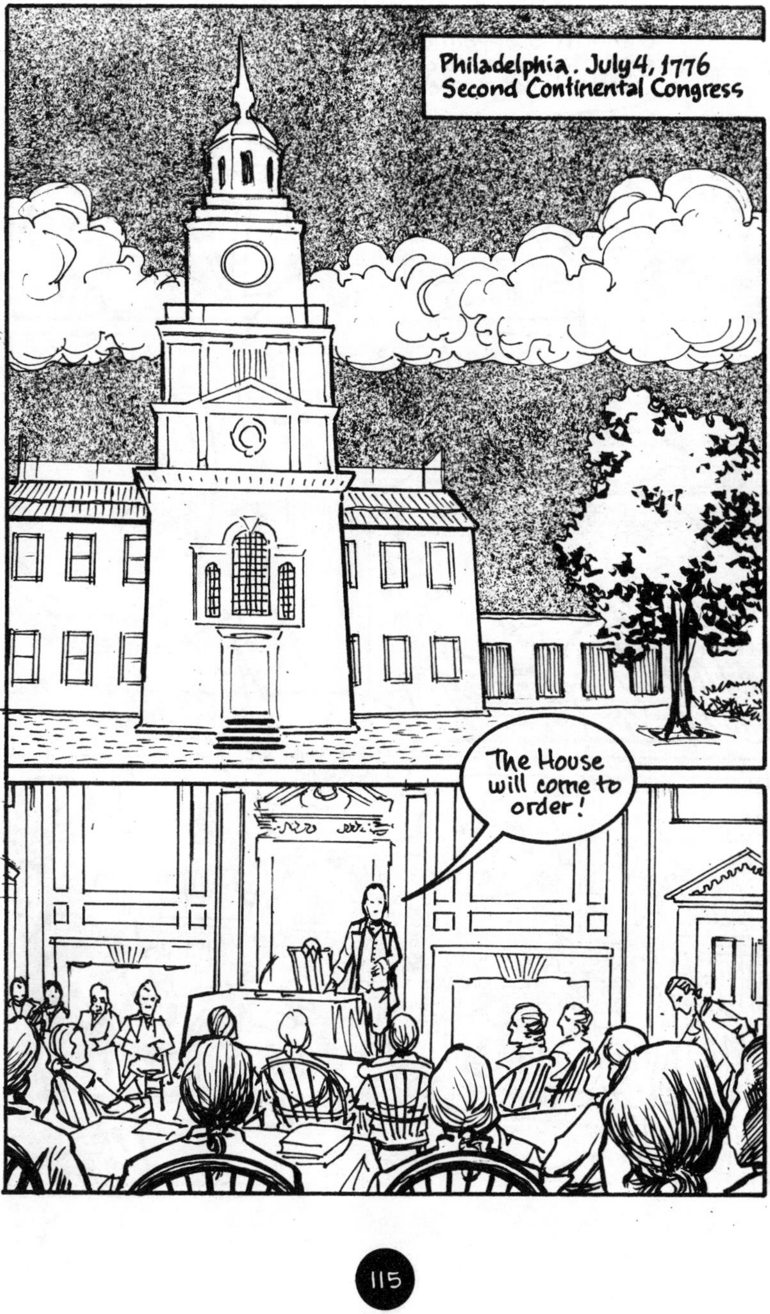
Philadelphia. July 4, 1776
Second Continental Congress
The House will come to order!

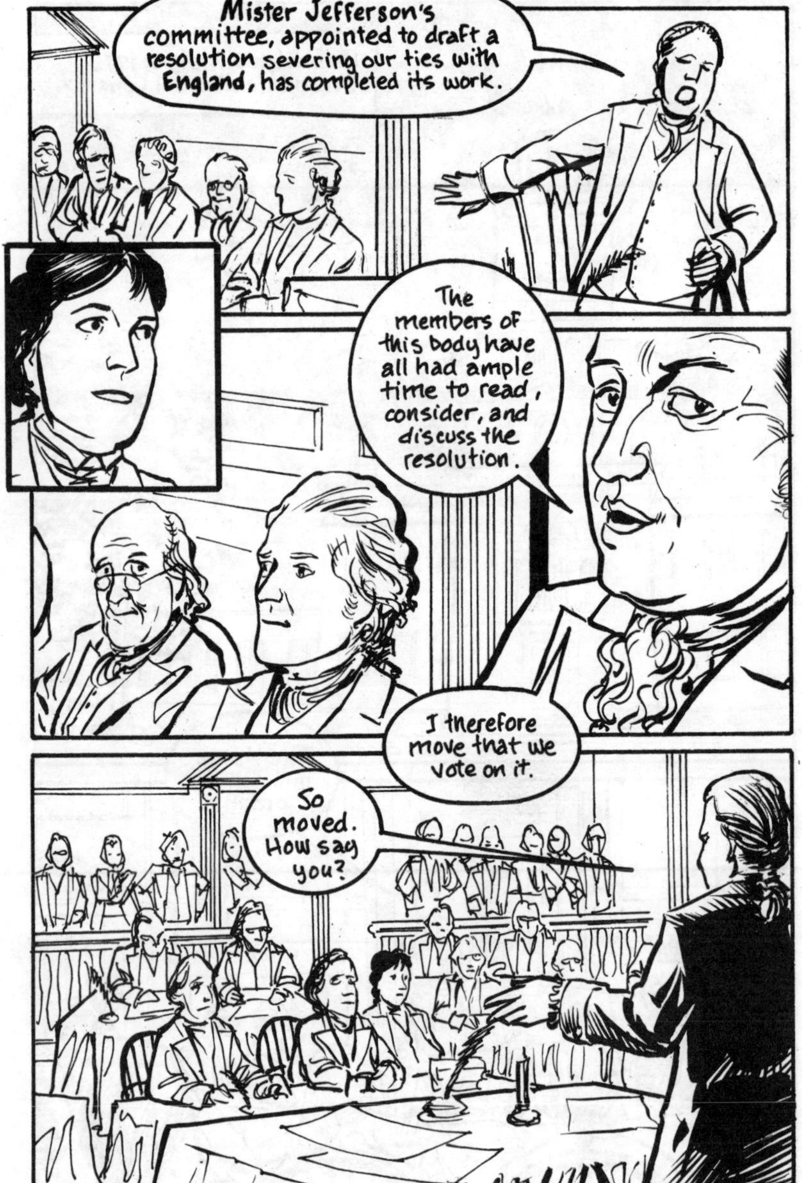
Mister Jefferson's committee, appointed to draft a resolution severing our ties with England, has completed its work.
The members of this body have all had ample time to read, consider, and discuss the resolution.
I therefore move that we vote on it.
So moved. How say you?

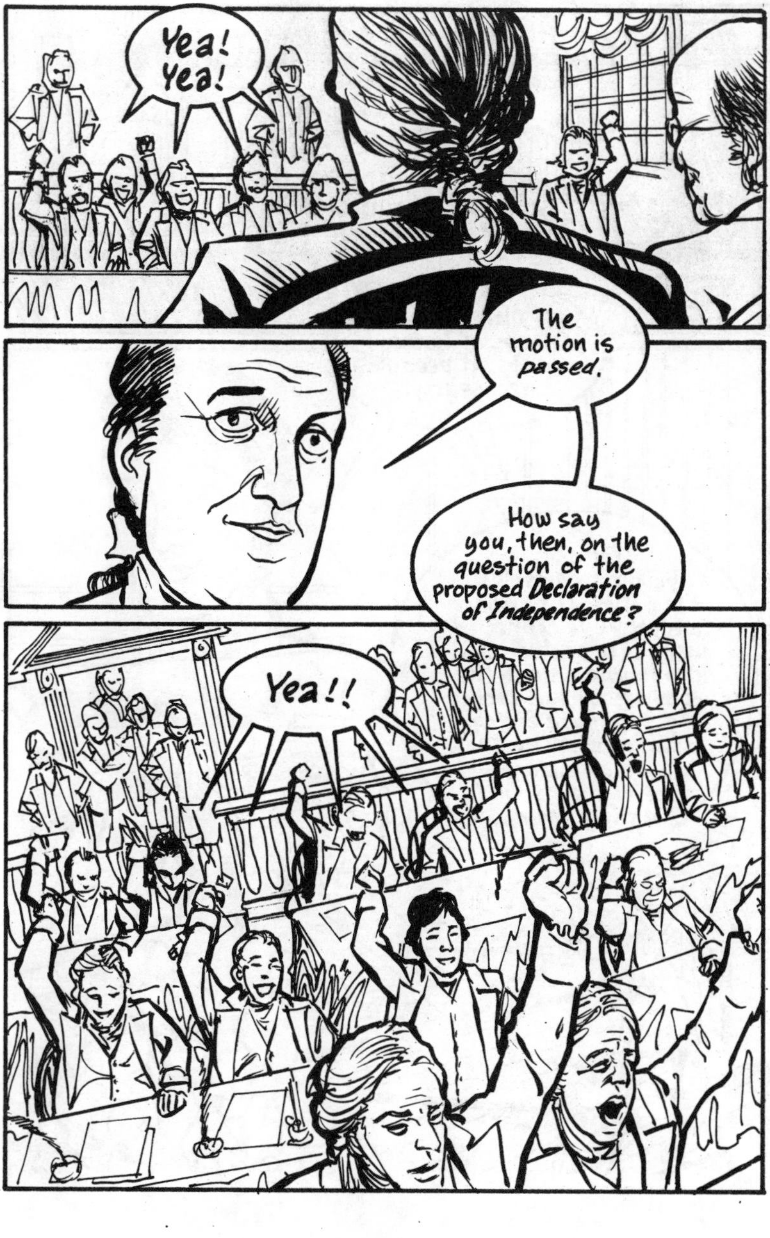
Yea! Yea!
The motion is *passed*.
How say you, then, on the question of the proposed *Declaration of Independence*?
Yea!!

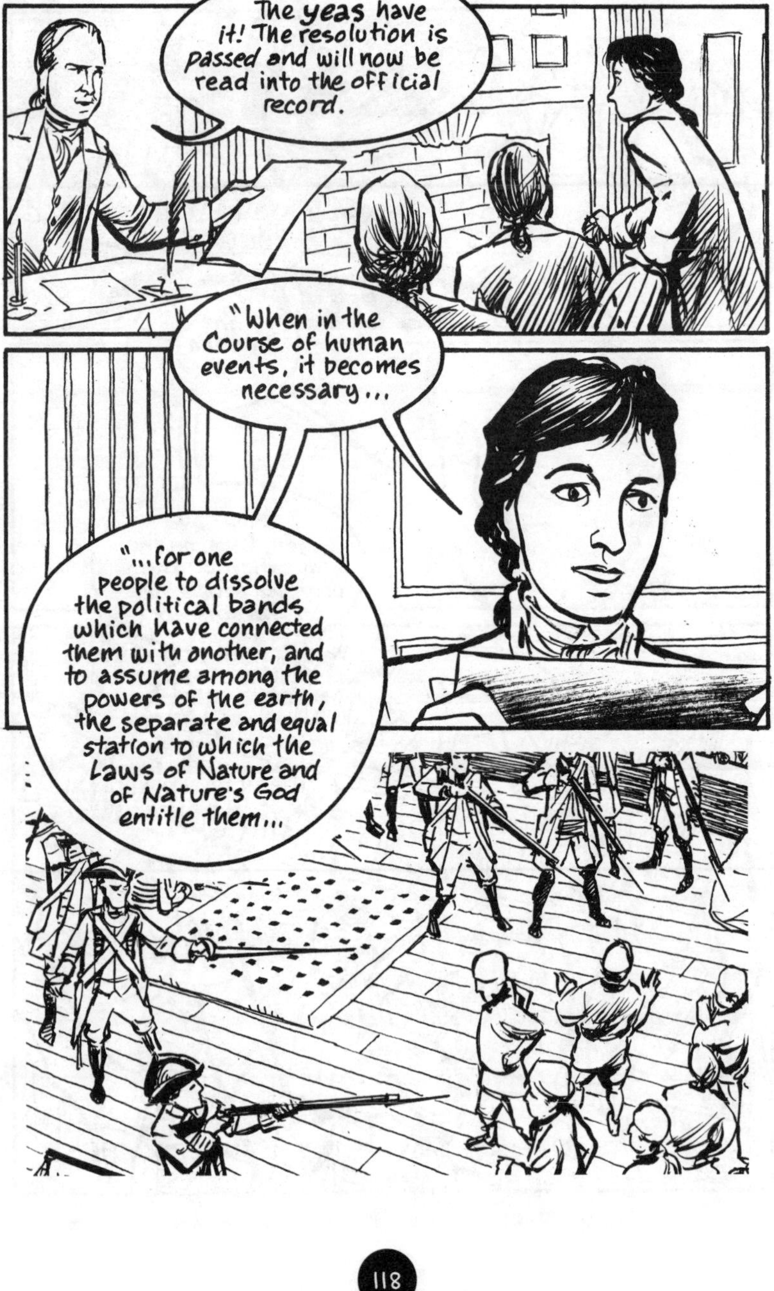
The yeas have it! The resolution is passed and will now be read into the official record.
"When in the Course of human events, it becomes necessary...
"...for one people to dissolve the political bands which have connected them with another, and to assume among the powers of the earth, the separate and equal station to which the Laws of Nature and of Nature's God entitle them...

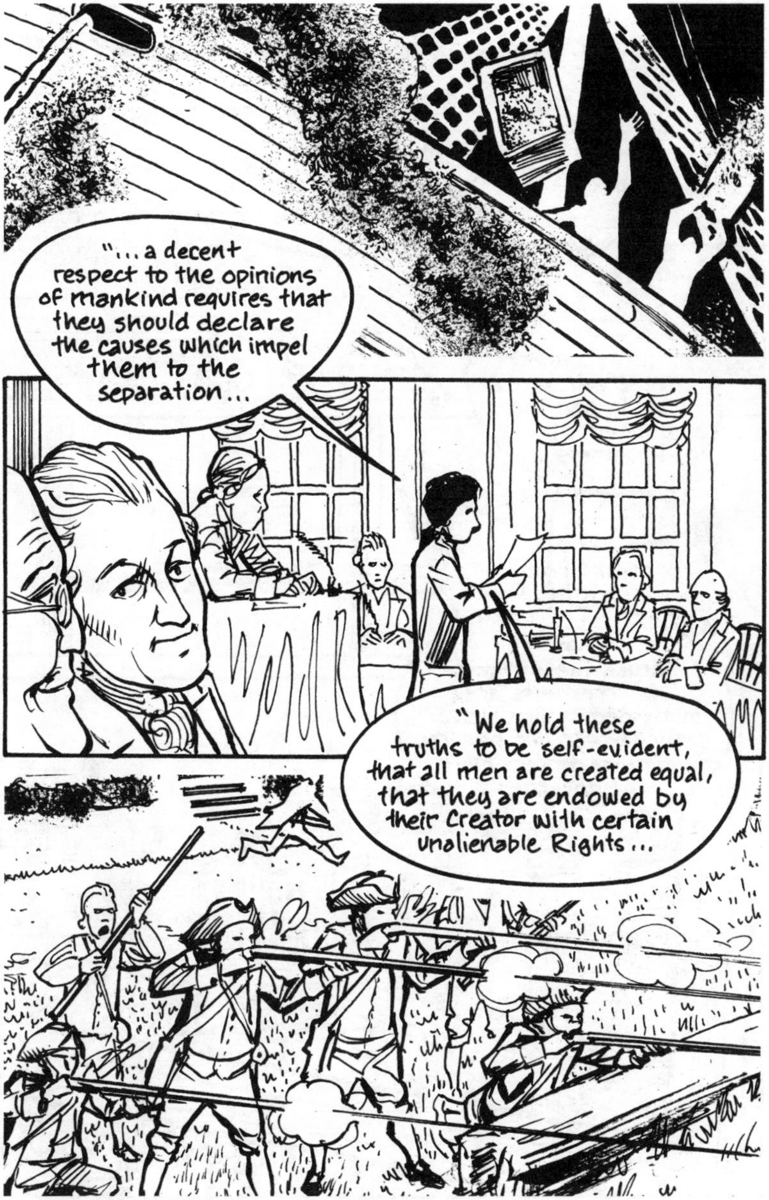
"... a decent respect to the opinions of mankind requires that they should declare the causes which impel them to the separation...
"We hold these truths to be self-evident, that all men are created equal, that they are endowed by their Creator with certain unalienable Rights ...

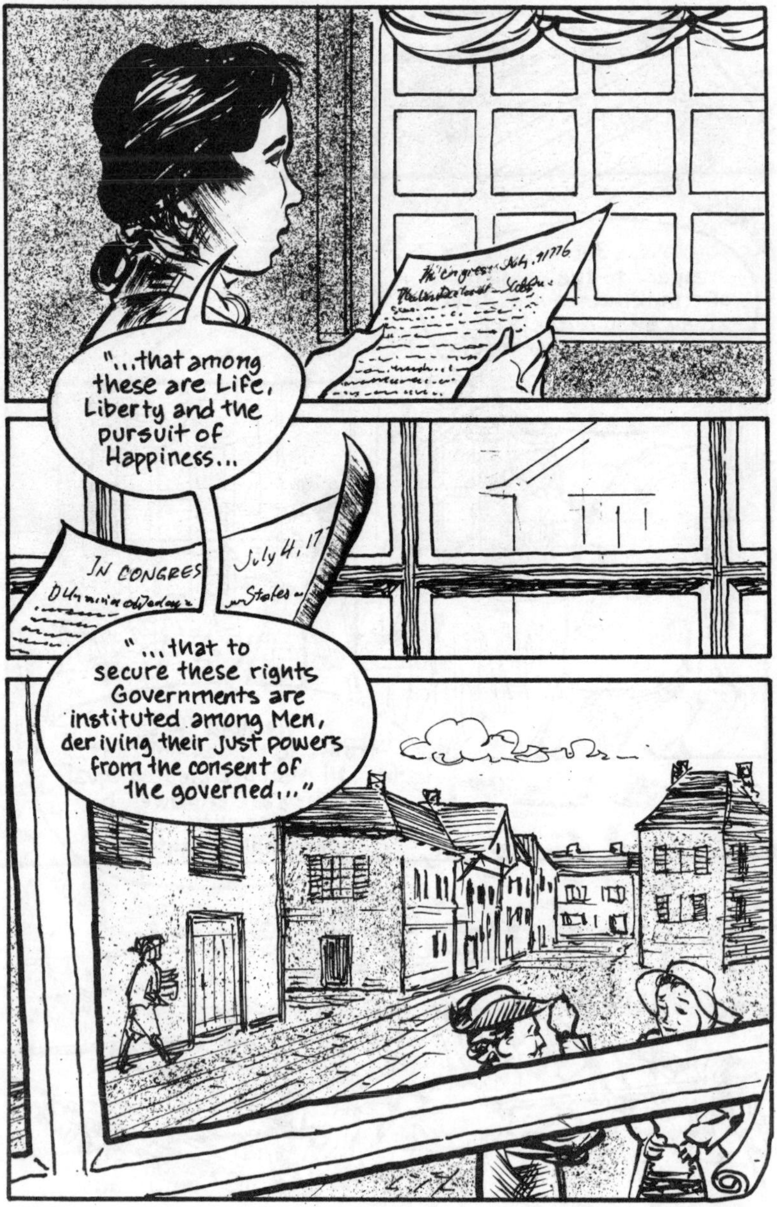
"...that among these are Life, Liberty and the pursuit of Happiness...
IN CONGRES
July 4, 17
"...that to secure these rights Governments are instituted among Men, deriving their just powers from the consent of the governed..."

MARSHALL POE

is an American historian and the author of many nonfiction works. He is currently a writer and analyst at the *Atlantic*. Marshall lives in Iowa City, Iowa.

LELAND PURVIS

is a Xeric Grant award-winning comics illustrator whose work has been published by companies such as Image and Dark Horse Comics. He lives in Brooklyn, New York.

ALADDIN GOES GRAPHIC...

don't miss any of Aladdin's exciting graphic novels!

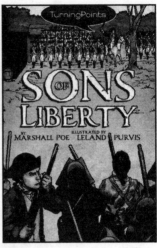